Supplementary Monograph of the Mollusca

SALZWASSER
VERLAG

John Lycett

Supplementary Monograph of the Mollusca

Reprint of the original, first published in 1863.

1st Edition 2022 | ISBN: 978-3-37500-204-6

Verlag (Publisher): Salzwasser Verlag GmbH, Zeilweg 44, 60439 Frankfurt, Deutschland
Vertretungsberechtigt (Authorized to represent): E. Roepke, Zeilweg 44, 60439 Frankfurt, Deutschland
Druck (Print): Books on Demand GmbH, In de Tarpen 42, 22848 Norderstedt, Deutschland

THE

PALÆONTOGRAPHICAL SOCIETY.

INSTITUTED MDCCCXLVII.

LONDON:

MDCCCLXIII.

SUPPLEMENTARY MONOGRAPH

ON THE

MOLLUSCA

FROM THE

STONESFIELD SLATE, GREAT OOLITE, FOREST MARBLE, AND CORNBRASH.

BY

JOHN LYCETT, M.D.

LONDON:

1863.

INTRODUCTORY EXPLANATION.

The introduction to the first part of the 'Monograph of the Great Oolite Mollusca' contained an intimation that, with increasing knowledge of the testacea of the Cornbrash and Forest Marble, it might eventually be desirable to give an additional monograph, or an Appendix to that work. The materials which have latterly been placed at the disposal of the writer are so considerable that he has been induced to endeavour to fulfil the anticipatory announcement made in 1850, and also to correct some errors, both textual and typographical, which occur in the former Monograph. In the execution of his task the writer begs thankfully to acknowledge the assistance he has received in the loan of specimens from gentlemen whose names will be found mentioned in connexion with each of the species illustrated, nor can he omit gratefully to mention the great advantages he has derived from the constant opportunities that have been afforded to him of comparing the Oolitic fossils of the southern counties with those of Yorkshire, contained in the very extensive and choice collection of Mr. Leckenby, of this place.

SCARBOROUGH; *September* 6, 1861.

SUPPLEMENT

TO

A MONOGRAPH

OF THE

MOLLUSCA FROM THE GREAT OOLITE.

CEPHALOPODA.

Ammonites Bullatus, *D'Orbig.* Tab. XXXI, fig. 1.

Ammonites Bullatus, *D'Orb.* Pal. Fr. Ter. Jurass., p. 412, pl. 142, figs. 1 and 2.
— — *Küdernatsch.* Abhand. K. K. Geol. Reich., 1 band., taf. iii, figs. 1—4—11.
— platystomus, *Quenst.*? Cephal., t. 15, fig. 3.
— Bullatus, *Oppel.* Juraform., p. 549.
— — *Quenstedt.*? Der Jura., t. 64, fig. 13, p. 479.

Testá bullatá, irregulari; anfractibus subinvolutis, latis, ultimo angustato, transversim late costato; costis inæqualibus; aperturá constrictá, semilunari. (D'Orbigny.)

Shell inflated, globose, variable in form throughout all the stages of its growth, ornamented with large, transverse, slightly elevated ribs, which pass from the umbilicus over the back to the other side, not straight, but curved forwards; these are separated by other shorter ribs, which alternate with the larger series of ribs in the adult state, but in the young state there are two and sometimes three short ribs between each of the longer ones. The volutions of the spire are irregular and embracing, forming a contracted umbilicus in the young state; subsequently the volutions are less contracted, which renders the shell unsymmetrical or deformed. The back is rounded, the mouth much contracted and prolonged in the middle part. The septa are very much complicated.

In England this Ammonite is very rare. The aged example figured is seven inches in diameter, the aperture having a height and breadth of two inches; its more advanced growth will account for the difference of figure when compared with those of D'Orbigny, Quenstedt, and of Kudernatsch; but in truth, the variability of figure extends not less to individuals than to the stages of growth, for in no instance does there appear to be a very near agreement of figure.

Geological Position and Localities. The sole specimen in my collection is from the Great Oolite, near Tiltups Inn, two miles south of Nailsworth; another specimen, apparently from the same locality, is in the collection of my friend, Dr. Wright, of Cheltenham. The foreign localities are St. Maixent, Deux-Sèvres; Masigny, Vendee; Nantua, Ain; Vezelay, Yonne; Wohnkammer, Swinitza.

AMMONITES DISCUS, *Sow.* Tab. XLI, fig. 8, 8 *a*.

NAUTILUS DISCUS, *Sow.* Min. Con., 1813, i, tab. 12.
AMMONITES DISCUS, *Sow.* Ibid., 1815, Suppl. Ind. to vol. i, p. 5.
— — *Morris.* Catal., 1854, p. 291.
— — *Oppel.* Juraformation, p. 472.

Testa discoidea, angusto umbilicato, dorse angusto acute carinatis, lateribus externe, valde compressis, lævigatis; apertura sagittæformi. Ætatê juniorí lateribus costis distantibus flexuosis.

Shell discoidal, with a narrow and deep umbilical cavity, the back acutely keeled; the sides of the volutions near to the back are much flattened and smooth; the aperture is sagittate, the margin of the umbilicus is rounded. In the young state, when the diameter does not exceed three inches, the sides are ornamented with regular distant, depressed, flexuose costæ.

The lobes are comparatively simple, with few ramifications, and have but little depth; the saddles are in a corresponding manner but little produced; they therefore differ altogether from the septa of *A. discus*, D'Orbigny, and from the *A. sub-discus*, of the same author; they are, however, more complicated than is seen in *A. discus*, Quenst. ('CEPHALOPODEN,' tab. viii, fig. 13); *A. Stauffensis*, Oppell, from the inferior Oolite of Boll, Balinger, &c. They also differ from the description given by Roemer ('Nord. Ool.,' p. 190) of an Ammonite attributed by him to *A. discus*, Sow., from the lower Coral Rag of Heersum.

The general figure is less discoidal than *A. Waterhousei*, Mor. and Lyc. (*A. discus*, D'Orb.); it differs also from that species by the absence of the flattening upon the inner portion of the sides of the volutions. From *A. sub-discus*, D'Orb., the general figure differs in the more acute back and in the smaller umbilicus.

The specimen figured in the 'Mineral Conchology,' is an adult shell, and smooth; the fine specimen selected for our illustration exhibits the septa, and also some traces of the falciform costæ proper to the young shell. I am obliged to Mr. Woodward, of the British

Museum, for information respecting it, and also for a careful drawing which exhibits its palæontological features; the specimen was obtained in the Bradford Clay of the Tetbury Road Railway Station, near Cirencester, by Professor Coleman, of the Royal Agricultural College.

Geological Positions and Localities. It has occurred at several localities in the Cornbrash, as at Wollaston, Chippenham, Trowbridge, and in Bedfordshire, but it is everywhere rare; to these positions must be added the single specimen above alluded to from the Bradford Clay, and another, in the British Museum, from the slate of Stonesfield.

GASTEROPODA.

BRACHYTREMA VARICOSA, *Lyc.* Tab. XLIV, fig. 27.

Testa parva ovata, gibbosa, spira anfractibus 5 *subplanis, costis transversalibus et longitudinalibus inæqualibus cruciatis; granulatis, granulis magnis, depressis, ultimo anfractu varicibus irregularibus duobus; apertura sinuosa, columella arcuata, canali breviusculo.*

Shell small, ovate, gibbose; spire elevated, obtuse, consisting of five, flattened volutions, with well-marked sutural depressions; encircling costæ five, of which the first and last are large, forming elevated bands, the three intermediate costæ being smaller, irregular, and unequal; they are decussated by very irregular, granulated, straight costæ, which occasionally form large varices, of which the last volution has two; these impart a distorted aspect to the lower part of the shell; the aperture is rather narrow and sinuated, the columella much curved, the canal short, the notch narrow and deep; the outer lip is thickened, but imperfect.

A short, ovate shell, with strongly marked and very irregular ornamentation; the varices are prominent only upon the two latter volutions; the straight costæ are very irregular, sometimes crowded, but occasionally very distantly arranged; the basal canal is unusually short, and curved forwards; the lips are without denticulations.

Geological Position and Locality. The Great Oolite of Minchinhampton Common; very rare, two specimens.

BRACHYTREMA BUCCINOIDEA, *Lyc.* Tab. XLIV, fig. 17.

Testa turriculata, ovali ventricosa, anfractibus 5—4 *convexis, suturis valde impressis, longitudinaliter costatis, costis* 14—16 *rectis, transversim finissime lineatis, anfractu ultimo magno, rotundo, basi attenuato, canali brevi, obliquo; apertura superne et inferne constricto.*

Shell turreted, ovately ventricose, volutions 5—4, convex, the sutures deeply impressed, longitudinally costated; the costæ, from 14 to 16 in a volution, are perpendicular, and not very strongly defined; they are decussated by fine, encircling lines; the last volution is large, rounded, attenuated at the base; the canal is short and oblique; the aperture is much contracted at the two extremities.

Geological Position and Locality. The Great Oolite of Minchinhampton, collected by E. Witchell, Esq., of Stroud.

Purpuroidea insignis, *Lyc.* Tab. XXXI, fig. 2, 2 *a*.

Purpuroidea insignis, *Lyc.* Cotteswold Hills Handbook, &c., pl. 7, fig. 8, *a*, *b*.

Testa turbinata, ovata, inflata, spira exserta, anfractibus 5 *subangulatis, tuberculis depressis* (9 *in ambitu*), *anfractu ultimo magno inflato, plerumque sine tuberculis; aperturâ magnâ ovatâ, canali leviter excavato*

Shell turbinated, ovate, inflated; spire half the length of the aperture; volutions (5) slightly angulated and flattened upon their upper surfaces, with nine small, depressed tubercles upon each volution; the last volution large, ventricose, rounded, the latter half of the circumference being destitute of tubercles, and having only oblique folds of growth; aperture ovate, columella with an umbilical groove; the basal notch is only slightly defined, the junction of the columellar and outer lips forming a gentle curvature. The shorter, angular spire, depressed tubercles, and ventricose figure of the last volution, serve to distinguish it from *P. nodulata*, the species to which it is most nearly allied. The expanded base, wide, shallow, or obsolete notch, and rounded columella, so constant in all the species of Purpuroidea, appear to me to justify a generic separation from the recent Purpura, to which they have been reunited by some French palæontologists of eminence. The genus Purpurina of D'Orbigny, exemplified by his type *P. Bellona*, is separated from Purpuroidea both by the figure of the aperture and by his description, in which the contracted basal canal is insisted upon; other so-called examples of Purpurina, in the 'Paléontologie Française,' as *Ornata*, *Bianor*, *Bixa*, and *Bathis*, have, together with a thin shell, a lengthened, subulate figure and an entire aperture; these should be placed with the Littorinidæ, and should range by the side of *Amberleya*, figured and described in the first part of this monograph. I am inclined to claim for *Amberleya* a more important position than that of a sub-genus.

The Great Oolite species of Purpuroidea have, however, been merged by Professor Morris ('Catalogue') and by Dr. Oppel ('Juraformation') with Purpurina.

Geological Position and Locality. The Great Oolite of Minchinhampton Common, associated with other species of the same genus.

Cerithium Bathonicum, *Lyc.* Tab. XLIV, fig. 19.

Testa parva subconica, apice obtuso, anfractibùs lâtis, paucis, plânis; costis (7) *rectis magnis, obtusis, striisque cingendis; apertura parva, cauda brevi.*

Shell small, somewhat conical; apex obtuse; volutions wide, few, flattened; costæ (7) straight, large, obtuse, encircled with regular striations; sutures of the volutions distinctly marked.

The costæ form straight, rounded elevations, which pass the whole length of the spire, and are only slightly interrupted by the sutures, the height of each volution being equal to about two thirds of its opposite measurement. It appears to be rare.

Length three lines, breadth half the length.

Geological Position and Locality. The upper beds of the Great Oolite near Bath, associated with numerous other minute testacea, collected by Charles Moore, Esq.

CERITHIUM BULIMOIDES, *Desl.* Tab. XLIV, fig. 3.

CERITHIUM BULIMOIDES, *Deslongchamps.* Mém. Soc. Linn. de Normand., 1848, vol. viii, pl. 11, fig. 40.
— — *D'Orb.* Prodr., i, p. 303.

Testa minima, elongato-turrita, acuta, anfractibus rotundatis, transversim striatis, longitudinaliter costatis, costis rectis, basi obliqua, transverse striata, apertura subrotunda, columella marginata, canali nullo. (Deslongchamps.)

Shell minute, elongated, turreted, acute; volutions (8) slightly convex, wide, transversely striated and longitudinally costated; costæ about 8 in a volution, perpendicular and obtuse; the sutures are deeply impressed, the aperture is oblique and rounded; there is no basal canal.

The costæ, which are large and elevated, are slightly knotted where they are crossed by three encircling lines in each volution; our specimen is imperfect at the base.

Geological Position and Localities. The Great Oolite of Minchinhampton, collected by E. Witchell, Esq. France, Luc.

CERITHIUM MULTIFORME, *Piette.* Tab. XLIV, fig. 20.

CERITHIUM MULTIFORME, *Piette.* Bull. Soc. Géol. Fr., 2 ser., t. 14, pl. 5, p. 553.

Testa parva elongato conica, anfractibus (9—10) *angustis, convexis, suturis valde impressis, costis subobliquis* (10 *ad* 12 *in ambitu*), *magnis, lineis cingendis* (5) *æqualibus; anfractu ultimo ad basin lineato, cauda brevi.*

Shell small, elongated, conical; volutions (9—10) narrow, convex, the sutures deeply impressed; costæ large, from 10 to 12 in a volution, longitudinal, but slightly oblique, and knotted by five rows of regular encircling lines, the last volution has encircling lines at the base; the canal is short.

The tumid, narrow volutions, large costæ, and deep sutures, afford strong distinctive characters, the height of each volution being only slightly greater than a third of its opposite measurement. The specimens figured by M. Piette vary much in the elevation of the spire, and consequently in the breadth of the volutions; the number of costæ likewise differ.

Geological Position and Locality. The Great Oolite of Kirklington, Oxon, collected by J. F. Whiteaves, Esq. Eparcy, France.

CERITHIUM? STRANGULATUM, *Archiac.* Tab. XLIV, fig. 2.

A shorter and less cylindrical variety of this species was figured in the first part of the 'Great Oolite' Monograph, plate ix, fig. 18. The present specimen, which agrees more nearly with the example figured by D'Archiac, has *seven* longitudinal costæ, which are conspicuous *even to the base;* the contracted, pupæform aperture, with its prominent lips, is alike in both varieties.

Cerithium strangulatum, C. Bulimoides, C. spiculum, and *C. exigua,* belong to a small group of minute, subcylindrical shells, with prominent, longitudinal costæ, and small, thickened, orbicular apertures, which have been referred to Cerithium and to Rissoa; perhaps eventually it may be deemed proper to separate them under a new generic appellation.

Geological Position and Locality. The Great Oolite of Minchinhampton Common; rare.

CERITHIUM UNDULATUM (var.), *Desl.,* sp. Tab. XLIV, fig. 6.

MELANIA UNDULATA, *Deslongchamps.* Mém. Soc. Linn. de Normand., 1842, vol. viii, pl. 11, fig. 58, var. *a.*

Testa turrita; anfractibus planis, transversim striatis, ad suturas crenulatis, longitudinaliter costatis, in ultimo anfractu costis subincurvis, basi obliqua, striata; apertura elliptica, obliqua, columella marginata; labro sinistro fissuram umbilicatem obtigente.

Var. a, testa breviori, costis et striis crassioribus, rariorisque. (Deslongchamps.)

Shell minute, turreted; volutions flattened, transversely striated, crenulated near to the sutures, and longitudinally costated; aperture elliptical, oblique.

Our example constitutes a small and short variety, with narrow volutions (about 8); the costæ are large, straight, and from 7 to 8 in a volution; they are most conspicuous near to their upper extremities, which project, forming a kind of coronary border immediately beneath the suture. Another minute specimen, apparently belonging to the same variety, has the first three volutions almost plain, and the costæ upon the succeeding volutions are but little prominent.

The typical form of the species figured by M. Deslongchamps has the costæ much more numerous and less prominent.

Geological Position and Locality. The Great Oolite of Minchinhampton, collected by E. Witchell, Esq.

RISSOA? EXIGUA, *Lyc.* Tab. XLIV, fig. 11.

Testa parva, ovato-conica, spira anfractibus (6) *plano-convexis, angustis, suturis valde impressis, costis longitudinalibus rectis, angustis,* 8—9 *in ambitu; apertura, parva, suborbiculari, labro externo simplici.*

Shell small, ovately conical; spire consisting of six flattened or slightly convex, narrow volutions, the sutures being strongly marked; longitudinal costæ elevated, narrow, perpendicular, 8 to 9 in a volution; aperture small, suborbicular, outer lip simple.

A minute lenticular shell, with about eight and a half costal spaces to a volution, the height of each volution being equal to the half of its transverse diameter; the apex is slightly obtuse, and the last volution is somewhat contracted.

Geological Position and Locality. The Great Oolite of Bussage, collected by Mr. Witchell.

CERITHIUM? SPICULUM, *Lyc.* Tab. XLIV, fig. 1.

Testa ovato-elongata, minuta, anfractibus (6) *latis subplanis, transversim striatis et longitudinaliter costatis; costis rectis* (6 *in ambitu*), *anfractu ultimo cylindrico, apertura parva, ovata, canali nullo.*

Shell minute, ovately elongated subcylindrical; volutions (6) wide, rather flattened, transversely striated, and longitudinally costated; costæ straight, six in a volution; the last volution is nearly cylindrical; the aperture is small, ovate; there is no canal.

The costæ, which have little prominence, appear to stretch continuously; the length of the shell only slightly interrupted by the sutures, which are not strongly marked; the aperture is pupæform; the general figure approximates to *C. strangulatum*, but more lengthened, and with higher volutions.

Geological Position and Locality. The Great Oolite of Minchinhampton.

CERITHIUM? COMPOSITUM, *Lyc.* Tab. XLIV, fig. 9.

Testa parva, elongato-conica, anfractibus (6) *angustis subplanis, transverse striatis et costatis; scilicet anfractu ultimo et penultimo costis crebris longitudinalibus rectis, circa* 18 *in ambitu; apertura parva, obliqua, ovata, depressa.*

Shell minute, conical, elongated; volutions (6) narrow, flattened, transversely striated, and longitudinally costated; but the costæ are limited to the two or three latter volutions, they are closely arranged, little elevated, and about eighteen in a volution; the aperture is depressed, oblique, and ovate.

Geological Position and Locality. The Great Oolite of Minchinhampton, collected by Mr. Witchell.

CERITHIUM? WITCHELLI, *Lyc.* Tab. XLIV, fig. 7.

Testa minuta subcylindrica, elongata, anfractibus (5—6) *subconvexis altis, suturis valde impressis, costis* (*circa* 15) *depressis subrectis, superne distinctis, inferne evanescentibus apertura ovata, labro externo simplici.*

Shell minute, subcylindrical, lengthened; volutions (5—6) high, rather convex, the sutures depressed and strongly defined; costæ (about 15 to a volution) depressed, distinct at the upper and vanishing towards the lower part of each volution; the aperture is of moderate size, ovate, the lips rather thickened.

The breadth of each volution is about one third more than its height; the costæ are only faintly marked; there are no traces of encircling striations or tubercles.

Geological Position and Locality. The Great Oolite of Minchinhampton, communicated by E. Witchell, Esq.

CERITHIUM? PULCHRUM, *Lyc.* Tab. XLIV, fig. 4.

Testa parva, crassa, turrito-subulata, anfractibus (8) *convexis, suturis valde impressis, costis transversis, obliquis, magnis* (*circa* 12 *in ambitu*), *lineis longitudinalibus decussatis, apertura parva ovata, canali nullo.*

Shell small, thick, elongately turreted; volutions 8, convex, the sutures deeply impressed; transverse costæ about 12 to each volution, oblique, large, decussated, and rendered nodulous by six narrow encircling lines; aperture ovate, rather contracted; no canal.

Allied to *Cerithium costellatum*, Desh., from which it differs in having fewer volutions, and in possessing encircling lines. *C. bulimoides*, Desh., with a similar general figure, has the costæ smaller, fewer, and perpendicular.

Geological Position and Locality. The Great Oolite of Minchinhampton Common, collected by Mr. Witchell.

NERINÆA GRANULATA, *Phil.*, sp. Tab. XXXI, figs. 12, 12 *a*.

TEREBRA GRANULATA, *Phil.* Geol. York., i, pl. 7, fig. 16, p. 173.
CERITHIUM GRANULATUM, *Mor.* Cat. Brit. Foss., 1854, p. 240.

Testa subulato-turrita, anfractibus numerosis angustatis, planis, sed inferne subconcavis, lineis subnodulosis irregularibus, inæqualibus (9-10) *cingendis; apertura obliqua, columella uno plicato.*

Shell elongated, turreted; volutions numerous (about twenty), narrow, flattened, but slightly contracted towards the base of each volution, and encircled with numerous (nine or ten) irregular, unequal, slightly nodulous lines; the aperture is small, subquadrate, and oblique, the columellar lip has a single strong plication.

The volutions are narrow, so that their height is little more than the half of their opposite diameters; the upper border of each is rendered prominent by the slight contraction towards the base of each volution; the single strong fold upon the pillar lip, and a trace of another mesial fold upon the outer lip, is all that can be ascertained from the single specimen at our disposal, which is also the type figured by Professor Phillips. Sixteen volutions are preserved, but probably four more would be required to render the spire perfect. *Nerinæa fasciata*, Voltz, approaches this species nearly, both in the general figure and in the ornamentation; judging, however, from specimens obtained in the Coral Rag of Yorkshire, the latter has the encircling lines more regularly disposed, and more constantly and regularly nodulous; the spiral angle also appears to be somewhat greater: it is therefore preferable to regard them as distinct species. The length of the imperfect specimen above referred to is an inch and a half, to which should be added two lines to perfect the spire; the transverse diameter of the last volution is three lines.

Geological Position and Locality. The sole example in the Scarborough Museum was obtained in the Cornbrash of that locality.

Ceritella minutissima, *Lyc.* Tab. XLV, fig. 5.

Testa minuta, elongata, spira anfractibus (4) *elevatis, subplanis; aperura ovato-elongata; columella contorta.*

Shell minute, elongated; spire with the volutions elevated, smooth, and flattened; the last volution is large, moderately convex, attenuated towards the base; the aperture is of moderate dimensions, ovately elongated; the columella is contorted at the base, as is usual in the genus.

The length of the aperture slightly exceeds one third that of the entire shell. It is allied to some of the varieties of *Ceritella parvula* (Actæonina), but is more subulate; it also approaches to *Tubifer Gerandoseus*, Piette, but is less attenuated than the latter shell.

Geological Position and Locality. Obtained, both by Mr. Witchell and myself, in the Great Oolite of Minchinhampton.

CERITELLA LYCETTEA, *Buv.*, sp., *Lyc.* and *Mor.*, sp.

> CERITELLA RISSOIDES, *Mor.* and *Lyc.* Gr. Ool. Monog., i, tab. 9, p. 7, 1850, non *Pleurotoma rissoides*, *Buv.* Mém. Soc. Verd., t. ii, pl. 6, fig. 9.
>
> ORTHOSTOMA LYCETTEA, *Buv.* Paléont. de la Mense Atlas, p. 32, 1852.
>
> TUBIFER PLICATUS, *Piette.* Bull. de la Soc. Géol. de France, 2 sér., t. xiii, pl. 13, p. 587, figs. 7—8, 1857.

I avail myself of the opportunity of giving another figure of this pretty species of Ceritella, as the magnified figure in Plate IX does not sufficiently exhibit the neatness and angularity of the volutions of the spire. M. E. Piette, in a memoir entitled "Description des Ceritheum enfouis dans les dépôts bathoniens de l'Aisne et des Ardennes," published in the work above quoted, rejects the claim of Ceritella to be regarded as a new genus; but figures the present and also another Minchinhampton species of Ceritella as examples of his proposed *new genus Tubifer*, under the names of *Tubifer plicatus* and *Tubifer Acteoniformis.* It is a satisfaction to discover this singular and unwitting testimony to the correctness of our appreciation of this generic form.

In the Atlas to the 'Palæontology of the Mense,' page 32, M. Buvignier shows that we were mistaken in supposing that our little Ceritella is the *Pleurotoma rissoides* of that author's memoir above quoted, and which he subsequently assigned to his proposed new genus *Orthostoma*; in this instance, also, our genus *Ceritella* has the priority.

CERITELLA MORRISEA, *Buv.*, sp. Pl. XLIV, fig. 22.

> CERITELLA LONGISCATA. Gr. Ool. Monog., i, tab. 9, fig. 14, p. 40, non *Pleurotoma longiscata*, Buvig., Mem. Soc. Phil. Verdun, pl. 6, fig. 8.
>
> ORTHOSTOMA MORRISEA, *Buvig.* Paléont. de la Mense Atlas, p. 32.

In this, as in the last species, the indifferent figures in the earlier memoir of M. Buvignier led to the error of assigning our Great Oolite shell to his *Pleurotoma longiscata*; the specific name proposed by that gentleman in his 'Palæontology of the Meuse' is here adopted.

CERITELLA FUSIFORMIS, *Lyc.* Tab. XLV, fig. 4.

Testa parva elongata, fusiformi, læve; anfractibus 5, *latis, subplanis, anfractu ultimo magno, subcylindrico, apertura elongata, angusta, antice et postice valde contracto.*

Shell small, elongated, fusiform, smooth; spire moderately elevated; volutions 5, wide and nearly flat, the last volution large and cylindrical; the aperture is elongated, narrow, and much contracted at both its extremities, its length slightly exceeding that of the spire.

More fusiform than other known English examples of the genus.

Geological Position and Locality. The Great Oolite of Minchinhampton, collected by Mr. Witchell.

NATICA HULLIANA, *Lyc.* Tab. XLI, fig. 2.

Testa ovata, subglobosa lævi; anfractibus 6 *valde convexis, suturis profunde impressis, spira elevato, acuto; apertura oblique ovali, antice rotundata postice angulata; columella callosa, umbilico nullo.*

Shell ovate, subglobose, smooth; volutions (6) very convex, the sutures deeply impressed; the spire is elevated, acute, the last volution being very large; the aperture is ovate, oblique, the anterior side rounded, the posterior side acute, the length exceeding a moiety of that of the entire shell; the columella is rounded, thickened, and there is no umbilicus.

Allied to *N. intermedia*, Tab. VI, fig. 1, but with a more elevated acute spire, more deeply depressed sutures, and a more globose ultimate volution; specimens vary somewhat in the figure of the last volution, but the acute, elevated, deeply sutured spire will always serve to distinguish it.

Geological Positions and Localities. I have obtained it in the Great Oolite of Minchinhampton, and in the Inferior Oolite of the same locality; Mr. Whiteaves has also kindly forwarded to me a specimen from the Great Oolite of Kirklington, Oxon; the latter, which is a young form, has the last volution slightly more globose than in the other examples.

EULIMA? LÆVIGATA, *Lyc.* Tab. XXXI, fig. 3.

Testa parva lævigata, subulata, acuta, anfractibus (*circa* 10) *planatis, angustis, suturis impressis; apertura suborbiculari obliquo, umbilico nullo.*

Shell small, smooth, elongated, apex acute; volutions (about ten) narrow, their sides flattened, the sutures distinct but not constricted; the aperture is obliquely orbicular; there is no umbilicus.

The height of each volution slightly exceeds the half of the opposite diameter; length, nine lines; diameter of the last volution, three lines.

Compared with *Eulima? communis*, the spire is more acute, the volutions more flattened, and the sutures are less deeply impressed.

Geological Position and Locality. It occurs rarely in the Cornbrash of Scarborough; the example figured is from the collection of J. Leckenby, Esq.

CHEMNITZIA VITTATA, *Phil.*, sp. Tab. XXXI, fig. 10.

MELANIA VITTATA, *Phil.* Geol. York., p. 116, pl. 7, fig. 15:
CHEMNITZIA VITTATA, *D'Orb.* Prodr., xi, et No. 29, p. 208.
— — *Mor.* Cat., 2nd edit., p. 242.
— — *Oppel.* Juraformation, p. 479.

Testa crassa, turrita, elongata, apice acuto, anfractibus (*circa* 10) *latis, in medio subdepressis, ad suturas elatis, carinis duobus instructis, suturis valde depressis; apertura, ovata basi angustata.*

Shell thick, smooth, turreted, elongated, apex acute; volutions (about 10) wide, rather depressed in their middle parts, elevated both above and beneath near to the sutures, forming two narrow, equal, cord-like carinæ; the sutures are deeply impressed; the aperture is ovate, rather small and contracted towards the base, where the extremity of the columella is conspicuous; the last volution is rendered somewhat angulated by the prominence of both the encircling carinæ; the surface is shining, with large plications of growth; a magnifier also discloses delicate, nearly regular, distantly arranged, encircling, granulated lines (about 20 to a volution), or when the surface has been slightly abraded, they appear as punctated striations.

Length, 4½ inches; transverse diameter of the last volution, 1 inch; the height of each volution is equal to 3-5ths of its transverse diameter.

The general figure is that of a lengthened cone, and the outline does not exhibit that step-like figure seen in some other allied species, as in *Chemnitzia turris* (Desl.), *C. coarctata* (Desl.), and *C. condensata* (Desl.). The two narrow and equally elevated cord-like cinctures which bound each volution, together with the somewhat angular figure of the last volution, separates it from the foregoing and all other known examples of the genus; perhaps the encircling granulated lines may also constitute a good distinctive character but it can only be discovered in very well preserved specimens. A *Chemnitzia*, in the Inferior Oolite of the Cotteswolds and of the south-western counties, which does not appear to have been figured or described, approaches near to *C. vittata*, and has sometimes been regarded as identical with it; there can, however, be no difficulty in separating specimens of the two forms, when they are well preserved. The Inferior Oolite shell is somewhat less conical, or more subulate; the sides of the volutions are more flattened; the upper cincture is rounded and distinct, but comparatively small; the lower cincture is angulated, and not cord-like; the last volution is destitute of the prominent lower cincture, which imparts an angularity to that part in the Cornbrash shell; the general figure of that volution is more lengthened and pyriform, so that the base of the aperture is wider and more produced. The Inferior Oolite shell also does not exhibit any trace of the encircling granulated lines; but possibly the test has not been preserved with sufficient delicacy to exhibit this feature, even if it originally existed; the plications of growth are also very large, so that in the latter volutions they render the carinæ distinctly nodulous; in *C. vittata* the carinæ are but slightly modified by this cause.

D'Orbigny, 'Prodrome,' has suggested that *Nerinæa suprajurensis*, D'Archiac, may be *C. vittata;* but, judging from the figure of D'Archiac, *N. suprajurensis* is more slender, with the volutions much more numerous and more narrow, the sutures are also destitute of that deeply indented figure which is so conspicuous in our Cornbrash shell. The general resemblance which *C. vittata* bears to some examples of the genus Nerinæa has led me to make a longitudinal section of it, and thus to ascertain with certainty that it cannot be assigned to that genus.

Geological Position and Locality. The Cornbrash of Scarborough and Gristhorp; it is not rare, but is very difficult to disengage from the hard limestone.

Kilvertia, *Gen. Nov.*

The views expressed on *Cerithium strangulatum*, p. 8, suggesting the propriety of erecting a new genus for the reception of that and other allied forms, have subsequently been strengthened by the examination of well-preserved specimens from the Forest Marble of Somerset and Wilts, in the collection of W. Walton, Esq., of Bath. I have now, therefore, no hesitation in proposing for these the new generic appellation Kilvertia, which will be found described in the Addenda.

Kilvertia constricta, *Lyc.* Tab. XLIV, fig. 8.

Testa parva turrita, elongata, anfractibus (8) *superne planalis, inferne ventricosis, suturis bene distinctis, lineis transversalibus et longitudinalibus, delicatissimis, cancellatis; apertura suborbiculari depressa, incrassato.*

The height of each volution is about equal to half its opposite measurement, the first encircling line beneath the suture is rather more prominent than the others; altogether there are six; their size and distances correspond nearly with the lines by which they are decussated; the aperture is imperfect at the outer lip, there is no umbilical chink.

Geological Position and Locality. A minute univalve, obtained by crushing shelly portions of the Great Oolite of Minchinhampton Common; Mr. Witchell has also kindly forwarded a specimen obtained by him at the same locality, and in the same manner.

Genus—Fibula, *Piette*, 1857.

Description des *Cerithium enfonis* dans les dépôts bathoniens de l'Aine et des Ardennes, par M. Ed. Piette, 'Bull. de la Soc. Géol. de France,' 20 Avril, 1857.

M. Piette has founded his proposed genus upon a small group of lengthened spiral univalves which possess characters intermediate and approximating them to Turritella and to Cerithium. A rounded, straight columella, with a rudimentary umbilical groove near the base, is combined with an arcuated outer lip slightly notched posteriorly at the suture; the base of the aperture forms a slight canal at its junction with the anterior extremity of the columella, or in other instances there is no canal, the base being rounded and entire, depending upon the exact period of growth at which the animal perished; the surface of the volutions is plain, or slightly ornamented with oblique costæ. The author has figured and described several species, and has characterised his genus in the following terms:—"Le principal charactère du ce genre est d'avoir une columella droite. Le bord libre est arqué, légèrement échancré à sa partie postérieure, près de la suture. L'ombilic n'est souvent que rudimentaire, à peine indiqué, et affectant seulement la columelle externe. D'autres-fois, il pénètre tout le spire. Un caractère très curieux que j'ai remarqué sur plusieurs espèces de ce genre, mais que je n'ai pu encore constater sur toutes, c'est que la columelle se termine parfois interieurement par un canal rudimentaire; que le mollusque forme ce canal et le rebouche tour à tour, pour le former ensuite de nouveau en grandissant. . . . . Ainsi il arrive souvent que parmi plusieurs *Fibula* d'une même espèce, les unes semblent se rapprocher des *Cerithium*, les autres des *Turritelles*. Cela dépend du moment où elles ont péri."

In admitting the generic value of Fibula, it becomes necessary to arrange with it the following Jurassic Testacea:—*Chemnitzia phasianoides* (Mor. and Lyc.), *Cerithium Roissii* (Mor. and Lyc.), *Turritella Roissii* (D'Arch.), and *Cerithium suturale* (Buvignier). The Great Oolite of Oxfordshire and of Minchinhampton has supplied the two following additional species.

Fibula variata, *Lyc.* Tab. XXXI, figs. 4, 4 *a*.

Testa turriculata, subventricosa; spira elongata, acuta, læve, anfractibus (11—12) *convexiusculis, angustis, suturis valde impressis; ultimo anfractu symmetrico-curvato; columella interdum ad basin subcanaliculato, aut integro, labro sinistro arcuato.*

Shell turriculated, somewhat inflated; spire lengthened, acute, smooth, consisting of 11 or 12 narrow, somewhat convex volutions, with deeply impressed sutures; the last volution is conformable with the others, and is symmetrically curved towards its anterior extremity; the aperture is oblique, contracted at the base, sometimes slightly channelled, in other instances entire and rounded; the outer lip is much curved and thin. Young specimens are less subulate, but the apex is delicately pointed, the volutions are more flattened and narrow, the sutures being less strongly marked; the latter two or three volutions in adult specimens are more inflated, and they acquire at the base a rudimentary umbilical groove.

It is nearly allied to *Fibula nudiformis*, Piette ('Bull. de la Soc. Géol. Fr.,' 1857, pl. 6, figs. 4, 5), from the Great Oolite of Rumigny, Eparcy, Poix, But, &c.; but, judging from the figures of M. Piette, his species has a shorter spire, with less strongly impressed sutures, and the last two volutions are more lengthened and cylindrical. Fibula = *Chemnitzia phasianoides*, which has the spine similarly subulate, has the volutions more flattened, and the sutures much less impressed; other recognised species are more lengthened, with flattened volutions.

Geological Position and Localities. Fibula variata has occurred rarely in the Great Oolite of Minchinhampton, and more commonly in the same formation at Kirklington, Oxon., from which place Mr. Whiteaves has kindly forwarded specimens. Examples are deposited in the British Museum, the Woodwardian Museum, Cambridge, in the collection of Mr. Whiteaves, of Oxford, and in that of the author at Scarborough.

Fibula eulimoides, *Whiteaves*, sp. Tab. XXXI, fig. 5.

Chemnitzia eulimoides, *Whiteaves*. MSS., 1859.

Testa turriculata, elongata, spira apice acuto, anfractibus (*circa* 12) *angustis, convexis superne vitta cingenda, suturis valde constrictis, ultimo anfractu rotundo; apertura obliqua, basi angusto subsinuato, columella umbilico rudimento; labro externo arcuato; anfractibus costis obliquis obscuris irregularibus.*

Shell turreted, elongated, acute; spire with about 12 volutions, narrow, convex towards their lower parts, and encircled with a narrow band at their upper borders; the sutures are deeply impressed; the last volution moderately large and rounded; the aperture is lengthened, oblique, narrow, and sinuated at the base; there is also a rudimentary umbilical groove; the outer lip is much arched; the surface has irregular, oblique, obscure costæ, which resemble lines of growth in the latter volutions.

Compared with *Fibula variata*, this species is more subulate, with a shorter last volution; the encircling band upon the upper border of each volution, the oblique costæ, and the convexity of the lower part of each volution, are also distinguishing features. *Fibula undulosa*, Piette, is more nearly allied to it, but the volutions are less narrow and more flattened or destitute of the swelling of the lower portions of the volutions which is a conspicuous feature in *F. eulimoides*. The height of each volution is equal to half of its opposite diameter.

Geological Position and Locality. The Great Oolite of Stonesfield, collected by Mr. Whiteaves.

RISSOINA WITCHELLI, *Lyc.* Tab. XLIV, fig. 12.

Testâ elongato-turrita, anfractibus 6, *latis, convexis, aut medio angulatis, longitudinaliter costellatis, costellis circa* 26—28, *rectis, simplicibus, crebris; apertura ovato-obliqua, labro extus incrassato.*

Shell elongately turreted; volutions 6, wide, convex, angulated at their middle part, and encircled with a slender band at the mesial angle; the longitudinal little ribs are very closely arranged; they are smooth, narrow, perpendicular, and are united to the mesial band; from 26 to 28 in a volution; the last volution is conformable with the others, both in figure and ornamentation; the aperture is of moderate size, it is oblique, ovate, but rather pointed at the two extremities; the columella is curved in its middle; the outer lip is thickened.

The angulated figure approximates to *Rissoina duplicata*, Sow., sp., 'Gr. Ool. Mon.,' i, p. 52); but the last volution is somewhat less expanded, the costæ upon the spire are less conspicuous, and nearly three times as numerous. Mr. Witchell, who discovered the species, has kindly communicated several specimens which agree with each other in all essential particulars.

Geological Position and Locality. The Great Oolite of Minchinhampton Common, associated with other minute testacea.

RISSOINA MILLERI, *Lyc.* Tab. XLIV, fig. 10.

Testa turrita subcylindrica, anfractibus (6) *subconvexis, angustis, longitudinaliter costellatis; costellis* 17—18, *rectis simplicibus; apertura ovato-semilunari, ad basim effusa; labro extus valde incrassato.*

Shell turreted, subcylindrical; volutions (6) convex in their middle part, narrow, but with the sutures only slightly impressed; longitudinally costellated; costellæ 17—18, perpendicular, not very prominent, and plain; aperture ovately semilunar, oblique, expanded at the base, the outer lip having a considerable thickening.

Allied to *Rissoina acuta*, Sow., but having the volutions more narrow and less convex, the sutures being less deeply impressed; the little ribs are much more numerous; the aperture is also larger and more effuse at the base.

Geological Position and Locality. One of a series of minute univalves obtained by Mr. Whiteaves in the Great Oolite of Minchinhampton Common. The name is an acknowledgment of the discrimination of the author of 'The Natural History of the Crinoidea,' who appears to have been the first person to discover the fossil riches of this locality, and whose strongly expressed opinion was originally the means of directing the attention of the present writer to it.

AMBERLEYA NODOSA, Tab. XLI, fig. 3; et Part 1, Pl. V, fig. 19, 1850.

This elegant shell was represented in so defective a manner at Plate V, fig. 19, as to render it desirable to give the present illustration, in which the aperture faces the spectator more directly. The examination of additional specimens has tended to confirm the views expressed in my manuscript of 1850, viz., that *Amberleya* should rank as a distinct genus of the *Littorinidæ*, separated from *Littorina* by the thin test, lengthened, almost turriculated, spire, and scarcely less so by the ornamentation of the volutions. Other examples of *Amberleya* will be found in *A. Jurassi*, Lyc. (the next species here described), *Turbo capitaneus*, Munst., *Turbo ornatus*, Sow., and some other allied Inferior Oolite species which have been figured by D'Orbigny as examples of *Purpurina*, but which are well distinguished from the type form of that genus (see the observations on *Purpuroidea insignis*). The generic appellation *Amberleya* was derived from Amberley Heath, which is a second name for Minchinhampton Common.[1]

AMBERLEYA JURASSI, *Lyc.* Part 1, Tab. IX, figs. 33, 33 *a*.

Testa turbinato-conicá, acutá, lineatá, anfractibus (6) *latis, tricarinatis, carina mediana, magna, subacuta, anfractu ultimo carinis* 8, *elevatis, subacutis, striis obliquis serratis, apertura magna, ovata basi subangulato, columella recta.*

Shell turbinated or conical; spire elevated, acute; volutions (6) high, with three elevated, subacute carinæ, of which the median carina is the most prominent. The last volution is large, with eight elevated carinæ, their edges being serrated by oblique, longitudinal striations; the aperture is large, ovate, somewhat angulated at the basal junction with the columella, which is straight.

Distinguished from *Turbo capitaneus*, Goldf., both by the characters of the general

[1] Subsequently to the completion of this Supplement, I have been favoured by M. Eugene E. Deslongchamps with a copy of his memoir, extracted from the fifth volume of the 'Bulletin of the Linnean Society of Normandy,' 1860, entitled "*Observations concernant quelques Gasteropodes, Fossiles, des Terrains Jurassiques places par l'auteur de la 'Paléontologie Fraçaise' dans les genres Purpurina. Trochus et Turbo. Note sur le genre Eucyclus.*" The latter proposed new genus is identical with our *Amberleya*, quoted in the memoir as *Abberleya*. The author has in this little work given an excellent critical analysis of the group of which he has proposed to constitute *Eucyclus;* these are *Purpurina Patroclus*, D'Orb., *P. Philiasus*, D'Orb., *P. ornata*, D'Orb., *P. bathis*, D'Orb., *Turbo Itys*, D'Orb., *T. niceus*, D'Orb., *T. Julia*, D'Orb., *T. capitaneus*, Munst., *T. castor*, Roem., *T. princeps*, Roem. He has also figured and described the following new species—*Eucyclus obeliscus* and *E. papyraceus*, from the Upper Lias; *E. pinguis* and *E. goniatus*, from the Inferior Oolite; the latter shell, in its general figure and plan of ornamentation has a considerable resemblance to *Amberleya nodosa*. *Eucyclus* is therefore a synonym of *Amberleya*.

figure, by the greater number of carinæ, and by the absence of tubercles upon them. *Turbo castor*, D'Orbigny, resembles it in the characters of the carinæ, but they are less numerous and less elevated; the spire is also much less produced.

Height 15 lines, transverse diameter of the last volution 11 lines.

Geological Position and Locality. The Great Oolite of Minchinhampton Common, in which it occurs rarely in the coarse volite or planking.

AMBERLEYA ARMIGERA, *Lyc.* Tab. XXXI, fig. 6.

Testa conica spira elata, apice acuta, anfractibus (5) *convexis, subangulatis, costis tuberculosis cingendis; costis duobus superioribus minoribus, inferioribus majoribus; anfractu ultimo basi carinis serratis* (5) *cingendis; umbilico nullo.*

Shell conical; spire elevated, pointed; volutions (5) convex, somewhat angulated, with four encircling costæ or carinæ, which are densely and delicately tuberculated, and decussated by fine striations, the two lower costæ being much larger than the upper, so that the lowest costa overhangs the upper part of the next volution; the base has five encircling, serrated costæ; there is no umbilicus.

Height 10 lines, length of the last volution 8 lines.

The encircling carinæ occupy nearly the entire height of each volution, leaving only narrow, deep, interstitial spaces; the lowest of the carinæ is the largest. The general figure approaches to *Turbo capitaneus*, Goldf., but the latter has the encircling carinæ much more elevated, narrow, more widely separated, and less numerous. *Turbo Phillipsi*, Mor. and Lyc., has a much shorter spire, with the volutions less ventricose or angulated; other species are more remotely allied.

Geological Position and Locality.—The Cornbrash of Scarborough, in which it is rare; from the cabinet of John Leckenby, Esq.

NERITA INVOLUTA, *Lyc.* Tab. XXXI, fig. 15.

Testa oblique ovata, lævigata, spira parva, depressa, sub-celata, anfractu ultimo per inflato; apertura ampla, labro interno convexo.

Shell oblique, ovate, smooth; spire (apparently consisting of two volutions) small, depressed, nearly concealed by the envelopment of the last volution, which is much inflated at the aperture; inner lip convex, smooth.

A plain species, distinguished by the great length and volume of the last volution; the apex of the spire is imperfect, but though quite depressed, probably it is not altogether concealed; the general figure is allied to *Neritina Staffensis*, Forbes, but the latter is more lengthened and more minute.

Geological Position and Locality. Collected by Mr. Whiteaves in the Great Oolite of Kirklington, Oxon.

Neritopsis Archiaci, *D'Arch.*, sp. Tab. XXXI, fig. 7, 7 *a*.

Turbo canaliculatus, *D'Archiac*. Mém. Soc. Géol. Fr., vol. v, pl. 29, fig. 6.
— Archiaci, *D'Orbigny*. Prodr., i, p. 300.

Testa ovato-depressa, spira elata, anfractibus tribus vel quarternis, angustis, inflatis, suturis profunde canaliculatis, anfractu ultimo costis transversis obscuris, inæqualibus, irregularibus, striisque crebris decussatis; striis tenuibus, regularibus, undatis; apertura ampla, suborbiculari.

Shell ovate, depressed; spire elevated, consisting of three or four volutions, which are narrow, inflated, their sutures deeply channeled; the last volution has some obscurely marked, irregular, and unequal transverse costa decussated by encircling striations; the striations are regular, very closely arranged, faintly impressed, with small, wave-like undulations; the aperture is large and rounded.

More depressed than *N. sulcosa* and *N. striata*, but with larger volutions, the sutures being also more deeply channeled; the ornamentation of the surface is so faintly impressed that it is scarcely perceptible without the aid of a magnifier.

Geological Positions and Localities. A rare species, from the Cornbrash of Scarborough, in the collection of Mr. Leckenby. Eparcy, France.

Trochus Guisei, *Lyc.* Tab. XLV, fig. 14.

Testa alta conica, apice acúto, anfractibus (6) *latis, leviter concavis, anfractû ultimó subangulató, basi convexo, concentrice striato; anfractibus, costis obscuris, obliquis, ad basin bi-cinctis; apertura depressa.*

Shell elevated, conical; volutions (6) wide, apex acute, slightly concave in their middle portions; the last volution angulated; the base convex, with fine, encircling striations; the sides of the volutions have delicate, obscure, oblique costæ, which are interrupted towards the base of each volution by two narrow, encircling bands; the sutures are delicate and faintly marked; the aperture is depressed.

The ornamentation of this little Trochus is regular and but faintly sculptured; the encircling bands are rendered slightly nodular by the decussating costæ.

The name in compliment to W. V. Guise, Esq., President of the Cotteswold Naturalists Club.

Geological Position and Locality. The Great Oolite of Minchinhampton, collected by E. Witchell, Esq.

Monodonta exigua, *Lyc.* Tab. XLIV, fig. 29.

Testa parva ovata, spira elata, obtusa, anfractibus tribus, subplanis, anfractu ultimo rotundo; striis tenuibus cingendis, costisque obliquis depressis, crebris, decussatis; apertura ovata, columella ad basin incrassato, subumbilicato.

Shell small, ovate; spire elevated, obtuse; volutions three, very slightly convex, the sutures distinctly marked; the last volution rounded with densely arranged, delicate, encircling striations, which are decussated upon the upper and middle portions of the volution by numerous depressed, oblique costæ, which are rendered somewhat granular by the striations; the aperture is ovate, the columella is thickened at its base, and there is a slight umbilical depression; the base of the last volution is destitute of costæ.

Geological Position and Locality. The Great Oolite of Minchinhampton Common, collected by Mr. Witchell.

Monodonta Lycetti, *Whiteaves*, MSS. Tab. XXXI, figs. 14, 14 *a*.

Testa subdepressa, spirà brevì, exserta; anfractu ultimo permagno lateribus planatis, costisque magnis, crenulatis, cingendis, basi constricta sulcò magnò.

Shell depressed; spire short and slightly mammillated, the last volution very large, angulated at its upper margin, flattened upon its sides, and slightly convex towards the base, which has a large, encircling furrow; the aperture is moderately large, wide above, contracted towards the base; the columella is rounded and very tumid.

The whole shell is encircled with rows of rope-like crenulated costæ, the upper border and flattened sides being formed by three costæ larger than the others; beneath these are five costæ diminishing symmetrically to the basal furrow; the upper surface, which is flattened, has three encircling costæ, within which rises a small, mammillated apex.

Lateral diameter one fourth greater than the height.

The large, rounded costæ, flattened sides, and depressed figure, readily distinguish it from allied species.

Geological Position and Locality. In soft, pale, gray, marly limestone (Bradford Clay?), Islip, Oxon., collected by J. F. Whiteaves, Esq.

Monodonta sparsistriata, *Lyc.* Tab. XLV, fig. 9.

Testa parva turbinata, depressa, spira anfractibus 4; convexiusculis, striis 6, cingendis; apertura ovata, basí subplanó, lævigato, umbilico nullo.

Shell small, turbinated, depressed; spire moderately elevated, consisting of four rather convex volutions, which are encircled with six regular striations; the aperture is ovate, the base somewhat flattened and smooth; there is no umbilical depression.

A small shell, with the last volution expanded and depressed; the striations are rendered slightly scabrous by very delicate, obtuse, decussating ornamentation, partially preserved, and which is only visible under a considerable magnifying power.

Geological Position and Locality. The Great Oolite of Minchinhampton Common, collected by Mr. Witchell.

MONODONTA COMPOSITA, *Lyc.* Tab. XLV, fig. 6.

Testa parva subdepressa, spira anfractibus 3—4 *angustis, angulatis, superne concavis; lineis angustis, regularibus subdistantibus cingendis, anfractu ultimo permagno, superne costulis depressis longitudinalibus lineis decussatis; aperturá magná ovatá, columella solida, dentata.*

Shell small, rather depressed; spire with the volutions (3—4), angulated in their middle part, narrow, delicate, and rather distantly arranged, the last volution is very large; the surface above the mesial keel is concave, and has closely arranged, depressed, longitudinal, little elevations or ribs, which are rendered nodulous in their upper parts by the encircling lines; the aperture is moderately large; the columella has a conspicuous thickening at its base; there is also a slight umbilical depression.

Geological Position and Locality. The Great Oolite of Minchinhampton Common, collected by Mr. Witchell.

SOLARIUM BATHONICUM, *Lyc.* Tab. XLV, figs. 27, 27 *a*, 27 *b*, 27 *c*.

Testa parva depressa, superne planata, inferné concavó, concentrice striató; anfractibus (3) *angustis tabulatis, externe subcarinatis nodulisque paucis, obscuris, coronatis; lateribus subconvexis striatis.*

Shell small, depressed, flattened above, concave beneath and concentrically striated; volutions (3) narrow, tabulated, externally slightly carinated, and with a few obscure coronary tubercles; the upper and lateral surfaces have encircling striations, the sides being slightly convex.

The specimen examined has a diameter of only two lines, the height being equal to about one third of the breadth.

Geological Position and Locality. The upper beds of the Great Oolite in the vicinity of Bath, collected by Charles Moore, Esq.

PLEUROTOMARIA GRANULATA, *Sow.*, sp. Tab. XXXI, fig. 8, 8 *a*.

TROCHUS GRANULATUS, *Sow.* Min. Con., t. 220, fig. 2.
PLEUROTOMARIA GRANULATA, *Deslong.* Mém. Soc. Linn., viii, pl. 16, figs. 6—8.
— — *D'Orb.* Prodrome, p. 267.
— — *Morris.* Cat. Brit. Foss., 1854, p. 271.
— — *Quenstedt.* Der Jura, p. 414, tab. 57, figs. 5—7.

Testa trochiformi subturrita, apice acuta, anfractibus convexiusculis, in medio angulatis, subgradatis, superne planiusculis, inferne convexiusculis, transverse et longitudinaliter striatis; sinu angusto, fascia sinus prominente,. transverse tenuissime striato, in medio anfractuum sita; ultimo anfractu ad basin subangulato, basi subconvexa, concentrice striata; umbilico minimo aut subnullo; apertura subquadrata labro sinistro crassiori reflecto.

Shell trochiform, subturreted; apex acute; volutions rather convex, angulated in their middle portions, or somewhat step-like, the upper half of each volution being flattened, the lower half rather convex; the surface is longitudinally and transversely striated, the decussations of the striæ forming granules or tubercles, of which there are usually five rows above and four beneath the mesial angle, the uppermost row having the tubercles more prominent and separated than the others; the sinus is narrow, and of moderate depth; the fascia of the sinus is prominent, with fine, transverse striations, and placed in the middle of the volution; the last volution has the base somewhat angulated; the base is convex, and concentrically striated; the umbilicus is very small or almost none; the aperture is subquadrate, the left lip being thickened and reflected.

A beautiful species, not very regular in the disposition of the longitudinal and transverse striations, but for the most part those beneath the mesial fascia are more strongly marked than above.

The height of the entire shell and diameter of the last volution are equal in the specimen figured; others have the height somewhat greater; 16 lines is a medium size.

Geological Positions and Localities. The Inferior Oolite of the south-west of England and the Cornbrash of the coast of Yorkshire. Our specimen is from Gristhorpe, in the collection of Mr. Leckenby. It is moderately abundant.

CYLINDRITES EXIGUA, *Lyc.* Tab. XLIV, fig. 14.

Testa parva, subcylindricâ, spira elata conica, apice obtuso, anfractibus 5, latis, paululum convexis, spira vero lateribus subconcavis; anfractu ultimo margine rotundato, apertura angustissimo.

Shell minute, subcylindrical; spire elevated, conical, its sides being, however, slightly concave, and its apex obtuse; the volutions are five in number, moderately wide and slightly convex; the last volution is lengthened, its upper margin is rounded; the aperture is very narrow.

More lengthened and attenuated, the spire more elevated, and its apex more obtuse, than in *C. acutus*, to which species it appears to be most nearly allied.

Geological Position and Locality. The Great Oolite of Minchinhampton, collected by E. Witchell, Esq.

CYLINDRITES TURRICULATUS. Tab. XLIV, figs. 26, 26 *a*.

CYLINDRITES TURRICULATUS, *Lycett.* Proc. Geol. Soc., 1853, p. 342, vol. ix, pl. 14, fig. 8.

Testâ elongatâ, subylindricâ; spirâ magnâ, acutâ; anfractibus (8) *convexis; suturis profunde impressis; anfratu ultimo ovato; apertura angustata.*

Shell elongated, ovately cylindrical; spire lengthened, its apex acute; volutions (8 in the adult state) convex, their sutures deeply impressed, the last volution ovately cylindrical; aperture narrow.

The general figure somewhat resembles *C. altus*, but the volutions are more numerous, and are not flattened, as in that shell; the subovate figure and elevated spire readily distinguishes it from other contemporaneous species. The length of the aperture is equal to three fifths of the entire shell.

Geological Position and Localities. Formerly collected at Ponton, Lincolnshire, by Professor Morris; recently it has been obtained in the Great Oolite of Minchinhampton by E. Witchell, Esq.

ACTEON BATHONICUM, *Lyc.* Tab. XLIV, fig. 16.

Testa parva ovata, spira elevata, anfractibus (4) *subplanis, ad suturam angulatis, suprâ angulam spiratis, tabulatis, ultimó anfractù striis regularibus tenuibus; apertura ovali, posticè angustatâ.*

Shell small, ovate, spire elevated, volutions (4) rather flattened upon the sides and elevated, their superior borders forming a sharply defined angle; above the angle is a flattened sutural area, the last volution has regular, delicate, encircling striations; the aperture is moderately large, ovate; the posterior extremity narrow; its length is more than half the height of the shell.

A minute but well-marked species, with a spire larger, more lengthened, more angulated and more pyramidal than *Auricula Sedgvici*, Phil.; it is more nearly allied to *Tornatella Aviothensis*, Buv., 'Pal., Mense,' pl. xxiii, figs. 32, 33; and to *Tornatella pulla*, Kock and Dunk., 'Ool.,' pl. xi, fig. 11; but these have the spire more lengthened and less flattened.

Geological Position and Locality. One of a series of minute and, for the most part, dwarfed testacea, collected by Mr. Moore from the upper portion of the Great Oolite in the vicinity of Bath.

Acteon phasianoides, *Lyc.* Tab. XLIV, fig. 28.

Testa parva ovato-elongata, sublæve, spira alta, turriculata afractibus 5, *superne convexis, inferne planatis, anfractu ultimo magno, ovato, basi tenerrime striato, apertura elliptia, columella recta, uniplicatá.*

Shell small, ovately elongated, nearly smooth; spire elevated, turreted; volutions 5, convex above, the sides flattened, and the sutures strongly defined; the last volution slightly exceeds half the entire length of the shell; it is ovate, its base having some delicate, regular spiral striations; the aperture is elliptical, the columella straight, having a single plication.

Possibly the entire surface may have had striations still more delicate than those at the base, but no traces of them remain; the spire is larger, and the volutions are more inflated, than is usually seen in this genus.

Geological Position and Locality. The Great Oolite of Minchinhampton, collected by E. Witchell, Esq.

Acteonina brevis. Tab. XLI, fig. 6.

Under the title of *Cylindrites brevis*, an immature and imperfect example was figured in the first part of the 'Great Oolite,' Monograph. Tab. VIII, figs. 13, 13, *a*; the fine example now figured was collected by Mr. Whiteaves in the Great Oolite of Kirklington, Oxon., and exhibits in the more advanced stage of growth a change in the last volution, whose upper margin rises higher than those of the preceding volutions, thus rendering the vertex slightly concave, a change with which recent conchology presents many analogous instances. The figure of the columella leaves no doubt that it is an *Acteonina*.

Acteonina Kirklingtonensis, *Lyc.* Tab. XLI, fig. 5.

Testa ovato-cylindrica, elongata, lævigata, spira obtusa, perspicua, anfractibus (4) *depressis, columella ad basin cortorta, apertura inferne elongata, ovata.*

Shell ovately cylindrical, elongated, smooth; spire obtuse, depressed, the upper margins of the volutions exposed and rounded; columella contorted at its base, forming with inner lip an umbilical depression; aperture narrow above, pyriform, lengthened, and rather pointed at its base.

A lengthened cylindrical *Acteonina*, with an exposed, obtuse spire, which does not rise higher than the upper border of the last volution; a small specimen is, in proportion, somewhat shorter. It is nearly allied to *Bulla? primæva*, Deslongchamps, 'Mém. Soc. Linn. de Normand.' t. 7., pl. x, figs. 23, 24; the latter is a larger shell, with the spire less exposed, and the aperture at the base much less lengthened and less pointed; it is therefore probably distinct. The elongation of the anterior part of the aperture appears also to separate it from *Acteonina convoluta*, Lyc., 'Cotteswold Hills,' p. 125, the left-hand figure, pl. iv. As three specimens of each form of different states of growth have been examined, we may rely upon the persistence of this distinctive feature.

Length 11 lines, opposite diameter 6 lines.

Geological Position and Locality. The Great Oolite of Kirklington, Oxon., collected by Mr. Whiteaves, who has obtained several specimens.

ACTEONINA LUIDII, *Luid.*, sp. Tab. XXXI, fig. 16.; Tab. XLI, fig. 18, *a*, *b*, *c*.

COCHLITES LUID. Lithoph. Brit. Ichnogr., 1699, 417.
ACTÆONINA LUIDII, *Mor.* Cat. Brit. Foss., 1854, p. 234.

Testa subcylindrica, antice mediocriter attenuato, postice truncato, anfractu ultimo superne angulato, lateribus planatis, spira depressa, anfractibus (4—5) *angustis, apice exserto.*

Shell short, subcylindrical, moderately attenuated anteriorly, truncated abruptly posteriorly; volutions (4—5) depressed, narrow, their upper margins exposed upon the flattened posterior surface; the apex is slightly elevated and obtuse; the last volution has its posterior margin angulated and its sides flattened. Casts exhibit the upper margin of the last volution somewhat rounded, and also the edges of the other volutions.

Height one third greater than the transverse diameter.

Geological Position and Localities. The Forest Marble of Kidlington, Oxon., collected by Mr. Whiteaves, and of Cirencester, Gloucestershire, collected by myself, at both of which localities it is rare.

ACTEONINA CANALICULATA, *Lyc.* Tab. XXXI, figs. 9, 9 *a*, 9 *b*.

Testa subcylindrica lævigata vel ovata, spira exserta, obtusa, anfractibus (7) *angustis, subplanis, superne convexis, et canaliculatis, ultimo anfractu subcylindrico, basi . . . . ?*

Shell subcylindrical, smooth, or ovate; spire elevated, obtuse, consisting of 7 narrow volutions, which have their sides flattened, their upper borders being rounded and deeply channeled; the last volution is nearly cylindrical, the aperture is not exposed, and the base is imperfect.

The characters of the spire, with its numerous narrow-channeled volutions, without angularity, appears to be sufficient to distinguish the species.

Geological Position and Locality. The Great Oolite of Kirklington, Oxon., obtained by Mr. Whiteaves.

Acteonina Scarburgensis, *Lyc.* Tab. XXXI, figs. 13, 13 *a.*

Testa ovata ventricosa lævigata, spira brevi obtusa, anfractibus (4) *convexis, anfractu ultimo ad suturam subcanaliculato; apertura angustata, columella ad basin marginata.*

Shell ovately ventricose, smooth; spire short, obtuse, consisting of four narrow, convex volutions; the last volution has the sides slightly convex, its upper margin rounded and slightly channeled at the suture; the aperture is narrow, somewhat expanded at the base, which is marginated at its junction with the columella.

A handsome ventricose shell, shorter and more tumid than *A. convoluta*, Lyc., which appears to approximate more nearly to it than other recognised species.

Length 14 lines, diameter of the last volution 10 lines, length of the aperture 11 lines. The specimen figured is from the fine collection of Mr. Leckenby; the test, which is thin, is partially preserved; it has a corneous aspect. A single specimen.

Geological Position and Locality. The Cornbrash of Scarborough.

Acteonina scalaris, *Lyc.* Tab. XLIV, fig. 18.

Testa parva, subcylindracea, spira brevi, acuta, anfractibus 4, *lateribus angustis planatis, marginibus acutis, superne tabulatis; aperturá elongatá, basi elliptico curvato.*

Shell small, subcylindrical; spire short, but elevated and acute, consisting of four narrow volutions, which are flattened upon their sides, their upper borders are acute, their upper areas are flattened; the aperture is moderately large and lengthened, its base is elliptically curved.

The length is 3 lines, the opposite diameter but little exceeds 1 line.

The upper angle of each volution is acute, and even slightly projects outwards, a character which is not seen in any other known species with an elevated spire. Possibly this is the young condition of a much larger species.

Geological Position and Locality. The Great Oolite of Kirklington, Oxon., collected by Mr. Whiteaves.

Dentalium entaloides, *Desl.* Tab. XXXI, figs. 11, 11 *a*, 11 *b.*

Dentalium ...., *Phillips.* Geol. York., i, pl. 4, fig. 37.
— glabellum, *Bean.* Cornbrash Fossils, Mag. Nat. Hist., 1839, without figure or description.
— entaloides, *Deslongchamps.* 1842. Mém. Soc. Linn., vii, p. 128, tab. vii, figs. 36—38.
— — *D'Orb.* Prodrome, i, p. 272, No. 205.
— Parkinsoni, *Quenstedt.* Handbook, t. 35, fig. 19.

DENTALIUM PARKINSONI, *Quenst.* Der Jura, p. 484, t. 65, figs. 5, 6.
— ENTALOIDES, *Oppel.* Die Juraformation, 1856-8, p. 390.
— ANNULATUM, *Bean, Leckenby.* Journ. Geol. Soc., 1858, vol. iv.

Testa crassa, tereti, subarcuata, sæpius nitida, striis tenuissimis densissimis paululim obliquis ornata. (Deslongchamps.)

Shell thick, tubular, round, smooth, shining, slightly curved; encircled with striations, which are somewhat oblique and strongly impressed towards the posterior or smaller extremity, anteriorly they are more faintly and densely arranged and ultimately disappear, the surface having some irregular annular folds of growth. Length of an imperfect Cornbrash specimen 24 lines, the larger diameter 2¼ lines. The Calcareous Grit examples have larger dimensions, they are of more advanced growth, and have the greater portion of their cylinder devoid of striations.

The Cornbrash imperfect specimens are less slender and more straight than the figures of *D. Parkinsoni* given by Professor Quenstedt, and more nearly accord with those of *D. entaloides*, Deslongchamps; but the specimens figured by Quenstedt differ also from each other in their attenuation and curvature. *Dentalium cinctum*, Goldfuss, has encircling striations, without obliquity; *D. undulatum* of the same author has the figure somewhat compressed; *D. tenue*, Goldf., is more slender and more nearly cylindrical.

Geological Position and Locality. Dentalium entaloides appears to have a considerable geological range; the Cornbrash of Scarborough has produced a few specimens; Mr. Leckenby has also obtained it in the Kelloway Rock and the Calcareous grit of the same locality. *D. entaloides* was obtained by M. Deslongchamps in the Inferior Oolite of Moutiers and Bayeaux; by Dr. Oppel in the beds with *Ammonites Parkinsoni* at Mont d'Or, near Lyons; in Swabia it occurs at the upper boundary of the Lower Oolite (Braun Jura e. Quenst.) at Ehningen and Balingen.

TROCHUS STRIGOSUS, *Lyc.* Tab. XLV, fig. 12.

Testa alta, conica, transversè costellatà, costellis granulosis æqualibus; anfractibus (5) *subplanis, quadricostatis et vitta striata anteriora; ultimo anfractu obtusè carinató; basi concava; columella obliqua; apertura sub-triangulari.*

Shell elevated, conical, transversely costellated; costellæ, four to a volution, granulated and equal; the anterior border of each volution has also a depressed, striated band; the volutions, about five in number, are flattened, and the last volution is rounded; the base has a few striations; the columella is oblique, and the aperture somewhat triangular.

The ornamentation is strongly marked and regular; the height and breadth are nearly equal; the sole specimen is rather imperfect at the apex.

Geological Position and Locality. The Cornbrash of Gristhorp Bay, near Scarborough, in the collection of Mr. Leckenby.

BIVALVIA.

GRYPHÆA MINUTA, *Sow.* Tab. XL, fig. 30.

GRYPHÆA MINUTA, *Sowerby.* Min. Con., tab. 547, fig. 4.
— — *Morris.* Catal. Brit. Foss., p. 186.

Testa parva, valva majora suborbiculata, umboni incurvo, lateré anticó sulcó breví instructó. Valva altera ignota.

Shell small; the larger valve subglobose, suborbicular; the beak produced, incurved, and nearly straight, only slightly roughened by the area of attachment; the anterior side with a short sulcation, but no distinct lateral lobe. The smaller valve is unknown.

A minute Gryphæa, of which several specimens have been obtained by Mr. Witchell in the Minchinhampton Great Oolite; it has no well-defined distinctive features, and would scarcely have been deemed worthy of notice had it not been figured by Mr. Sowerby from Ancliff.

PLACUNOPSIS SEMISTRIATUS, *Bean*, sp. Tab. XXXIII, figs. 9, 9 *a*.

ANOMIA SEMISTRIATA, *Bean.* Mag. Nat. Hist., 1839, p. 61, fig. 21.

Testa, valva majora convexa, subobliqua, ovato rotundata, apice submarginalí, acutá, lamellís concentricís, irregularibús, superne lævigata, inferne lineis radiantibus subæqualibus nodulosis ornata. Valva affixa ignota.

Shell with the larger valve ovate, slightly oblique, convex; the apex pointed, and placed near to the margin; the surface has numerous irregular, concentric lamellæ; the lower portion has numerous radiating lines, which are nearly equal, granulated, and undulated. The attached valve has not been obtained.

The test appears to be less delicate than is found in some other examples of the genus, and is usually affixed to another shell, more especially to *Terebratula lagenalis*, so that it is scarcely possible to obtain a specimen whose figure has not been affected by some extraneous body. The general aspect has much resemblance to *Placunopsis Jurensis* ('Gr. Ool. Monog. Biv.,' tab. i, fig. 13), but the latter has the ornamentation of the surface much more strongly defined, with larger and more densely arranged radiating lines. In *P. semistriatus* these can only be discerned with a magnifier.

Geological Position and Locality. The Cornbrash of the Yorkshire Coast, at Gristhorpe and Scarborough, where it is moderately rare. The upper portion of the Inferior Oolite in the Cotteswold Hills has a species probably identical with this Placunopsis, and possessing a similar kind of ornamentation.

PECTEN RIGIDUS, *Sow.* Tab. XL, fig. 16.

PECTEN RIGIDUS, *Sow.* Min. Con., t. 205, fig. 8.
— — *Morris.* Catal., 1854, p. 177.
— — *D'Orb.* Prodr. Et., xi, p. 314.
— — *Oppel.* Juraformation, p. 492.

Testa ovato-orbiculari, sub-æquivalvi, plano-convexa, reticulata, costis depressis, crebis, sub-regularibus, divergentibus, lamellis concentricis angustis, hinc inde decussatis; auriculis inæqualibus, transverse lamellosis, lamellis elevatis, crebris.

Shell ovately orbicular, equivalve or subequivalve, moderately convex; costæ diverging, depressed, slightly unequal, sometimes undulating and closely arranged, crossed by narrow, irregular, concentric lamellæ, which are sometimes elevated upon the ribs, and in other instances form only narrow lines across the interstitial spaces, giving to them a punctated aspect; auricles large, unequal, with numerous transverse, narrow, elevated lamellæ.

Geological Positions and Localities. It is not uncommon in the upper portion of the Great Oolite, in the Forest Marble, and in the Cornbrash of many localities, as at Castle Combe; Stanton, near Chippenham; Kidlington, Oxon.; Rushden, Northamptonshire; Luc, France.

PECTEN GRIESBACHI, *Lyc.* Tab. XXXIII, figs. 6, 6 *a*.

Testa, valva sinistra crassa subæquilaterali acuta, compressá, auriculis magnis subæqualibus, radiatim costata et concentricè striatá, costis (circa 26) superne angustis subæqualibus transverse striatis, inferne obsoletis; striis concentricis, regularibus tenuissimis; auriculis transverse plicatis. Valva altera compressa interne lævigata.

Shell with the left valve thick, subequilateral, compressed, acute; auricles large, nearly equal, and transversely plicated; the surface is ornamented with about twenty-six very delicate, radiating costæ, which are striated, narrow, nearly equal, and regular; they are distinct towards the apex, but are only faintly traced towards the middle and lower part of the valve; the concentric striations are very fine and regular over the whole surface; a few faintly marked plications of growth are visible towards the lower border. The external surface of the right valve has not been exposed; its convexity is about equal to that of the other, its inner surface being smooth, without traces of the exterior ornamentation.

Geological Position and Locality. The Great Oolite of Wollaston, Northamptonshire, in the cabinet of the Rev. A. W. Griesbach.

PECTEN INÆQUICOSTATUS, *Phil.* Tab. XXXIII, figs. 1, 1 *a*.

PECTEN INÆQUICOSTATUS, *Phil.* Geol. York., i, pl. 4, fig. 10.
— — *D'Orb.* Prodrome, p. 373.
— OCTOCOSTATUS, *Roemer.* Ool., p. 69, pl. 3, fig. 18.
— INÆQUICOSTATUS, *Mor.* Cat. Brit. Foss., 1854, p. 176.
— — *Oppel.* Juraformation, p. 607.

Testa ovato-acuta, convexa, longitudinaliter, 8 *costata, concentrice lineata, costis convexis latis sulcis conformibus in dorso hinc inde dentatis, duobus mediis latioribus, lineis exilibus confertis sublamellosis auriculis subæqualibus longitudinaliter lineatis.* (*Roemer pro valva dextra.*) *Valva sinistra costis* (8) *angustis, elevatis rotundis asymmetricis, subnodosis, interstiis latis irregulariter concentrice striatis.*

A convex, subæquivalve, acute-pointed Pecten, with large, nearly equal auricles; the surfaces of both the valves having irregular, concentric striations and several large folds of growth. The right valve has broad, slightly elevated costæ (8), which are unequal and slightly defined towards the posterior side, separated by narrow and but little depressed sulcations, which are distinct upon the inner surface of the valve; the left valve has eight narrow, elevated, but rounded costæ, of which those upon the sides are small and unsymmetrical; the intervening spaces are broad upon the middle of the valve, and very narrow laterally; the auricles are obliquely lineated.

Geological Positions and Localities. Rarely in the Cornbrash and Kelloway Rock of Scarborough, more commonly in the Coralline Oolite of Malton, but it is seldom well preserved at either of these geological positions; Roemer makes a similar statement respecting its occurrence at Lindner Berges.

PECTEN ARTICULATUS, *Schloth.* Tab. XXXIII, fig. 12.

PECTEN ARTICULATUS, *Schloth.* Petref., pp. 227, 228.
— — *Goldf.* Petref., p. 47, tab. 90, fig. 10.
— — *Roemer.* Verst., p. 68.

Testa ovato-acuta convexa, costis angustis acutis, subæqualibus cingulatis acuminatis, sulcis duplo latioribus concavis subtillissime transversim striatis, auriculis inæqualibus lamelloso-lineatis costulisque virgatis. (Goldfuss.)

Shell ovately pointed, convex; radiating costæ elevated, narrow, acute, more or less unequal, with acute transverse lamellæ; interstitial sulcations wider than the costæ, concave, with delicate transverse striations; auricles unequal, with radiating ribs crossed by lineal lamellæ. The more numerous ribs (about twenty-four), their irregularity and inequality, will distinguish it from *P. vimineus*, Sowerby, a species which abounds in the Inferior Oolite.

Geological Positions and Localities. Pecten articulatus occurs in the Cornbrash of the Yorkshire coast, and more frequently in the Calcareous Grit and Coralline Oolite of the same county.

PECTEN RUSHDENENSIS, *Lyc.* Tab. XXXIII, figs. 4, 4 *a*, 4 *b*, 4 *c*.

Testa æquivalvi, suborbiculari, acuta, auriculis inæqualibus (auricula antica majora), valvis plano-convexis rugis concentricis elevatis, crebris, inferne squamatis, squamis brevibus, regularibus delicatissime instructis.

Shell equivalve, suborbicular, acute, moderately convex; auricles unequal (the anterior one being the larger); the valves have a few plications of growth, and very densely arranged, elevated, concentric rugæ, which are slightly wrinkled towards the apices, but towards the middle of the valves become short, regular, scabrous elevations, disposed checker-wise with those above and beneath, so that when viewed obliquely the ornamentation resembles that of an engine-turned watch; this is more especially the case with the surface of the right valve, which has the concentric rugæ more delicate and closely arranged, and also the scabrous elevations; in other respects the valves are alike in the design of their ornamentation.

A beautiful suborbicular species; the minute scabrous elevations arrest the finger when it is passed upwards over the surface. It is very rare.

Geological Position and Locality. The Cornbrash of Rushden, Northamptonshire, in the collection of the Rev. A. W. Griesbach.

PECTEN WOLLASTONENSIS, *Lyc.* Tab. XXXIII, figs. 2, 2 *a*, 2 *b*, 2 *c*.

Testa ovato-orbiculari compressa, æquivalvi, auriculis inæqualibus transverse plicatis et radiatim costatis; valva dextra concentrice striata et radiatim costata; striis tenuissimis, inferne lamelloso-rugosis; costis inæqualibus nodosis; numerosis, inferne evanescentibus; valva sinistra striis subtillissimis concentricis regularibus.

Shell ovately orbicular, slightly convex, equivalve, with unequal auricles, the anterior one being the larger; they have numerous transverse plications and two or three radiating costæ; the surface of the right valve has concentric striations and radiating costæ; the striations are very fine and irregular; the middle and lower portion of the valve is occupied by irregular, scabrous, concentric plications; the radiating costæ are very numerous, irregular, and knotted; they gradually disappear towards the middle of the valve. The left valve has very delicate, regular, concentric, densely arranged striations.

This rare Pecten differs from *Pecten Dyonisius*, Buv., chiefly in being equivalve, and in the dissimilarity of the ornamentation in the opposite valves.

Geological Position and Locality. The Great Oolite of Wollaston, Northamptonshire, in the cabinet of the Rev. A. W. Griesbach.

PECTEN MICHELENSIS, *Buvignier*. Tab. XXXIII, fig. 3.

PECTEN CANCELLATUS, *Bean*, on Cornbrash Fossils, Mag. Nat. Hist., 1839 (no figure or description).
— MICHELENSIS, *Buvignier*. Paléont. de la Meuse, Atlas, p. 24, pl. 32, fig. 7.

Testa orbiculari, depressa maxima, concentrice rugosa et obsolete lineis subpunctatis irregulariter radiata, ad umbones costulis convexis, distantibus, regularibus radiantibus et concentricis decussata; umbonibus acutis; auriculis inæqualibus, transverse costellatis. (Buvignier.)

Shell orbicular, depressed, large, rugose in the adult state, with slightly defined, irregular, radiating lines and large, irregular, concentric lamellæ; the umbones are acute, the auricles are unequal, the posterior auricle with large, rugose, transverse striations; the surface near to the umbo has regular, radiating costæ, slightly knotted where they are decussated by the concentric costæ, which are nearly regular, and somewhat less closely arranged than those which radiate.

The foregoing description applies to the right valve; the change which the surface undergoes in acquiring its adult condition is very striking, and is slightly indicated by the few last lamellæ upon the specimen figured; a very fine example in the Scarborough Museum, from the Coralline Oolite of Malton, shows that it ultimately acquired the aspect of Hinnites, thus losing all regularity in its ornamentation, and having very large, irregular, squamose lamellæ; the left valve has not been obtained.

Pecten retiferus ('Gr. Ool. Monogr. Biv.,' p. 9, tab. i, fig. 15) approaches to it in the kind of ornamentation, but has the radiating costæ larger and more distant, as are also the concentric lamellæ; the umbones are less acute, and the auricles, which have a different figure, are more nearly equal. Under the name of *Pecten cancellatus*, it was inserted by Mr. Bean in his list of Cornbrash fossils, but without either figure or description. The splendid work of M. Buvignier on the 'Palæontology of the Meuse' exemplifies an aged specimen, together with the progressive changes which the ornamentation of the surface underwent.

Geological Positions and Localities. The specimen figured is from the Cornbrash of Scarborough; it occurs also in the Coralline Oolite of Malton; M. Buvignier has recorded it in the same formation at St. Mihiel and at Donaument.

PECTEN ANISOPLEURUS, *Buv.* Tab. XXXIII, figs. 5, 5 *a*.

PECTEN ANISOPLEURUS, *Buvignier*. Paléont. de la Meuse, Atlas, p. 23, pl. 19, figs. 31—35.

Testa subrotunda, depressa, inæquivalvi; valva sinistra subplana, quinquecostata, lamellis concentricis, fibrosis, interdum interruptis, subtextis, ornata; costis distantibus, convexis, squamatis, intervallis, triplolatioribus; costis extremis minoribus; auriculis subæqualibus, transverse lamellosis. Valva dextra convexiori quinquesulcata, concentrice tenuiter lamellosa; sulcis concavis, costis alteræ valvæ respondentibus; costis latioribus convexis, subdivisis. (Buvignier.)

Shell suborbicular, inequivalve, depressed. The left valve nearly flat, with fine radiating ribs, separated by very wide intervals; the costæ have large, squamous plications, rather irregular, and nearly disappearing as they approach the apex, the costæ near to the margins being the smaller; the intervals between the costæ have five regular, concentric, squamous plications; the auricles are nearly equal, they are transversely lamellated. The right valve is convex, with five radiating sulcations, corresponding to the five costæ of the other valve; the whole surface of the valve is covered with delicate, regular, concentric, closely arranged lamellæ. The interior of the valves present an appearance corresponding with the ornamentation of the exterior.

Height rather greater than the breadth, and thrice the diameter through both the valves.

Geological Position and Locality. The Cornbrash of Scarborough and of Northamptonshire; the collections of Mr. Leckenby and of the Rev. A. W. Griesbach contain fine specimens. M. Buvignier quotes the species from the lower ferruginous beds of the Oxford Clay, Ardennes and Meuse.

HINNITES GRADUS, *Bean*, sp. Tab. XXXIII, figs. 10, 10 *a*.

PECTEN GRADUS, *Bean*. Mag. Nat. Hist., 1839.

Testa valva sinistra, ovato orbiculari convexo-plana, radiatim undulato costata et concentrice lineata; umboni acuto submediano, auricula antico magno, oblique radiatim lineatis; auricula postica subnullo; costulis radiantibus numerosis, costa una majora et minora alternatim instructis, semel varicibus duobus radiantibus magnis. Lineis decussantibus densis regularibus; valva affixa ignota.

Shell with the left valve ovately orbicular, somewhat convex, the surface irregular, with unequal, undulating, radiating costæ and concentric lines; umbo acute, mesial straight, the anterior auricle large, with oblique radiating lines, the posterior auricle scarcely produced; the surface of the valve has very numerous, unequal, radiating, rounded costæ, in two series, a larger and a smaller costæ being arranged alternately; there are also two elevated, irregular, large, radiating varices upon the middle of the valve, as in *Hinnites abjectus*. The costæ are about equal in width to the intercostal spaces; the entire surface of the shell has densely arranged, very regular, concentric lines, which are scarcely visible without the aid of a magnifier. The other valve is unknown.

Nearly allied, both in figure and aspect, to *Hinnites abjectus*, from which it is distinguished by the regularity and smoothness of the costæ and by the regular, concentric lines crossing both the costæ and the intercostal spaces; the latter are equal in width to the costæ, whereas *H. abjectus* cannot be said to have any intercostal spaces, every part of the surface being occupied by unequal, crowded, nodose costæ; the two large, radiating, nodose, elevated varices are alike in both species.

The specimen figured is the original example, which belonged to Mr. Bean; it has lost a portion of the surface near to the lower border, and also a portion of the apex, nor will it appear remarkable that only a single specimen of a shell so thin and fragile should have been disengaged from a rock so intractable as the Cornbrash of Yorkshire.

Geological Position and Locality. The Cornbrash of Scarborough, in the collection of Mr. Leckenby.

AVICULA CLATHRATA, *Lyc.* Tab. XL, figs. 7, 7 *a*, 7 *b*.

Testa parva suborbiculari, convexo-plana, valva sinistra auriculis subæqualibus magnis; superficie costis radiantibus (*circa* 24) *acutis, regularibus et nodosis, lineis concentricis distantibus decussatis; valva altera subplana, lævigata, inornata.*

Shell small, suborbicular; the left valve with a low convexity, with large and nearly equal auricles; the surface of the valve has about twenty-four regular, acute, and slightly knotted radiating costæ, which are decussated by a few distantly arranged, concentric, elevated lines; the costæ radiate equally over the auricles and the middle of the shell. The right valve is more flattened, it is smooth and destitute of ornamentation. Diameter, about three lines.

Geological Position and Locality. The Great Oolite of Minchinhampton; a single specimen.

AVICULA SUBCOSTATA, *Roemer*, sp. Tab. XL, fig. 24.

MONOTIS SUBCOSTATA, *Roemer*. Nord. Ool., p. 75, t. 4, p. 7.

Testa orbiculari subobliqua, convexa, longitudinaliter costulata, subtillissime concentrice striata, costulis (10—14) *remotis superne evanescentibus, inæqualibus, auricula lævi, umbonibus minimis antrorsum incurvis. Valva sinistra.* (Roemer.)

Shell orbicular, rather oblique, convex, longitudinally costulated, and with very delicate concentric striations; costellæ (10—14) acute, distinct, rather unequal, and disappearing towards the umbo; auricles plain; umbo small, curved forwards. The right valve is not known.

A small shell; much less convex, less oblique, with a shorter hinge-line and more delicate ribs than *A. costata*, Sow.

Geological Position and Locality. The Great Oolite of Minchinhampton Common, at which place it is very rare.

GERVILLIA TORTUOSA, *Sow.*, sp. var. Tab. XL, fig. 25.

GASTROCHÆNA TORTUOSA, *Sow.* Min. Con., t. 526, fig. 1.
— — *Phil.* Geol. York., t. 11, fig. 36.
GERVILLIA TORTUOSA, *Mor.* Catal. Brit. Foss., 1854, p. 168.
— — *Oppel.* Juraformation, p. 418.

Testa elongata, antice tortuosa, postice recto, attenuato, umboni perobliquo, subterminali; linea cardinis obliquissimo; margine antico undulato, plicis concentricis læviter instructis. Valva dextra subconcava, tortuosa; facies interna ignota.

Shell elongated, convex, and contorted anteriorly, straight and attenuated posteriorly; umbo very oblique, with a small anterior auricle; hinge-border very oblique, anterior border undulated; the surface of the valve has five irregular, concentric plications upon its anterior side. The right valve is twisted conformably with the left valve; it is somewhat concave. The cardinal ligamentary pits have not been exposed in the present variety. Compared with the Inferior Oolite forms of *Gervillia tortuosa*, this variety is more narrow and less contorted, having the posterior extremity nearly straight; the umbo is also more acute, and the surface is destitute of the large, rugose, concentric plications which are conspicuous upon well-preserved examples of the typical form. So much variability, however, is seen in the contorted species of Gervillia that I prefer to regard the present as pertaining to *G. tortuosa*, but constituting a well-marked variety.

Geological Position and Locality. It occurs rarely in the Cornbrash of Scarborough; from the collection of Mr. Leckenby.

GERVILLIA ISLIPENSIS, *Lyc.* Tab. XL, fig. 35.

Testa, valva sinistra crassa, obliqua, convexa, linea cardinis elongata, auricula postica permagna, falciformi, dorso angulo obtuso obliquo instructo; plicis incrementi paucis. Valva altera et foveolis interni ignotis.

Shell with the left valve thick, inflated, very oblique, with a lengthened hinge-line and falciform posterior auricle; the anterior border is slightly excavated, and there is an obtuse, oblique angle, which extends from the umbo to the posterior extremity of the valve, which is curved backwards; the folds of growth are few and prominent; the surface is destitute of ornament. The other valve is not known, nor has the hinge been exposed.

The general figure much resembles that of *G. crassicosta*, Mor. and Lyc., but it is more inflated; it has a greater posterior curvature, and is destitute of the oblique costæ. The length of our largest example is 2 inches, that of the hinge-line 1⅓ inch.

Geological Position and Locality. The Cornbrash of Islip, Oxon., also the Great Oolite of Stonesfield; collected by Mr. Whiteaves.

Perna foliacea, *Lyc.* Tab. XXXVII, figs. 3, 3 *a*.

Testa ampla subæquivalvi, subplana, umbonibus prominulis acutis; latere antico excavato, margine posteriore et inferiori elliptico curvato; lateribus rugis concentricis paucis irregularibus. Foveolis interni ignotis.

A large, subæquivalve, depressed shell, with prominent, pointed umbones, excavated and thickened anterior border, the hinge-line short, the posterior and inferior borders elliptically rounded, the general figure being mytelliform, the left valve being somewhat more convex than the other; the test is thin, with delicate margins.

Dimensions. Length, 4½ inches; opposite diameter, 2½ inches; the hinge-area has not been exposed.

Geological Position and Locality. The Great Oolite of Minchinhampton Common; a single fine specimen of each valve is in the collection of the author, who is not cognizant of any other examples.

Inoceramus quadratus, *Sow.*, sp. Tab. XXXVIII, figs. 1, 1 *a*, 1 *b*.

Perna quadrata, *Sow.* Min. Con., t. 492, non Phil. non Goldf.
— — *Lycett.* Ann. and Mag. Nat. Hist., 1855.

Testa tenue subquadrata, transversa, inæquivalvi, valde inæquilatera, valva sinistra antice oblique inflato, postice compresso; umboni magno, subinvoluto, antrorsum instructo; linea cardinali subhorizontali elongato; latere anteriore truncato, infra umbonem concavo, basi subrecto, superficie rugis concentricis paucis irregularibus. Valva dextra planata umboni parvo antico. Foveolis interni parvis numerosis.

Shell thin, subquadrate, transverse, inequivalve. The left valve inflated anteriorly, with a large, subinvolute, projecting beak, and a steep, truncated and excavated slope beneath it; the posterior side is very thin, compressed, and expanded; the hinge-line is lengthened and nearly horizontal; the base is lengthened and nearly straight. The right valve is flattened; the umbo is small, pointed, and anterior. The internal hinge-pits are placed upon a narrow, lengthened plate; they are small and numerous. The surfaces of the valves are smooth, with a few irregular, concentric plications.

The diagnosis in the 'Mineral Conchology' is as follows:—"Quadrilateral, one side shorter than the other three; valves gibbose, unequal, the shorter side very concave, bounded by two obtuse carinæ."

The figure in the 'Mineral Conchology' has the right or smaller valve facing the spectator; the contour of the larger or convex valve is not seen; even the outline is not perfect, as there seems to be a portion of the lower (right) border wanting, and thus forming an angle at its anterior extremity, which would be rounded in the perfect shell; but the whole is stated by the author to be little better than a cast. With such an illustration it is not surprising to find that in the plates to the 'Geology of Yorkshire,' and in the 'Petrefacta' of Goldfuss, two very different species of Perna (flattened, equivalve, and rugose) were figured for the *Perna quadrata* of Sowerby.

The convexity of the left valve, little remarkable in young specimens, becomes very considerable with advance of growth; the test upon the anterior side is moderately thick, but the posterior side is delicate and is rarely preserved entire. Upon the smaller of the specimens figured the portion denuded of the test exhibits obscure, concentric, and radiating striations in the convex valve; the same feature is also visible upon the surface of the cast of the smaller valve figured by Mr. Sowerby; it must therefore have existed upon the inner surface of the very thin, nacreous layer of the test, which has not been preserved; the exterior surface of the test is quite destitute of ornamentation.

Dimensions. Length of our largest specimen, in the direction of the hinge-line, 5¼ inches; height, 3¾ inches; convexity of the larger valve, 2¼ inches.

Geological Positions and Localities. Mr. Sowerby's specimen was obtained in the Cornbrash at Bulwick, Northamptonshire, and, as far as can be ascertained, no second example has been obtained from that locality. In the Inferior Oolite of the vicinity of Nailsworth the present author has procured specimens at several quarries, in a single bed; its position being the highest bed of the white building-freestone, and immediately underlying the bed of hard, cream-coloured limestone with Nerinæas, which appears to be special to the Nailsworth valley. *Perna quadrata* does not appear to be very uncommon; but owing to the thinness of the fibrous test, it can only be disengaged from the Oolite by a tedious and difficult process; more frequently, however, the shell is found to have been crushed or imperfectly preserved at its posterior side.

LIMA PECTINIFORMIS, *Schloth.* Tab. XXXVI, fig. 1. Part II, Tab. VI, fig. 9.

In figuring a larger and more characteristic example of this shell some additional remarks may be allowed. It is widely diffused, abundant and of large dimensions in the upper portion of the Inferior Oolite, rare and delicate in the Great Oolite, rare in the Cornbrash, in the Kelloway Rock and Oxford Clay; it reappears in considerable numbers in the Coralline Oolite, assuming all its pristine varieties of form; these are sufficiently remarkable. In its young condition it was gregarious, and probably was attached by one of the valves to the ground; such, at least, seems an easy explanation of the fact that the upper surface of a slab of stone covered with the species usually discloses only the inner surfaces of single valves, the other valves having probably been removed by marine action in their dead state; but although young and thin, the specimens in this condition often attained to the full dimensions of the species, the radiating flutings of the external surface being almost equally strongly marked upon the inner surfaces, in which state, also, the muscular scar is not distinguishable, and when the valves are closed the umbones touch each other. In old specimens, owing to a continual deposition of shell upon the inner surface, more especially towards the umbones, the triangular sub-umbonal area is large and oblique, so that the umbones then are widely divergent; the internal radiating flutings have gradually disappeared, or are only visible at the lower border of the valves; the muscular scar is conspicuous; ultimately, each valve acquired at its umbonal extremity a thickness of two inches and a half, the cavity of the interior became much smaller, the outer surface ceased to be extended at its borders during this internal accretion of shell; we may also infer, from its solid, ponderous mass, and from the frequency with which it became perforated by the Lithophagidæ, that, unlike the common Limæ and Pectens, its habits were sedentary; doubtless these perforations may have been made in dead shells, but they are not to be discovered in any other of the Jurassic Limæ.

The test consists of two very distinct layers; the outer layer is always thin and semi-transparent, the inner layer is white, opaque, laminated, and received continual additions to its thickness; in brief, the structure and mode of growth agrees with that of the genus Spondylus as fully as does the external aspect of the imbricated rugæ and the tubular, spine-like processes; it is, in truth, *an equivalve Spondylus, destitute of hinge-teeth.* The variations of figure are also considerable; sometimes sub-orbicular, with no more obliquity than a Pecten or Spondylus, with the sides nearly equal, the radiating costæ undulating and irregular, as in Hinnites; in other instances it is oblique, with a steep anterior slope; add to this latter figure a greater lengthening of the valves, a compression of the posterior side, and the aspect becomes strictly that of Lima, as in *L. squammicosta*, Buv., which appears to be only the young condition of this variety.

Few shells differ more in the convexity of the valves; occasionally an example will be found so much inflated that its figure can only have resulted from having been moulded upon and remained closely adherent to a convex surface, to which the missing valve probably remained attached.

The shell is not inæquivalve, although such an appearance is often imparted to it from a depression, or an irregularity in the convexity of one of the valves; as, however, the borders of the valves are found to fit perfectly, this distortion cannot be owing to the effects of fossilization.

Even from the earlier days of palæontology this shell has been a source of doubt and perplexity. Schlotheim referred it to Ostracites, as also did Ziethen. Mr. Sowerby, in the 'Mineral Conchology,' placed it with Lima, but expressed doubts as to the genus; more recently, Professor Quenstedt, in his 'Jura,' after alluding to the features which distinguish it from the ordinary Limæ, divides it into two varieties, one having a thick and the other a thin shell; he concludes by assigning it to the genus Ostrea, but without offering any proofs that it would be correctly placed with the latter genus. The change from the thin to the thick shell has already been explained, and the structure of the test is distinct from that of Ostrea.

Lima pectiniformis may be placed at the head of a group of Jurassic Limæ which are nearly allied, both in their external characters, shell structure, and mode of growth; these are the following: *L. Elea*, D'Orb., from the Supraliasic Sands; *L. Electra*, D'Orb., from the Supraliasic Sands and the Inferior Oolite; *L. Hector*, D'Orb., Inferior Oolite; *L. Luciensis*, D'Orb., Great Oolite; *L. rudis*, Sow., Coralline Oolite; *L. rotundata*, Buv., Coralline Oolite; *L. angusta*, Buv., Coralline Oolite.

LIMA PUNCTATILLA, *Lyc.* Tab. XL, fig. 32.

LIMA PUNCTATILLA, *Lyc.* Ann. and Mag. Nat. Hist., 1853, p. 420.

Testa parva, inflata, ovato-oblonga, auriculis parvis subæqualibus, lateribus leviter excavatis; costis radiantibus (circa 24) elevatis, granulatis, interstiis angustis, striis concentricis crebris decussatis.

Shell small, inflated, ovately oblong; auricles small and nearly equal, the sides of the valves steep and slightly excavated; radiating (costæ about 24), elevated, granulated; large upon the centre of the valves, and degenerating upon the sides into lines, decussated by closely arranged concentric striations.

The general figure resembles *Lima gibbosa*, but more convex, and with radiating lines or delicate costæ upon the sides, which increase in size symmetrically towards the middle of the valve, each rib being ornamented with a minute line of granules. The specimen figured is of less dimensions than others, but it has only occurred very rarely.

Geological Position and Locality. The Great Oolite of Minchinhampton; the Inferior Oolite of Leckhampton Hill, in the shelly freestone.

LIMA HELVETICA, *Oppel.* Tab. XXXIII, figs. 8, 8 *a*.

LIMA GIBBOSA, *Goldfuss.* Pet., t. 102, fig. 10, p. 86, non Sow.
— HELVETICA, *Oppel.* Juraformation, p. 489.

Lima testa fornicata ovata subobliqua antice declivi, costis (25—27) subacutis adpressis et linea laterali notatis, sulcis conformibus, lunala lævi convexa. (Goldfuss.)

Shell ovately oblong, convex, slightly oblique; anterior slope lengthened, steep; posterior slope more gradual and flattened; umbones acute, straight; anterior and posterior auricles equal and but little produced, forming a short horizontal hinge-line; radiating costæ upon the middle portion of the valves narrow, sub-acute, 25—27 in number at the lower border, 14—15 near to the umbo, the additional costæ near to the lower border consisting of smaller intervening costæ or lines, unequal in size, and rather irregularly arranged; the larger costæ towards the sides of the valves appear as if compressed upon the shell. The anterior sides of the valves are nearly smooth, but each side has a few very delicate radiating lines; the entire surface of the valves has very delicate, closely arranged, concentric, irregular striations, which impress the costæ, and are very conspicuous upon the wide, flattened intercostal spaces; the valves are close fitting and thin.

Geological Position and Localities. It occurs rarely in the Cornbrash of Scarborough. Dr. Oppel records it in the same geological position at Marquise, near Boulogne; also at Egg, near Aarau, Switzerland. Goldfuss records it at the latter locality, and at Basel.

LIMA RIGIDULA, *Phil.*, sp. Tab. XXXIII, figs. 7, 7 *a*.

PLAGIOSTOMA RIGIDULUM, *Phil.* Geol. York., i. t. 7, fig. 13.

Testa elongata, convexa, per-obliqua, umbonibus obliquis, acutis, auriculis parvis subæqualibus; latere antico elevato, excavato, postico elliptico curvato; valvis costulis radiantibus angustis, rotundatis, regularibus, sed undulatis et granulatis; interstiis duplo latioribus subtillissime transversè striatis, striisque regularibus instructis.

Shell elongated, convex, very oblique; umbones small, pointed anterior; auricles small, nearly equal; anterior side very convex, with a steep, excavated border; posterior side curved elliptically; the entire surface has delicate but rounded, elevated, and finely knotted radiating costæ, gently waved and separated by interstitial spaces twice the breadth of the costæ; the spaces have very fine, regular, and closely arranged transverse striations; the plications of growth are few, but become prominent near to the lower border.

One of the most elongated and oblique of the Jurassic Limæ. The general figure and ornamentation would much resemble *Lima ovalis*, Sow., if the convexity of the anterior side were not much greater, and the costæ more elevated, in the Cornbrash shell; the striations are so densely arranged that the spaces do not present a punctated aspect, as is usually seen when the striations are more distant, and larger.

Dimensions. Length, 20 lines; breadth, 12 lines; diameter through both the valves, 10 lines.

Geological Position and Locality. The Cornbrash of Scarborough, in which it is abundant.

MODIOLA GIBBOSA, *Sow.* Tab. XXXIII, figs. 11, 11 *a*.

MODIOLA GIBBOSA, *Sow.* Min. Con., t. 211, fig. 2.
— RENIFORMIS, *Sow.* Ib. fig. 3.?
— — *D'Orb.* Prodr., i, p. 282.
— GIBBOSA, *Mor.* Catal., 1854, p. 210.

Testa elongato-ovato, convexa subreniformi umbonibus curvatis acutis sulco obliquo antico; latere antico inferne sinuato, latere postico elliptico curvato; lateribus plicis magnis concentricis distantibus.

Shell ovately elongated, very convex; umbones pointed, curved forwards; an oblique sulcation proceeds downwards and forwards to the lower part of the anterior border, which is sinuated; the anterior side has a large, rounded, but compressed lobe; the posterior border is very convex, and is curved elliptically; the surfaces of the valves have a few large, irregular and distant plications.

The length is twice the breadth, and two fifths greater than the convexity of the united valves.

The very inflated figure, the curvature of the valves, and the distinct anterior broad sulcation, distinguishes it from other Jurassic species; some specimens, smaller and apparently younger, cannot perhaps be distinguished from *Modiola reniformis*, Sow., for the species varies in the length, curvature, and convexity.

Geological Positions and Localities. This species is figured upon the authority of specimens in the Museum of Practical Geology, which are stated to have been collected in the Cornbrash of Melbury Osmond. It is common in the Inferior Oolite of the southern counties.

CUCULLÆA CORALLINA. Tab. XXXIX, fig. 3.

CUCULLÆA OBLONGA, *Phil.* Geol. York., i, t. 3, fig. 34, non Sow.
— CORALLINA, *Damon.* Geol. Weymouth, Suppl., pl. 4, fig. 8.

Testa inflata, subrhomboidali, subæquilaterali, umbonibus magnis medianis acutis, incurvis, latere postico abbreviato abrupte truncato, area cardinis brevi, superficie lineis longitudinalibus crebris, irregularibus aliis radiantibus subobsoletis decussata.

Shell much inflated, subrhomboidal, nearly equilateral; umbones large, mesial, incurved, elevated, slightly oblique, and nearly in contact.

The anterior side is produced and rounded, the posterior side is very short, abruptly truncated, slightly excavated, and separated from the other portion of the surface by a strongly defined subacute angle; the hinge area is short and not wide; the surface has densely arranged, irregular, longitudinal lines, decussated by others radiating, but much less clearly defined.

Dimensions.—Height, three fourths of the length.

A very short, tumid, abruptly truncated Cucullæa, possessing these characters in a greater degree, and less oblique than any of the shorter examples of *C. oblonga*, Sow.; the latter shell has also several large, widely separated, radiating lines upon the anterior side, of which our species is destitute. It appears to be identical with *Cucullæa oblonga*, Phil., from the Coral Rag, at least with the more short examples of that species, for the Coral Rag shell presents great variability in its general figure, more especially in that of the posterior side, and it is easy to obtain specimens which insensibly connect the shorter with the more lengthened and oblique forms; it rarely happens that the surface ornamentation can be discovered, but the portions of the surface obtained agree with that of the Cornbrash shell.

Geological Positions and Localities. Cucullæa corallina occurs rarely in the Cornbrash of the Yorkshire coast, but is abundant in the Coral Rag of Pickering and of Oxfordshire.

CUCULLÆA CLATHRATA, *Leck.* Tab. XXXIX, figs. 4, 4 *a*.

CUCULLÆA CLATHRATA, *Leckenby*. Journ. Geol. Soc., 1858, vol. xv, pl. 3, fig. 4.

Testa subrhomboidali inflata, umbonibus antemedianis magnis, valde separatis, area ampla, excavata, lanceolata, basi subrecto; valvis rugis longitudinalibus, irregularibus, lineisque radiantibus, crebris tenuibus, dorso angulo obtuso et obliquo.

Shell subrhomboidal, inflated; umbones large, placed anterior to the middle of the valves, separated by a large lanceolate area; there is an oblique obtuse angle upon the posterior side, separating a concave posterior space from the middle portion of the valves; the surface has large, longitudinal, irregular, rugose plications crossed by closely arranged, delicate, radiating lines; the lower border is nearly straight, and slightly sinuated.

The shorter posterior side and larger umbones distinguish it from *Arca lata*, Dunker, to which in other respects it has a considerable resemblance.

Dimensions.—Length, 26 lines; height, 14 lines; diameter through both the valves, 16 lines; space separating the points of the umbones, 3 lines.

Geological Position and Locality. The Cornbrash of Scarborough, also in the Kelloway Rock of the same locality. In the collection of Mr. Leckenby.

NUCULA MENKEI, *Roem.* Tab. XXXIX, fig. 2.

NUCULA MENKEI, *Roemer*. Nordd. Ool., t. 6, fig. 10, p. 98.

Testa ovata, medio ventricosa concentrice striata, antice brevissima acuta oblique truncata, cordato-subexcavata, posterius producta rotundata, basi subarcuata, umbonibus crassis incurvis, aream lanceolatam haud efformantibus. (Roemer.)

Shell ovate, anterior side very short, somewhat excavated, and pointed at its lower extremity; posterior border lengthened, curved, sloping obliquely downwards, its lower extremity rounded, base slightly curved elliptically, umbones large, incurved, area very slightly defined; the middle portion of the valves is moderately convex, with a few distant plications of growth, and delicate concentric striations obscurely defined.

Nucula variabilis, Sow., approximates to this species, but is without the anterior excavation, and has a more lengthened posterior side. *Nucula nuclens*, Desl., is shorter and more globose.

Geological Positions and Localities. Roemer records *Nucula Menkei* in the Portland Limestone of Wendhausen. Mr. Whiteaves has collected it in the Great Oolite of Kirklington, and in the Cornbrash of Islip, Oxon.

Genus—Isoarca, *Munster*.

Shell equivalve, ventricose; umbones large, anterior or antero-mesial, sometimes more or less spiral, ligament external; hinge-border lengthened, curved, with two series of small transverse teeth, which decrease in size towards the centre; pallial impression simple.

Isoarca Scarburgensis, *Lyc.* Tab. XXXIX, figs. 5, 5 *a*.

Testa tenui, ovato-oblonga, tumida, umbonibus magnis subanticis, prominentibus, latere antico brevi, curvato, postico elongato, oblique declivi, sulcis duobus evanescentibus; margine inferiore subrecto; valvis striis concentricis irregularibus, inferne semel granulis irregularibus instructis.

Shell thin, ovately oblong, somewhat inflated; umbones large, prominent, placed anterior to the middle of the valves, directed obliquely forwards; anterior side short and curved elliptically, posterior side lengthened, the margin sloping obliquely downwards with two slightly impressed oblique furrows, which are distinct towards the umbo; the lower border is lengthened and nearly straight; the surface has fine irregular, concentric striations, and the sides have towards their lower border irregular, rounded granules, rather distantly arranged.

Dimensions.—Length, 24 lines; height, 16 lines; diameter through the valves, 12 lines.

A fine and rare example of a genus which seldom occurs in the Jurassic rocks of this country. It is much less inflated, and the umbones are more prominent than in *Isocardia transversa*, Munst., less oblong, and with the anterior side more produced than in *Isoarca Lochensis*, Quenst., and *Isoarca eminens*, Quenst. Other Jurassic species more remotely allied and approaching the orbicular figure are *Isoarca subspirata*, Munst., *Isoarca texata*, Munst., *Isoarca decussata*, Munst., and *Isoarca cordiformis*, Quenst. The general figure resembles Cypricardia, but when the hinge cannot be exposed, the genus may be distinguished by the granulations upon the surface, and by the tenuity of the test.

Geological Position and Locality. The Cornbrash of Scarborough, in the collection of Mr. Leckenby.

Leda Anglica, *D'Orb.* Tab. XXXIX, fig. 7.

Nucula lachryma (obtuse variety) *Phil.* Geol. York., i, pl. 9, fig. 25.
Leda Anglica, *D'Orb.* Prodr., p. 275.

Testa lævigata parva, inflata, subtrigona, umbonibus medianis obtusis incurvis depressis, latere antico curvato, oblique-declivi, latere postico abrupte declivi, acute carinata, carina obliqua promimula; valvis striis longitudinalibus obscuris et plicis incrementi paucis impressis.

Shell small, inflated, short, subtrigonal; umbones depressed, mesial, obtuse and incurved; the anterior border is rounded, sloping downwards and uniting with elliptical curvature of the lower border; the posterior side slopes abruptly downwards, it has an oblique posterior carina, which becomes conspicuous and raised towards its lower extremity; it separates a posterior, depressed, lanceolate area from the sides of the shell. The surface has obscure longitudinal striations, and several folds of growth.

The inflated figure, short posterior side and projecting oblique posterior carina, distinguish it from *Leda lachryma*, Sow., and also from other species of the Lower Oolites.

Geological Positions and Localities. The Cornbrash of Scarborough, in which it occurs rarely. Professor Phillips records it in the lower stage of the Inferior Oolite (Dogger), and in the gray limestone or upper stage of the same formation upon the coast of Yorkshire.

TRIGONIA ELONGATA, *Sow.* Tab. XXXIX, figs. 6, 6 *a.*

TRIGONIA ELONGATA, *Sow.* Min. Con., t. 431.
— — *D'Orb.* Prodr., vol. i, p. 338.
— — *Morris.* Catal., 1854, p. 228.
— — *Oppel.* Juraformation, p. 525.
— — *Damon.* Geol. Weymouth, Suppl., pl. 2, figs. 1, 2.

Testa subtrigona, alta, convexa, antici brevissima truncata, costis, magnis, subhorizontalibus, leviter undulatis; umbonibus prominentibus acutis incurvis; area cardinali lata, ornatissima, distincte tripartita, carinis prominentibus, denticulatis.

Shell subtrigonal, very convex and lengthened; anterior side short, its border abruptly truncated with numerous large, nearly horizontal and slightly undulated costæ; the umbones are elevated and much incurved; the posterior area (which nearly equals in size the other portion of the surface) is very wide, and is separated into three distinct parts by as many prominent denticulated carinæ; the marginal carina is very large and nearly straight; the mesial and inner carinæ though smaller are likewise conspicuous in both the valves; the space between the mesial and inner carina is much depressed and its ornamentation is very delicate; the superior or post ligamental space is short and wide, it has a few elevated perpendicular plications. The convexity of the united valves is somewhat greater than the breadth of the shell, and equal to two thirds of the length of the marginal carina.

The general figure and other characters are so strongly defined that it will not readily be mistaken for any other example of the group of the *Costatæ;* the figure of the Cornbrash specimens agrees with those from the Oxford Clay, but the sculpture upon the area is less strongly marked in specimens from the latter formation, which are also usually smaller. Compared with other examples of the same group of species, *T. elongata* is remarkable for the short, widely-separated horizontal costæ, for the great size and straightness of the marginal carina, for the prominence of the sculpture upon the tripartite area, and more especially for the shortness and great breadth of the superior or post-ligamental space, which, when the valves are united, becomes cordate rather than lanceolate. D'Orbigny (Prodrome) believes it to be identical with *T. cardissa*, Agassiz, it is, however, only necessary to compare the marginal carina in the two forms to perceive their distinctness.

Geological Positions and Localities. It is abundant in the Oxford Clay of the southern counties, more especially at Radipole near Weymouth, and in the Cornbrash of the coast of Yorkshire, at Gristhorp, and at Scarborough. The foreign localities cited are France, Dives, Villers (Calvados), Clucy, Mont Orient, near to Salins (Jura), Montsec, near to St. Mihiel (Meuse), Marault, near to Chaumont (H. Marne), Beaumont, Pizieux, Chauffour (Sarthe).

TRIGONIA TUBERCULOSA, *Lyc.* Tab. XL, fig. 6.

TRIGONIA TUBERCULOSA, *Lycett.* Ann. and Mag. Nat. Hist., 1850, p. 12, t. 11, fig. 9.
— — *Morris.* Cat. Brit. Foss., 1854, p. 229.

Testa ovato-trigona, subdepressa, umbonibus parvis, recurvatis, marginè anteriorè et inferiorè rotundo, marginè posticó excavató, area augustata, transverse plicata, plicis magnis acutis; carina marginali delicati nodulois; carina interna varicibus magnis regularibus ornata; area lanceolata varicibus paucis obliquis; valvis lateribus costis numerosis concentricis et dense tuberculosis, tuberculis crebris elevatis, compressis.

Shell ovately trigonal, depressed; umbones small, mesial and recurved, anterior and lower borders rounded, superior border rather excavated; area narrow, with two oblique carinæ, and with transverse acute plications, every second plication forming a varix upon the inner carina; the marginal carina is delicately tuberculated; the post ligamental lanceolate space is small, with several oblique varices; the sides of the valves have very numerous, closely arranged, concentric tuberculated, costa; the tubercles are much elevated, and compressed laterally, imparting to them a club-shaped figure, the lower extremity of each extending to the succeeding costa.

A pretty little species, remarkable for the delicacy and salient features of its ornamentation. The characters of the tubercles upon the sides of the valves closely resemble those in *Trigonia elathrata* Ag., but in other particulars the two species are widely separated; the close contiguity of the extremities of the tubercles between row and row gives to them, when viewed from the posterior side, the appearance of forming a series of vertical costæ; the tubercles are, however, very well separated in the rows, and towards the lower border they project considerably from the sides of the valves; eighteen rows of costæ may be counted in a specimen whose length is only nine lines.

Geological Positions and Localities. The specimen figured is from the cabinet of the Rev. A. W. Griesbach, and was obtained by him from the Cornbrash of Rushden; it is silicified, and is a beautiful object for the delicacy of its ornamentation; the original specimen figured by me in the 'Annals and Magazine of Natural History,' was obtained by the Rev. P. B. Brodie in the shelly freestone of the Inferior Oolite at Leckhampton Hill; at each locality it ranks as one of the more rare productions.

TRIGONIA CLYTHIA, *D'Orbigny*. Tab. XXXVII, fig. 2; Tab. XL, figs. 5, 5 *a*.

TRIGONIA CLYTHIA, *D'Orbigny*. Prodr. de Paléont., i, p. 309.

"*Coquille singulière par ses côtes concentriques formant de deux en deux un angle sur la region anale, independamment de la area costulée en travers.*" (D'Orbigny.)

Testa subtrigona, convexa, transversim costata, costis numerosis, crebris, curvatis, postice alternatim angulatis, carina marginali lævigato, elevato, areá planatá transversim costatá, costis magnis, depressis.

Shell subtrigonal, convex, transversely costated; costæ numerous, small, closely arranged, curved, convex upon their lower and concave upon their upper sides; the first few costæ are united to the marginal carina, the succeeding costæ are bent suddenly upwards at their posterior extremities, forming a series of angles, one of which proceeds from every second costa; the marginal and inner carinæ are smooth and elevated; the area is moderately wide, flattened, traversed transversely by a few large depressed and waved costæ, which are interupted by an oblique mesial furrow.

The general figure is nearly triangular; the umbones are mesial, much elevated and pointed; the anterior border is nearly straight, sloping obliquely downwards, but slightly sinuated immediately beneath the umbones; the posterior border is short and oblique.

Dimensions.—The height and the lateral diameter are nearly equal; the diameter through both the valves is one fifth less.

The costæ upon the sides of the valves are so closely arranged that about twenty occur in a specimen seven lines in height.

Geological Positions and Localities. The Great Oolite of Minchinhampton and Bisley Commons, also in the upper zone of the same formation near to Bath. Luc (Calvados).

TRIGONIA SCARBURGENSIS, *Lyc*. Tab. XXXVII, fig. 1.

Testa ovato-trigona subdepressa, elongata, umbonibus recurvatis, margine antico rotundo, postico excavato, producto; area angusta, elongata, carinis tribus delicatissimis ornato; valvis costis tuberculatis, magnis per series leviter arcuatis, antice parvis, irregularibus, postice magnis curvatis.

Shell ovately trigonal, rather depressed, elongated; umbones recurved; anterior side rounded and produced; posterior slope somewhat concave, lengthened; the area is narrow, flattened, with irregular transverse striations, and ornamented with three very delicate knotted carinæ, the lanceolate, post-ligamental space is much lengthened, smooth, and excavated. The costated portion of the shell has the rows at first regular and concentric, with regular, distinct tubercles; subsequently the costæ become more ridge-like and the tubercles less separated; anteriorly they are small, and the rows are broken and confused; posteriorly they are large and more regular, curving upwards slightly, but their extremities are well separated from the marginal carina.

This is the shell attributed by Messrs. Young and Bird to *T. clavellata*, and subsequently also by Professor Phillips, Professor Williamson, and Mr. Bean, in their lists of Cornbrash fossils.

Trigonia signata, Ag., figured in the second part of the Great Oolite Monograph under the name of *Trigonia decorata*, is also an elongated shell, but is destitute of the recurvature of the umbones and of the produced anterior side; the rows of costæ likewise differ; the posterior portions are not larger than the anterior, and there is wanting that arrest in the continuity of the rows always conspicuous in the Cornbrash shell, and which imparts to the anterior portion of the latter form a broken, irregular character. *Trigonia clavellata*, Lhwyd, Parkinson, and Sowerby, so abundant in the Lower Calcareous Grit of England, France, and Switzerland, has a much shorter and more convex figure, the umbones are not recurved, features which will suffice to distinguish them irrespective of the ornamentation of the surface. *T. perlata*, Ag., and *T. Bronnii*, Ag., from the same beds, appear to be only varieties of *T. clavellata*. *Trigonia Scarburgensis* is also allied to that beautiful and well-known Oxford Clay representative of the *Clavellatæ* so long procured at Weymouth, and of which a good figure is given in Mr. Damon's 'Geology of Weymouth,' Suppl., pl. ii, fig. 3; the latter, in addition to the unusual elongation of its posterior side, has a wide diagonal space, destitute of ornament, separating the posterior extremities of the costæ from the marginal carina.

Geological Position and Locality. *Trigonia Scarburgensis* is moderately common in the Cornbrash of the Yorkshire coast; it may also occur in the same rock of the southern counties, but the condition of the specimens is such that it has not been ascertained with any confidence.

TRIGONIA CASSIOPE, *D'Orb.* Tab. XXXVII, fig. 10.

TRIGONIA CASSIOPE, *D'Orb.* Prodrome de Paléont., 1, p. 308.

Testa ovato-trigona, transversè elongata, subdepressa, costis transversis, subhorizontalibus, numerosis, lævigatis, gracilibus curvatis, antice rotundata, postice producta; area tricarinata, carina marginali et interna crenulata, carina mediana parva; carinarum intervallo costellis longitudinalibus granosis, confertis, ornatis; area postica lanceolata, delicatè reticulata.

Shell ovately trigonal, transversely elongated, somewhat depressed; transverse costæ

7

numerous, smooth, slender, nearly horizontal, and gracefully curved; the anterior border is rounded; the area is lengthened, narrow, and slightly excavated, having three carinæ, of which the marginal and inner carinæ are conspicuous, curved, and crenulated; the median carina is small; the spaces between the carinæ have longitudinal, delicate, closely arranged, granulated little costæ; the post-ligamental lanceolate space has a very delicately reticulated surface.

A transversely lengthened, large, and gracefully curved form, much less convex than *T. costata*, with more depressed umbones, and having the anterior side greatly more rounded and produced. The costated portion of the shell is very large; the costæ are numerous, not much elevated; their direction is nearly horizontal, excepting near to the apex, where they have an elegant sigmoidal curvature. The length upon the marginal carinæ is one fourth greater than the opposite measurement; the diameter through both the valves is somewhat less than half the height. The area is very narrow and lengthened, the ornamentation of its surface is minute and delicately sculptured, the general figure is depressed, which, together with the small prominence of the umbones, the excavated posterior side, and the large, rounded anterior side, will, in the aggregate, serve to distinguish it from other allied forms.

Geological Position and Localities. It is moderately abundant in the Cornbrash of the coast of Yorkshire. The foreign localities quoted by D'Orbigny are Luc (Calvados), Vezelay (Yonne), Grange-Henry, near Nantua.

TRIGONIA COMPTA, *Lyc.* Tab. XL, fig. 1.

Testa ovato-trigona, subdepressa, umbonibus obtusis, depressis, latere antico brevi, rotunda, postico producto; area planata, carinis tribus delicatissimis et striis transversis tenuissimis instructis, costis (circa 12) posticè nodulosis, interruptis, antice rugis obliquis instructis.

Shell ovately trigonal, rather depressed; umbones obtuse, depressed, not recurved; anterior side short, rounded, posterior side more produced, its border straight, sloping obliquely downwards; area flattened, with three very delicate, tuberculated carinæ, and fine transverse striations, lanceolate; post-ligamental space narrow, lengthened, and smooth. The other portion of the surface has about twelve rows of costæ, which become large, horizontal, nodulose, interrupted varices posteriorly, and form small, oblique, rather imperfectly tuberculated, but continuous costæ anteriorly, so that all the costæ reach the anterior border in an oblique rather than in a concentric direction.

The diagnostic characters are not very strongly marked, but in the aggregate are sufficiently distinctive. The delicately ornamented area separates it from *T. Moretonis*, Mor. and Lyc., and the posterior, interrupted varices from *T. impressa*, Sow. From *T. Goldfussii*, Ag., it is distinguished by the smaller oblique costæ, more especially of their posterior extremities, where they do not form large, continuous varices, bent upwards at a considerable angle, as in the latter species. *T. costatula*, Lyc., is more convex, the costæ are more regular, smooth and concentric, the area also is much larger, which imparts a subquadrate figure to the outline; other species are more remotely allied.

Geological Position and Locality. The slate of Collyweston, Northamptonshire, in which the specimens are usually compressed.

TRIGONIA CLYTHIA, *D'Orb.* Suppl., p. 48, Tab. XXXVII, fig. 2; Tab. XL, fig. 5.

Some fine specimens received subsequently to the printing of page 48 have enabled the artist to illustrate the more adult aspect of this species. Tab. XL, fig. 5 *a* exhibits the nodulous character of the posterior extremities of the costæ, their anterior portions remaining regular and concentric; fig. 5 is an aged specimen, exhibiting further changes. In common with many other of the Jurassic Trigoniæ in the ultimate stage of growth, the smooth costæ are no longer regular or concentric; they become less distinctly marked, broken, undulating or wrinkled, constituting the approach to the period when all ornamentation ceases.

TRIGONIA TRIPARTITA, *Forbes.* Tab. XL, fig. 4.

TRIGONIA TRIPARTITA, *Forbes.* Journ. Geol. Soc., vii, tab. 5, fig. 11.
— — *Morris.* Catal., 1854, p. 229.

Testa ovato-trigona, subdepressa, umbonibus obtusis sed recurvatis, latere antico rotundo, postico subconcavo obliquè declivi, antice costis lævigatis parvis obliquis crebris, posticè aliis (7—8) *obliquis magnis depressis, nodulatis; area subconcava, sulco mediano obliquo, costis transversalibus penes apicem instructis.*

Shell ovately trigonal, rather depressed; umbones obtuse, but recurved; anterior margin rounded; posterior margin somewhat concave, sloping obliquely downwards; the anterior side has numerous (about thirty) delicate, oblique, smooth costæ, which are interrupted posteally by others which cross them nearly at right angles; the latter costæ (about seven or eight) are large, nodulous and depressed, the two latter only reach the lower border; the marginal carina is but little conspicuous; the area is somewhat concave, it is transversed by a mesial furrow, and has a few transverse costæ near to the apex. Our specimen is slightly imperfect at the apex and at the inferior border.

Geological Positions and Localities. A single example from the Cornbrash of Chippenham, in the collection of W. Walton, Esq. This pretty species was also obtained by the late Professor E. Forbes in a stratum of yellowish, crumbly limestone and shale, beneath the Oxford Clay at Lock Staffin, in the Isle of Skye, associated with fresh-water and marine testacea, which are believed to represent estuary conditions, a geological horizon which possibly is not very dissimilar to that of our specimen.

TRIGONIA ARATA, *Lyc.* Tab. XL, fig. 2.

Testa ovato-trigona, subdepressa, umbonibus antemedianis, obtusis depressis, latere antico brevi, rotundo, postico obliquè declivi, area planata, oblique irregulariter, striatis, carina marginali subnullo, lateribus costis antice obliquis, posticè angulatis, depressis, simplicibus. Testa ætate juniori costis concentricis simplicibus.

Shell ovately trigonal, somewhat depressed; umbones anterior to the middle of the valves, obtuse and depressed; anterior side short, rounded; posterior side sloping obliquely down; area flattened, with transverse, irregular striations; marginal carinæ not conspicuous, and obsolete posteriorly; the sides of the valves with numerous closely arranged, oblique, plain costæ, which are bent upwards posteriorly at an obtuse angle, and meet the area at a right angle.

The costæ are rounded and rather depressed; they become more distantly arranged posteriorly, but only slightly increase in size. The young shell has the costæ regular and concentric; the marginal carina is small, but forms a distinct elevation; a specimen more aged than the one selected for our figure has the posterior portions of the costæ slightly nodulous; anteriorly they become waved and irregular.

Geological Positions and Localities. A rare species; Mr. Walton's specimens are from the Forest Marble of Farleigh, near Bath; it has also occurred in the same position near to Cirencester.

TRIGONIA BATHONICA, *Lyc.* Tab. XL, fig. 3.

Testa subtrigona, depressa, umbonibus altis medianis, latere antico et postico subrecto, obliquè declivi, lateribus costis elevatis, angustis, crebris, subundulatis, et spinulosis, obliquè instructis; area parva planata obliquè striata, carina marginali minimo, subnullo.

Shell subtrigonal, short, depressed; umbones elevated, mesial, and not recurved; anterior and posterior borders nearly straight, sloping obliquely downwards, the surface with numerous (about twenty-four) narrow, elevated, spinose, and somewhat undulated oblique costæ, which are directed from the marginal carina anteally downwards, and all reach the lower margin; the area is narrow and obliquely striated; the marginal carina is very small, and rather indistinct.

The narrow, ridge-like costæ have numerous minute, obtuse spines, which impart roughness to the surface; they are distinct, rather irregular, and therefore very different from the serrated, elevated, regular costæ of *T. striata*, Miller, and its allied species; the general aspect resembles *T. duplicata*, Sow., but it has no bifurcating costæ near to the lower border, and is also destitute of concentric costæ near to the apex. The sole specimen at our disposal is imperfect at the posterior extremity; it has twenty costæ, and would require about four others to complete its surface. Possibly *Trigonia Cybele*, D'Orb., from the Great Oolite of Luc, may not differ from this species, but the seven words allotted to it in the 'Prodrome' of that author are insufficient to characterise it.

The figure is nearly that of an equilateral triangle, each of the sides having a length of about an inch.

Geological Position and Locality. In rubbly, hard, ferruginous Oolite (Great Oolite) from the Box Tunnel; communicated by W. Walton, Esq.

CARDIUM LINGULATUM, *Lyc.* Tab. XXXIII, figs. 2, 2 *a*; Tab. XXXV, figs. 11, 11 *a*.

Testa ovato-oblonga, mediocriter convexa, umbonibus prominentibus, medianis, subacutis, valvis marginibus ellipticis curvatis, rugis concentricis irregularibus, striisque tenuibus, delicatè impressis; postice striis obliquis regularibus decussatis.

Shell ovately oblong, moderately convex; umbones prominent, mesial, and subacute; the anterior, posterior, and inferior margins of the valves are elliptically curved; the surface has numerous irregular, concentric rugæ, and delicate, regular striations; the posterior side has some regular, oblique striations, which decussate those which are concentric. The height and the transverse diameter are equal.

Allied to *Cardium cognatum*, Phil., but the latter has much greater convexity, it has larger and less pointed umbones, its surface is also destitute of the concentric rugæ and striations.

Geological Position and Locality. The Great Oolite of Kirklington, Oxon., collected by J. F. Whiteaves, Esq.

CARDIUM INCERTUM, *Phil.* Tab. XXXV, figs. 14, 14 *a*.

CARDIUM INCERTUM, *Phil.* Geol. York., i, pl. 11, fig. 5.
UNICARDIUM INCERTUM, *D'Orb.* Prodrome, i, p. 279, No. 323.
CARDIUM INCERTUM, *Morris.* Catal., 1854, p. 192.

Testa suborbiculari convexa, lævi, umbonibus submedianis elevatis subacutis incurvis, margine antico concavo, lunula subnulla; latere postico planato angulo obliquo formante, margine postico subrecto inferne angulato; lateribus plicis concentricis paucis, irregularibus et tenuibus.

Shell suborbicular, moderately convex, smooth; umbones mesial or slightly antero-mesial, elevated, acute, and incurved; anterior border concave and rounded; lunule scarcely defined; posterior side forming a flattened area, well separated from the other portion of the surface by a clearly defined, oblique, and acute angle; the posterior border, at first curved, slopes suddenly downwards, nearly in a straight direction, forming an angle at its junction with the lower border; the surface has a few faintly marked, irregular, concentric plications.

Dimensions.—Length, 13 lines; height, 11½ lines; diameter through both of the valves, 8 lines. The hinge has not been examined.

Geological Positions and Localities. The fine specimen figured was collected by J. F. Whiteaves, Esq., in the Great Oolite of Kirklington, Oxon. It occurs rarely in the Inferior Oolite of Blue Wick; it was also collected in the roe stone of the Inferior Oolite at Leekhampton Hill by the Rev. P. B. Brodie.

CARDIUM COGNATUM, *Phil.* Tab. XXXVI, figs. 3, 3 *a*.

CARDIUM COGNATUM, *Phil.* Geol. York., i, t. 9, fig. 14.
— COGNATUM, *Morris.* Catal., 1854, p. 192.
UNICARDIUM COGNATUM, *D'Orb.* Prodr., Et. x, No. 324.
— — *Oppel.* Juraformation, p. 410.
CARDIUM — *Leckenby.* Journ. Geol. Soc., xv, pl. 3, fig. 8.

Testa ovato-orbiculari, convexa, umbonibus magnis, medianis, subrectis, margine antico et postico, elliptico curvato, lunula nulla; valvis striis concentricis, crebris, instructis; postice striis radiantibus obliquis decussatis.

Shell ovately orbicular, convex; umbones large, prominent, mesial, straight, or directed slightly forwards; the anterior and posterior margins of the valves are curved elliptically; there is no lunule; the whole surface has very densely arranged, delicate, concentric striations; the posterior side is not compressed, but has some oblique, faintly marked striations, which produce a roughened surface where they decussate the concentric striations.

The specific characters are not strongly defined, and reside more in the general figure than in the ornamentation of the surface; the Cornbrash specimens have a thin, shining test, and the striations can scarcely be distinguished without the aid of a magnifier; the posterior side is scarcely so much produced as the other, and the greatest convexity of the valves is placed a little posterior to the mesial line; the Kelloway Rock examples are smaller.

Cardium cognatum is nearly allied to an inferior Oolite species, casts of which are very common in the Cotteswold Hills; the latter fossils are more ovate, the muscular scars more strongly impressed; the test is much more thick; the striations, both concentric and oblique, are more strongly defined, especially the oblique striations upon the posterior side, which deeply indent the shell, and are therefore always conspicuous. The *Cardium cognatum* of Goldfuss is a very different shell, having a posterior angle and oblique umbones. D'Orbigny ('Prodrome') has arranged our species with his genus *Unicardium*, in which he has been followed by Dr. Oppel ('Juraformation'); but, having examined the muscular impressions and also those of the hinge, I can affirm that Professor Phillips correctly discriminated the genus.

Geological Positions and Localities. The specimens figured are from the Cornbrash of Scarborough; it occurs also in the Kelloway Rock of the same neighbourhood and in Wiltshire.

CARDIUM WITCHELLI, *Lyc.* Tab. XL, fig. 36.

Testa parva ovato-trigona, convexa, umbonibus magnis prominentibus medianis, subacutis, latere posteriore angulo obliquo et area postica planata, in medio sulco obliquo instructo; dorso striis tenuissimis concentricis regularibus.

Shell small, ovately trigonal, convex; umbones mesial, prominent, and somewhat pointed; the anterior and lower margins are rounded; the posterior margin is somewhat angulated at its lower extremity; the posterior side has a conspicuous, oblique angle, separating a flattened, smooth, posterior area, which is traversed by a mesial, oblique furrow; the other portion of the surface has very fine, regular, concentric striations. The height and length are equal; the diameter through both the valves is somewhat less.

The abruptness of the posterior angle, the flattened, smooth area, with its mesial groove, appear to separate it from other allied Jurassic species. Possibly it may be a dwarfed representative of a much larger form.

Geological Position and Locality. The Great Oolite of Bussage, near Bisley Common; the process of crushing shelly portions of the white Oolite has yielded this little species to Mr. Witchell.

CYPRICARDIA CAUDATA, *Lyc.* Tab. XXXVI, figs. 8, 8 *a*.

Testa transversa, subtrigona, obliqua, subdepressa, umbonibus magnis, elevatis, subinvolutis, incurvis, latere postico oblique declivi, obtusangulo instructo; lunula depressa; valvis striis longitudinalibus tenuissimis, inæqualibus, latere antico semel striis radiantibus tenuissimis decussatis. Nucleo striis obscuris radiantibus et concentricis.

Shell transverse, subtrigonal, oblique, rather depressed; umbones large, elevated, and subinvolute; the posterior side slopes obliquely downwards, and has a slightly defined, obtuse angle; the anterior side is moderately produced; the lunule is strongly defined;

the lower portion of the anterior border is elliptically curved; the base is nearly straight; the inner borders of the valves are crenulated; the surface has closely arranged, delicate, unequal, longitudinal striations, which are decussated upon the anterior side by others which radiate from the umbones, and when the outer layer of the test has been removed a series of strongly marked, radiating striations are exposed over the whole of the valve; both kinds of striations are also impressed more or less distinctly upon the nucleus.

This delicately ornamented Cypricardia might at the first glance be mistaken for a depressed variety of *Cypricardia cordiformis*, Desh., a shell which in the young condition possesses great differences of figure; it will be found, however, that *Cypricardia caudata* is more depressed, more trigonal, the anterior side more lengthened, and the posterior angle much less defined, so that the portion of the surface posterior to it is even somewhat convex; but in *Cypricardia cordiformis* it is flattened or often slightly concave in some instances; the entire absence of ornamentation, both upon the test and the nucleus, is another distinctive feature. The fine specimen figured has the area delicately preserved, and exhibits the ligament; the test is of moderate thickness, and the inner borders of the valves are crenulated; an exposed portion of the nucleus has striations corresponding to those upon the inner layer of the test.

Geological Position and Locality. The Cornbrash of Northamptonshire; also in the Forest Marble of Wiltshire, obtained by W. Walton, Esq.

ISOCARDIA MINIMA, *Sow.* Tab. XXXVI, figs. 1, 1 *a*.

ISOCARDIA MINIMA, *Sow.* Min. Con., t. 295, fig. 1.
— — *Phillips.* Geol. York., i, t. 7, fig. 6.
— — *Morris.* Catal., 1854, p. 204.
— — ? *Quenstedt.* Der Jura, p. 443, pl. 60, fig. 17.
Non ISOCARDIA MINIMA, *Goldf.* Pet., p. 211, t. 140, fig. 18.

Testa crassa, lævigata, tumida, umbonibus parvis submedianis incurvis, margine dorsali oblique-curvato, lunula excavata; lateribus striis concentricis crebris æqualibus, tenuissimis instructis.

Shell thick, smooth, convex; umbones small, somewhat oblique, and placed a little anterior to the middle of the valves; dorsal border curved obliquely; lunule excavated; the surface of the valves with very delicate, closely arranged, concentric striations.

A smooth, short, rounded, and moderately convex shell, with rather small umbones, quite different from the casts figured by Goldfuss and attributed by him to this species, but which probably belong to the genus Cardium.

The single figure given by Quenstedt is much more inflated, with larger umbones, and is probably also distinct; it is from a lower geological position, associated with *Trigonia signata*, Ag., and other Inferior Oolite fossils of that stage.

Another shell erroneously attributed to our species is *I. minima*, Damon ('Geol. Weymouth,' Suppl., pl. iv, fig. 7), from the Coral Rag of Weymouth; it is much more oblique, with produced umbones.

The figures given in the 'Mineral Conchology' and in the 'Geology of Yorkshire' may each be objected to for the great prominence of the umbones and the large excavation of the lunule. The Yorkshire examples, which are very well preserved, differ somewhat from each other in the degree of their obliquity; some have a slightly defined, oblique, posterior angle. The height and length are usually equal, the diameter through the valves being one fourth less.

Geological Position and Locality. The Cornbrash of the Yorkshire coast, in which it is not uncommon.

Isocardia tenera. Tab. XXXVIII, figs. 5, 5 *a*, 5 *b*.

Isocardia tenera. Gr. Ool. Monog., t. 7, fig. 1, part 2, p. 66.
— — Ibid., t. 38, fig. 5, Supplement.

As the figures given in the former portion of this Monograph represent a specimen deprived of the test, a fine example in a perfect condition is now given, together with a magnified figure of the ornamentation of the surface. The Cornbrash and the Lower Calcareous Grit of Yorkshire yield specimens with the test very beautifully preserved, brown and shining. One from the former rock has been selected; the valves have delicate, regular, concentric striations; and when a portion of the external lamina of the test has decomposed, the striations are decussated by others radiating from the umbones, as is also seen in *Isocardia nitida;* these radiating striations belong only to the inner layer of the test.

Isocardia nitida, *Phil.* Tab. XXXVIII, figs. 6, 6 *a*, 6 *b*.

Isocardia nitida, *Phil.* Geol. York., i, pl. 9, fig. 10.
— triangularis, *Bean.* Mag. Nat. Hist., 1839, p. 60, fig. 20.
— nitida et I. triangularis, *Morris.* Catal., 1854, p. 204.

Testa crassa, nitida, inflata, ovato-trigona, umbonibus medianis, altis, acuminatis, sub-involutis, latere postico angulo obliquo acuto et area postico subconcavo; basi postice sinuato; valvis striis regularibus, longitudinalibus, crebris; nucleo lævi.

Shell thick, shining, moderately inflated, ovately trigonal; umbones mesial, elevated, acuminated, subinvolute; the posterior side with an oblique, acute angle, which separates a slightly concave, posterior area; the base is sinuated posteriorly; the sides of the valves have closely arranged, regular, delicate, longitudinal striations. The nucleus is smooth.

The anterior side is more produced and less inflated than *Isocardia tenera*, Sow., from which, also, it differs in having an acute posterior angle. When the external shining surface has been abraded, it becomes the *Isocardia triangularis* of Bean, with radiating striations, which indent the longitudinal ridges, a feature of which there are analogous examples in some species of Ceromya, Pecten, &c. The inner border of the valves is crenulated, and the ultimate stage of growth is distinguished by a deeply grooved, longitudinal fold.

Length, 14 lines; height, 11 lines; diameter through the valves, 10 lines.

Geological Position and Locality. The Cornbrash of Scarborough, in which it is not uncommon.

Lucina striatula, *Buv.* (var.). Tab. XXXVIII, fig. 7.

Lucina striatula, *Buvignier*. Paléont. de la Meuse, Atlas, p. 12, pl. 12, figs. 6, 7, 8.

Testa orbiculari, depressa, striis concentricis, tenuibus, interdum majoribus et striis radiantibus obsoletis decussata; cardine subbidentato; impressione musculari anteriore longa, angusta, posteriore obovata; impressione palleali rugosa, substriata, sulco obliquo incurvo notata. (Buvignier.)

Shell suborbicular, depressed, inequilateral; anterior margin horizontal and nearly straight; outline of the borders of the valves rather irregular; the surface with very delicate, densely arranged, and a few distant, large, concentric striations, decussated by numerous faintly marked, longitudinal lines; anterior muscular impression lengthened, narrow, the posterior one obovate; the pallial impression rugose, with an obliquely curved sulcus. Height and transverse diameter equal.

The original of our figure is less transverse than that of M. Buvignier, but in other particulars strictly agrees with it; it is much less convex then *L. rotundata*, Roem., and the surface ornamentation is quite distinct, but the outline of the two species is very similar.

Geological Positions and Localities. Collected in the Great Oolite of Kirklington, Oxon., by Mr. Whiteaves. M. Buvignier records it from the Upper Coral Rag of the Meuse. Casts which are not uncommon in the Coral Rag of the southern counties of England appear to belong to the same species.

Lucina ? Burtonensis, *Lyc.* Tab. XL, figs. 20, 20 *a*, 20 *b*.

Testa suborbiculata, depressa, umbonibus subangulatis antrorsum curvatis, latere postico area depressiuscula, superficie striis tenuibus concentricis crebris notatis.

Shell suborbicular, depressed; umbones antero-mesial, angulated at their extremities, and curved forwards; the posterior side has a depressed, oblique area, without any angle; the surface has very delicate, closely arranged, regular, concentric striations; the hinge-border is short, and slightly curved.

As the hinge has not been exposed, some doubt may exist whether it is really a Lucina; the umbones are more produced than is commonly seen in that genus.

Geological Position and Locality. The Forest Marble of Burton Bradstock, Dorset, in the collection of W. Walton, Esq.

Lucina Beanii, *Bean*, sp. Tab. XXXVIII, fig. 3.

Astarte rotundata, *Bean.* Mag. Nat. Hist. 1839, *non* Roemer.

Testa tumida ovato-obliqua, umbonibus antemedianis, magnis, incurvis, margine cardinali oblique-declivi, curvato, margine antico brevi, arcuato curvato; valvis striis irregularibus, plicisque semel instructis.

Shell somewhat inflated, oblique, ovate; umbones prominent, obtuse, incurved, placed anterior to the middle of the valves; hinge-margin lengthened, curved, sloping obliquely downwards; anterior margin short, rounded; lunule very slightly excavated; the surface of the valves has irregular, concentric striations, and also a few large plications of growth. The interior has not been exposed, but neither the hinge-margin nor the anterior border possesses the usual characters of Astarte, the lunule being nearly obsolete. It is shorter and more convex than *Lucina crassa*, nor does it nearly resemble any other contemporaneous species.

Height and lateral diameter nearly equal; diameter through both the valves, one third less.

Geological Position and Locality. The Cornbrash of Scarborough, in the collection of Mr. Leckenby.

Corbis Neptuni, *Lyc.* Tab. XXXV, fig. 19.

Testa transverse ovali subæquilatera, concentrice costata, margine cardinali curvato, oblique declivi, lunula magna excavata, umbonibus medianis subdepressis, antrorsum curvatis; costis concentricis regularibus angustis, striisque interstitiis instructis.

Transversely oval, convex, nearly equilateral; umbones rather depressed, curved forwards; lunule large, excavated; hinge-border curved and sloping downwards; the extremities are rounded and the base curves elliptically; the concentric costæ are regular, narrow, elevated, the interstitial spaces having delicate longitudinal striations. The convexity is moderate beneath the umbones, the extremities of the shell being rather compressed; the general figure approaches to *C. Leymerii*, Buv., but that species has the posterior side shorter and less rounded. The present shell is more lengthened than is usual with the Jurassic species, and the concentric costæ are less conspicuous.

Length, 19 lines; height, 12 lines; diameter through the valves, 9 lines.

Geological Position and Locality. The upper portion of the Great Oolite, near Minchinhampton, in pale, buff-coloured Oolite; few specimens have been obtained, and these, for the most part, are only casts.

CORBIS ELLIPTICA, *Whiteaves*, MSS. Tab. XXXV, fig. 1.

Testa ovato-elongata, depressa, umbonibus parvis medianis, margine antico subhorizontali, postico oblique declivi; basi elliptico curvato; superficie rugis longitudinalibus regularibus, magnis, elevatis, crebris.

Shell ovately elongated, rather depressed; umbones small, but little elevated, mesial; anterior margin nearly horizontal; posterior margin sloping obliquely downwards; the two extremities of the shell are rounded, and the base is curved elliptically; the surface is ornamented with large, elevated, longitudinal, regular, and closely arranged rugæ.

Length, 7½ lines; height, half the length.

A small, depressed, and unusually lengthened Corbis, which will not readily be mistaken for any other known Jurassic species.

Geological Position and Locality. The Forest Marble of Kidlington, Oxon., collected by Mr. Whiteaves.

CORBIS ROTUNDA, *Walton*, MSS. Tab. XL, fig. 17.

Testa crassa, ovato rotundata, umbonibus magnis medianis antrorsum curvatis, lateribus sub-æqualibus postice subcompressa, superficie rugis concentricis magnis, crebris, subæqualibus; ætate adulto rugis obsoletis; cardo dente antico laterali magno.

Shell thick, ovately orbicular, subglobose; umbones large, mesial, curved forwards; the sides nearly equal, but the posterior side is slightly compressed and shortened; the surface with large, closely arranged, concentric, but somewhat unequal rugæ, which degenerate in the adult state and nearly disappear.

It has sometimes been mistaken for *Sphæra Madridi*, but it is more orbicular, and the umbones are larger; the concentric rugæ will also at once distinguish it, as the young shell of *S. Madridi* is smooth.

Geological Positions and Localities. The Great Oolite of Hampton cliffs; the Cornbrash of Laycock. In the collection of W. Walton, Esq.

OPIS LECKENBYI, *Wright.* Tab. XXXVII, figs. 9, 9 *a.*

OPIS LECKENBYI, *Wright*, in Proc. Geol. Soc., vol. xvi, part 1, 1860.

Testa crassa, trigona, obliqua, fornicata, inæquilatera, cordiformi, transverse regulariter costata, postice acute carinata, umbonibus magnis elevatis, anticis, involutis, latere antico brevissimo, postico subrecto oblique declivi; lunula magna profunda, marginibus obtusis, striatis; costis transversis, regularibus, angustis, subacutis; valvis striis longitudinalibus et decussantibus subtillissimis instructis.

Shell thick, trigonal, oblique, very convex, and inæquilateral, cordiform, with transverse, regular costæ; a large, flattened, posterior area is separated from the other portion of the shell by an elevated, acute carina, anterior and parallel to which is a slight depression; the umbones are large, elevated, much inclined forwards, and involute; the anterior side is very short, having a large and deep lunule, whose margin is rounded and striated; the costæ upon the sides of the valves are regular, narrow, subacute, and not much elevated; the wide, posterior area has large, oblique striations; the costated portion is covered with extremely fine perpendicular and decussating striations, which are only distinguishable under a magnifier.

Height, 15 lines; length, 15 lines; diameter through both the valves, 13 lines.

A large and elegant species, distinguished from *Opis lunulatus*, Sow., by the more convex figure, the rounded margins of the lunule, and by the more acute and more densely arranged costæ; the posterior carina and bordering sulcation are also very prominent features; the costæ under a magnifier exhibit a beautifully decussated surface.

Geological Position and Locality. The Cornbrash of Scarborough; a single specimen in the collection of Mr. Leckenby.

OPIS PULCHELLA, *D'Orb.* Part II, Tab. VI; fig. 3, p. 80.

OPIS PULCHELLA, *D'Orbigny.* Prodrome, i, p. 307.
— LUNULATUS, var. Great Ool. Mon., Pal. Soc., part 2, pl. 6, fig. 6, p. 80.

Espèce voisine de l'O. lunulata, mais bien plus courte et moins oblique, presque carrèe ornèe de còtes concentriques." (D'Orbigny.)

The experience derived from a multitude of examples leaves no room to doubt that the

Minchinhampton Opis allied to *O. lunulatus* is distinct from the typical Inferior Oolite shell, and that D'Orbigny has correctly indicated its distinctive characters in the brief sentence above quoted; our figures in Part II, Tab. VI, faithfully represent the Great Oolite species.

OPIS LUCIENSIS, *D'Orb.* Tab. XL, figs. 19, 19 *a*.

OPIS LUCIENSIS, *D'Orbigny*. Prodrome, i, p. 307, No. 106.

Testa subtrigona, postice acute carinata, umbonibus prominentibus acutis, lunula permagna, profunda, lævigata, inferne rostrata, area posteriora sulco obliquo instructo; superficie striis tenuibus concentricis, interdum obsoletis.

Shell subtrigonal, short, posteriorly acutely carinated, with a conspicuous, oblique sulcus upon the post-carinal area; the umbones are elevated, acute, moderately incurved; the lunule is very large and deeply excavated, occupying the entire anterior side; the surface is smooth, with an acute, plain margin, its lower extremity forming a rostrated projection; the posterior surface of the valves has very delicate, concentric striations, which are only partially visible.

It is allied to *O. pulchella*, but is shorter, less convex, the umbones are more prominent and less incurved, the lunule is very much larger, the posterior keel more acute, the surface more smooth.

Geological Position and Locality. The Great Oolite of the Box Tunnel, near Bath, in the collection of W. Walton, Esq.

CORBULA ATTENUATA, *Lyc.* Tab. XXXVII, figs. 6, 6 *a*.

Testa convexa, parva, subæquilatera, transversa, longitudinaliter, subtillissime striata; latere posteriore attenuato, rostrato, producto; angulo obliquo instructo; basi leviter curvato, postice subsinuato.

Shell small, convex, nearly equilateral, transverse, longitudinally very finely striated; anterior and posterior borders sloping obliquely downwards; the posterior side is attenuated; it has an oblique angle, which separates a narrow posterior space; its lower extremity is rostrated; the anterior lower extremity is elliptically curved; the lower border is lengthened, slightly curved, and posteriorly somewhat sinuated; the umbones are small and somewhat pointed. The figure is more elongated and has less convexity than the other Great Oolite species of the genus; the striations upon the posterior slope are bent upwards at a right angle to their direction across the valve.

Height, equal to two thirds of the length, and a third greater than the diameter through both the valves.

Geological Positions and Localities. This well-marked little Corbula has been kindly forwarded by J. F. Whiteaves, Esq., from the Great Oolite of Kirklington, Oxon.; also by W. Walton, Esq., from the Forest Marble of Laycock, Wilts.

CORBULA INVOLUTA, *Munst.* Tab. XXXVII, figs. 4, 4 *a.*

CORBULA INVOLUTA, *Goldf.* Pet., t. 151, fig. 14.
CYPRINA — *D'Orb.* Prodrome, i, p. 278, No. 309.

Testa crassa, parva, perinflata; concentrice subtillissime striata; umbonibus magnis obtusis, submedianis; latere antico rotundo, postico rostrato, obtuse carinato et attenuato.

Shell small, thick, greatly inflated, with very delicate, concentric striations; umbones large, obtuse, submesial; anterior side short, rounded, posterior side attenuated, rostrated, its margin concave, and forming at its lower extremity an acute angle; the posterior slope has delicate, transverse striations; it is somewhat flattened, very narrow, and is only obscurely separated from the dorsal portion of the shell by an obtuse angle; the lower border is nearly straight.

Length, one third greater than the height and the diameter through both the valves.

The foregoing description will serve to distinguish it from a small, thick, but less inflated species, abundant in the Great Oolite of Minchinhampton, and which was formerly regarded by me as *C. involuta* of Munster, and figured under that title in Part II, Tab. VI, of the 'Great Oolite Monograph,' and described in Part II, p. 97; it had previously been figured and described by Professor Buckman, in Sir R. Murchison's 'Geology of Cheltenham,' 2nd ed., p. 97, pl. 3, fig. 4, under the title of *Corbula striata;* but as that name had already been appropriated by Lamarck for an Eocene Corbula, it becomes necessary to change it to *C. Buckmani,* under which name it is refigured, Tab. XXXVII, fig. 8, thrice magnified.

Geological Position and Locality. The Great Oolite of Kirklington, Oxon.; collected by J. F. Whiteaves, Esq.

CORBULA ISLIPENSIS, *Lyc.* Tab. XXXVII, fig. 7.

Testa parva, inflata, umbonibus medianis, magnis, erectis, latere anteriore rotundo, posteriore brevi, abrupte truncato, angulo obliquo instructo; valvis longitudinaliter striatis, striis magnis regularibus, lineis angustis separatis; lunula excavata; basi subrecto.

Shell small, inflated, but subquadrate or cuculæform; umbones large, mesial, erect; anterior side rounded, its lunule excavated; posterior side short, abruptly truncated, with an oblique and subacute angle separating a posterior smooth and slightly concave area; the lower border is nearly straight; the dorsal surface has large, regular, longitudinal striations, separated by elevated, narrow lines, which disappear at the posterior angle.

The height, length, and diameter through the united valves are nearly equal; the test is thick.

The shortness of the posterior side, its angle, and the greater prominence of the umbones, will distinguish it from *C. striata*, Buck. (*C. Buckmanii*, nobis, Pl. XXXVII, fig. 8). *Corbula involuta*, Munster, has the posterior side more lengthened and rostrated, and is almost destitute of the posterior angle; the striations upon the surface are much more delicate and faintly traced, they are oblique rather than concentric or longitudinal. *Corbula cuculæformis*, Kock and Dunker, is also allied to it, but with the figure less inflated and with more pointed umbones; it is therefore, probably, distinct. Possibly *C. amata*, D'Orb., may be identical with our species, but unfortunately the few words of description in the 'Prodrome' of that author are insufficient to characterise it; the same remark will also apply to his *C. Aglaya* and *C. Alimena*.

Geological Position and Locality. The Bradfordian beds of Islip, Oxon.; collected by J. F. Whiteaves, Esq.

CORBULA HULLIANA, *Mor.* Tab. XXXVII, fig. 5.

CORBULA HULLIANA, *Morris*. Hull. Mem. Geol. Surv., Cheltenham, 1857, pl. I, fig. 6.

Testa crassiuscula, inflata, ovato-trigona, subæquivalvi, subæquilaterali, antice producta, rotunda, postice attenuata, sulco obliquo et carina marginali obtuse; umbonibus magnis subacutis incurvis; basi subarcuato aut subrecto; lateribus costis obliquis angustis, elevatis, regularibus postice undulatis; striis radiantibus decussatis.

Shell of moderate thickness, much inflated, ovately trigonal, subæquivalve, subæquilateral; umbones large, incurved, and pointed; anterior side produced and rounded, posterior side more attenuated, with an oblique groove and submarginal, obtuse, rugose keel, the base arcuated, or in other specimens nearly straight and slightly irregular; the surface of the valves with prominent, oblique, regular, narrow costæ, which are slightly undulated posteriorly; occasionally the left valve exhibits towards the middle of its lower portion a few perpendicular striations, which decussate the costæ and render the lower margin dentated.

The largest of the British Oolitic Corbulæ, with the hinge-characters strongly marked; the valves are less thick than usually obtains in the genus; it is also apparently equivalve; a well-preserved specimen of the left valve is destitute of the perpendicular striations.

Geological Position and Localities. The specimen figured in the 'Memoirs of the Geological Survey of Great Britain' was obtained in the Forest Marble near to Northleach; it occurs in the same position at Hinton, at Farleigh, and at Kidlington, Oxon., specimens have been forwarded to me by Mr. Walton and by Mr. J. F. Whiteaves; at the Oxfordshire locality, the specimens are small and usually compressed.

CORBULA AGATHA, *D'Orb.* Tab. XL, figs. 28, 28 *a.*

CORBULA AGATHA, *D'Orb.* Prodrome, i, p. 307, No. 100.

Testa parva, subglobosa, lævigata, nitida, umbonibus magnis, obtusis, medianis, erectis, latere anteriore rotundo; lunula magna, concava, cordata; latere posteriore brevi, subcarinata, truncata.

Shell small, globular, smooth, shining; umbones large, obtuse, mesial, erect; anterior side rounded, lunule large, cordiform, concave; posterior side very short, with a faintly marked oblique carina, and a truncated posterior border; the surface has a few delicate, irregular folds of growth; it appears to be equivalve.

The diameter through both the valves is equal to the height, and somewhat less than the length.

Corbula Deshaysea, Buv., is also a smooth species, but less short, the posterior border being also slightly sinuated. *Corbula Macneillii,* Mor., another smooth shell, is much more oblique, and more produced posteriorly. *Corbula obscura,* Sow., appears to be less convex, and to have the posterior side more produced.

Geological Position and Locality. The Forest Marble of Cirencester and of Wiltshire.

Genus—SOWERBYA, *D'Orb.*, 1850.

ISODONTA, *Buv.* Bull. Soc. Géol. de Fr., sér. 2, t. 8, p. 353, 1851.

Shell equivalve, subequilateral, the valves close fitting; hinge in the right valve, with two oblique, diverging, symmetrical cardinal teeth separated by a mesial trigonal pit, and two lamellar lateral teeth separated from the hinge-border by longitudinal grooves. The left valve with a projecting conical tooth between two oblique pits; lateral teeth two, longitudinal, lamellar, projecting and united to the superior border. Ligament external. Muscular impressions small, rounded, deeply marked; palleal impression emarginated posteriorly.

M. D'Orbigny in his 'Prodrome de Paléontologie,' vol. i, 13 Et., p. 362, characterised his genus Sowerbya as follows:—"*Sowerbya,* D'Orb., 1847.—Coquille voisine des *Mactra* par son sinus, mais avec des dents laterales énormes, et une fossette interne ligamentaire simplement creusée."

It appears from the above quotation that M. D'Orbigny was acquainted only with the hinge of the right valve of his *Sowerbya crassa*, upon which species the genus was founded, and that he mistook the mesial dental pit for a fosse destined to receive an internal ligament. In 1851, M. Buvignier having worked out the details of the generic characters from specimens obtained in the upper ferruginous Oolite of the Oxfordian strata of Ornes (Mense), and Launoy (Ardennes), gave them to the public in the 'Bulletin of the Geological Society of France,' sér. 2, t. 8, p. 353, under the new generic designation of *Isodonta*. It is to the researches of M. Buvignier, therefore, that we are indebted for a full and accurate description of *Sowerbya*. The same author states that M. Terquem has discovered one nearly allied to the typical form in the Bradfordian beds of the Mozelle.

The Jurassic rocks of England contain upwards of five species of Sowerbya:—1, *S. triangularis*, from the Oxfordian and Lower Oolites of Yorkshire; 2, *S. Woodwardi*, from the Great Oolite of the Minchinhampton district; 3, a small abruptly truncated species from the Coral Rag of Yorkshire and Oxfordshire; 4, a small subæquivalve shell, with a posterior strongly marked oblique angle from the Coral Rag of Bullingdon; 5, an internal cast of a large species determined by Mr. Woodward, and figured by Mr. Damon in his 'Geology of Weymouth,' from the Portland Oolite, under the name of *S. Dukei*.

Sowerbya triangularis, *Phil.*, sp. Tab. XXXV, figs. 3, 3 *a*, 3 *b*.

Cucullæa triangularis, *Phil.* Geol. York., i, pl. 3, fig. 30.
Arca triangularis, *D'Orb.* Prodr., i, p. 369.
Cucullæa triangularis, *Mor.* Catal., 1854, p. 197.

Testa transverse, oblonga, inflata, subæquilatera, postice oblique carinata, umbonibus parvis postero-medianis, margine inferiore angulo formante; superficie plicis longitudinalibus paucis magnis et striis longitudinalibus subtillissimis ornata.

Shell transverse, oblong, inflated, slightly inæquilateral; the posterior side the shorter, with a posterior oblique angle, separating a posterior slightly excavated surface which terminates downwards in a conspicuous angle; the anterior side is produced and curved elliptically; the umbones are placed a little posterior to the middle of the valves; they are small and contiguous. The surface has one or two large folds of growth, and is ornamented with longitudinal, regular, closely arranged striations, which disappear upon the posterior excavated slope.

The height is about equal to the diameter through both the valves, and to three fifths of the length.

The species exhibits much variability in the general figure, in the degree of convexity, in the prominence of the posterior angle, and in the length; differences which are not limited to a single formation or locality, as it occurs in the Yorkshire Oolites in the

Dogger, the Gray Limestone, the Cornbrash, the Kelloway Rock, and the Coral Rag; numerous specimens are also in the Tessonian collection from Normandy, now in the British Museum. Some of these examples are almost destitute of the posterior angle, and approach so nearly in the general figure to *Sowerbya crassa*, D'Orb. = *Isodonta Deshaysea*, Buv., that they might fairly have been assigned to that species, if we had not the assurance of M. Buvignier that his specimens from two localities are in a good state of preservation, and that they are destitute of ornamentation—a feature which is always discoverable in good examples of *S. triangularis*, whether British or Foreign.

Mr. Whiteaves has figured a small species of Sowerbya, 'Ann. and Mag., Nat. Hist.,' August, 1861, under the name of *S. triangularis*, Phil. Having had the advantage of comparing the original specimen, through the kindness of Mr. Whiteaves, with various Yorkshire specimens of *S. triangularis*, I feel unable to coincide in the opinion that it is identical with the species of Professor Phillips; the new Oxfordshire form is much smaller, less inflated, destitute of ornamentation; and the posterior side is so short that '*truncata*' would be an appropriate name: it is from the Coral Rag of Oxfordshire. I have also found it in the Calcareous Grit at Scarborough Castle.

The second small species figured by Mr. Whiteaves upon the same plate under the name of *S. Deshaysea*, Buv.? also appears to be distinct from each of the foregoing examples; the general figure is more compressed, the anterior slope is excavated, which renders its lower extremity pointed; the whole aspect somewhat resembles a *Nucula*.

Our specimen figured is from the Cornbrash of Scarborough.

SOWERBYA WOODWARDI, *Lyc.* Pl. XL, figs. 27, 27 *a*, 27 *b*, 27 *c*.

Testa ovato-trigona subdepressa, subæquilatera, latere posteriore breviori, planata, lævigata angulo obliquo diviso, dorso et latere antico striis longitudinalibus regularibus crebris, delicate instructis.

Shell ovately trigonal, rather depressed, subequilateral, the posterior side being the shorter; the umbones are not very prominent nor large; the anterior and posterior borders slope obliquely downwards; the extremities of the valves are rounded; the surface has delicate, closely arranged regular longitudinal or concentric striations, which are separated from the smooth and flattened posterior side by a distinct angle.

It is much smaller, more depressed, more lengthened, and the umbones are much less elevated than in *S. triangularis*. Our right hand figure is imperfect at the posterior extremity, and the posterior oblique angle is not clearly shown; the left hand figure has the anterior extremity too obtusely rounded, the specimen wanting a little of its border.

Geological Position and Locality. The Great Oolite of Bussage, near to Bisley

Common, collected by E. Witchell, Esq. A specimen has also been brought under my notice by S. P. Woodward, Esq., but its locality is uncertain.

TANCREDIA GIBBOSA, *Lyc.* Tab. XXXV, fig. 7. Tab. XXXVI, fig. 11.

TANCREDA GIBBOSA, *Lyc.* Cott. Hills Handb., p. 121, pl. 7, fig. 4.

Testa subtrigona, tumidula, umbonibus medianis acutis, latere antico attenuato, postice tumido subangulato; dorso lævigato, plicis incrementi, paucis irregularibus.

Shell subtrigonal, tumid; umbones elevated, pointed, and placed a little anterior to the middle of the valves; the anterior side is rather attenuated and pointed at the lower extremity; the posterior side slopes obliquely downwards, it is somewhat tumid, and has an oblique angle slightly defined; the surface is smooth, but with a few plications of growth towards the lower border.

Height, 10 lines; length, 13 lines; diameter through both the valves, 6 lines.

It is distinguished from other Great Oolite species by the combination of a trigonal outline with a tumid figure.

Geological Position and Locality. It occurs rarely in the Great Oolite shelly weatherstones of Minchinhampton Common, and the Forest Marble of Farleigh, Somerset.

TANCREDIA MACTRÆOIDES, *Whiteaves*, MSS. Tab. XXXV, fig. 4.

Testa ovato trigona, convexa, umbonibus submedianis elevatis, incurvis; margine antico breviore, læviter excavato, margine postico oblique declivi, angulo oblique læviter instructo, basi elliptico curvato.

Shell ovately trigonal, convex, with a few concentric plications; umbones antero-mesial, elevated, and incurved; anterior border the shorter, slightly concave; the extremity pointed; posterior hinge-border sloping obliquely; there is also a posterior oblique angle faintly marked.

Tancredia gibbosa, Lyc., approximates to this species, but is more convex, with a more elevated and rounded posterior slope. *T. axiniformis*, Phil., from the Inferior Oolite of Yorkshire, is more flattened, with more pointed umbones and acute posterior angle. Height two thirds of the length.

Geological Position and Locality. The Great Oolite of Stonesfield, Oxon., where it appears to be rare; collected by J. F. Whiteaves, Esq.

TANCREDIA SIMILIS, *Whiteaves*, MSS. Tab. XXXV, fig. 9.

Testa ovato elongata, umbonibus antemedianis, latere antico attenuato, breviore; postico convexo, angulo obtuso obliquo; basi elliptica curvata.

Shell ovately elongated; umbones placed anterior to the middle of the valves, rather depressed and obtuse; anterior side the shorter, its upper margin slightly excavated, its lower extremity pointed; posterior side larger, more convex, with an oblique obtuse angle; the hinge-border is moderately lengthened and horizontal; the surface is smooth, the lower border is elliptically curved.

T. extensa, Lyc., 'Gr. Ool. Mon.,' p. 93, approximates to the present form, but has a much larger anterior side, with the umbones more elevated and mesial.

The height slightly exceeds half the length.

Geological Position and Locality. The Great Oolite of Kirklington, Oxon., collected by Mr. Whiteaves.

CORBICELLA SUBÆQUILATERA, *Lyc.* Tab. XXXV, fig. 12.

CORBICELLA SUBÆQUILATERA, *Lycett.* Cotteswold Hills Handbook, p. 126.

Testa ovato-obliqua lævigata, umbonibus parvis, antero-medianis, lunula angusta, sulco ligamenti angusto, margine superiore oblique curvato.

Shell oblique, ovate, smooth; umbones not prominent, placed a little anterior to the middle of the valves; anterior border slightly depressed, lunule narrow; superior border curved obliquely; ligamental sulcus narrow and lengthened; surface of the valves smooth, the lines of growth being only faintly impressed. The height is equal to two thirds of the length; the diameter through both the valves is equal to about half the height.

This shell presents an example of a remarkable series of Jurassic bivalves, whose characteristic features are intermediate between Corbis and Tancredia, and which may usually be discriminated without reference to the hinge; compared with Corbis, the more depressed form, the smallness of the anterior side, and the surface destitute of ornament, will always distinguish it; from Tancredia by the more ovate form, and by the absence of the posterior oblique angle. The hinge is figured upon Pl. XII, fig. 15, of the 'Great Oolite Monograph;' but the artist has scarcely extended the hinge-lamina sufficiently to exhibit the depressed posterior lateral lamellar process; the absence of the anterior lateral tooth, and the figure of the cardinal dentition, is also distinct from Corbis, and is more nearly allied to Tancredia, from which it differs chiefly in possessing a lengthened hinge-lamina and depressed remote posterior lateral tooth; these distinctive features are remarkably persistent in every example of Corbicella, and tends greatly to strengthen its claims to a generic distinction.

Under the name of *Corbis lucida* our species was included in Mr. Bean's list of Cornbrash Fossils, published in the 'Magazine of Nat. Hist.,' 1839, but was not accompanied by any figure or description.

Geological Positions and Localities. The specimen figured is a fine example from the

Cornbrash of Scarborough, in which rock it is rare. The lower grit of the upper portion of the Inferior Oolite at Rodborough Hill, near Stroud, has produced a considerable number of specimens, for the most part smaller, and sometimes more nearly equilateral; it also occurs in the same position at Leckhampton Hill; at each of these Inferior Oolite localities it is associated with a larger, more lengthened, and more depressed species. (*C. complanata*, Lyc.). *Corbis depressa*, Desh., from the Oxfordian strata of Viel, St. Remy, approaches nearly to it in the general outline, but is more depressed and somewhat less ovate.

CORBICELLA SUBANGULATA, *Lyc.* Tab. XL, fig. 9.

Testa ovata sub-compressa, transversa, umbonibus antemedianis, mediocri magnitudine, margine cardinali oblique declivi, latere postico angulo oblique instructo, margine antico subconcavo, superficie plicis incrementi magnis irregularibus.

Shell ovate, somewhat depressed, transverse; umbones of moderate size, placed anterior to the middle of the valves; hinge-border of moderate length, sloping obliquely downwards; the posterior side has an oblique angle; the anterior border is slightly concave; the surface has numerous plications of growth, which become large and irregular towards the lower border.

Allied to *C. complanata*, Lyc., from which it is distinguished by the strongly marked posterior angle, and by the larger umbones; our specimen is imperfect at the posterior extremity.

Geological Position and Locality. The Forest Marble of Laycock; in the collection of W. Walton, Esq.

CYPRINA ISLIPENSIS, *Lyc.* Tab. XXXV, fig. 13.

Testa ovato-transversa, convexa, lævi, obliqua, umbonibus antemedianis magnis, incurvis, lunula magna, excavata, area parva lanceolata; latere postico compresso, angulo obliquo formante; basi elliptica curvata; striis concentricis tenuibus, irregularibus, subobsoletis.

Shell ovately transverse, convex, smooth, oblique; umbones large, incurved, placed anterior to the middle of the valves; area small, lanceolate; posterior side compressed and slightly concave, forming an oblique and well-defined angle with the other portion of the surface; lower border curved elliptically, forming an angle at its junction with the posterior border. Nearly allied to *Cyprina Loweana*, Mor. and Lyc., from which it is distinguished by the larger umbones; larger lunule, by the posterior flattened or concave area, and by the well-defined oblique and acute angle, which renders the posterior extremity somewhat rostrated.

Geological Positions and Localities. The specimen figured was obtained by Mr. Whiteaves in the Great Oolite of Kirklington, Oxon.; it has also occurred rarely in the same formation at Minchinhampton Common, and in the Cornbrash of Islip, Oxon.

CYPRINA BELLA, *Lyc.* Tab. XL, figs. 15, 15 *a.*

Testa ovato-orbiculari lævigata, subdepressa, umbonibus mediocris, antero-medianis, margine cardinali recto, subhorizontali, postice subangulata, lunula angusta vix depressa; superficie angulo postico obliquo instructo; striis incrementi crebris, irregularibus.

Shell transverse, ovately orbicular, smooth, rather depressed; umbones of moderate size, but little elevated, placed a little anterior to the middle of the valves and curved forwards; hinge margin straight, nearly horizontal, and slightly angulated posteriorly; the lunule is narrow, and but slightly impressed; the exterior surface has an oblique angle, posterior to which the surface is flattened; the striations of growth, and delicate, numerous and irregular.

The depressed form, posterior subhorizontal straight hinge border, and oblique posterior angle, are the features that will serve to distinguish it from allied contemporaneous forms. The numerous specimens placed at my disposal include examples from two to nine lines in length, which measurements usually exceed the height by one fifth.

Geological Position and Localities. The Forest Marble of Laycock and Pound Pill. In the collection of W. Walton, Esq.

CYPRINA DAVIDSONI, *Lyc.* Tab. XXXVI, figs. 6, 6 *a.*

Testa ovato-orbiculari crassa, convexa, obliqua, umbonibus obtusis submedianis antrorsum inflectis, marginibus arcuatis curvatis, latere postico area subplanata, angula obtuso obliquo interdum instructo, aut nullo; lunula vix excavata, inconspicua, superficie striis concentricis irregularibus.

Shell ovately orbicular, thick, convex, oblique, but varying much in the length and obliquity; umbones obtuse, submesial, directed forwards; margins of the valves curved elliptically and close fitting, lunule not conspicuous and scarcely excavated; the posterior side has a narrow, oblique, flattened space, sometimes separated from the other portion of the surface by an obtuse angle; in other instances there is no distinct angle; the surface has numerous irregular concentric and faintly marked plications.

Dimensions of a large specimen of medium figure; length, 17 lines; height, 15 lines; diameter through the valves, 11 lines.

It is liable to be mistaken for *Cyprina Loweana,* compared with which our shell is shorter, more convex, the test thicker, the umbones larger, less oblique, and more obtuse; the posterior flattened area is also a distinguishing feature when it is present.

Geological Position and Localities. The Forest Marble of Laycock and Farleigh, in the collection of W. Walton, Esq., of Bath.

Astarte ungulata, *Phil.*, sp. Tab. XXXV, fig. 20.

Astarte lurida, *Phil.* Geol. York., i, pl. 5, fig. 2, p. 137, non *A. lurida*, Sow.
— — *Williamson.* Trans. Geol. Soc., 2d ser., vol. vi, p. 149.
— — *Bean*, on Cornbrash Fossils, Mag. Nat. Hist., 1839.
— — *Leckenby*, on Kelloway Rock Fossils, Journ. Geol. Soc., 1858.

Testa suborbiculari aut subquadrangulari, depressa, inæquilatera, ad peripheriam concentrice costellata, costellis elevatis, subangularibus, concentrice subtillissime striatis; costellis inferne evanescentibus; margine cardinali curvato, lunula subnulla.

Shell suborbicular or somewhat subquadrangular, depressed, inequilateral; umbones small and only slightly produced; posterior and inferior margins rounded, lunule, obsolete; the surface near to the umbo with elevated acute concentric rugæ, which are impressed with very delicate concentric striations; the rugæ disappear towards the middle of the valve, the lower portion having only some plications of growth.

The character of the surface has a considerable resemblance to *Astarte Wiltoni*, 'Gr. Ool. Monogr.,' Tab. IX, f. 16; but the latter has the umbo much more produced, it has a distinctly excavated lunule and is more convex; other depressed species are sufficiently separated by their ornamentation.

Astarte lurida, Sow., which occurs in Gloucestershire at Nailsworth in gray shale near to the upper boundary of the Upper Lias, and in the lower portion of the overlying Supraliassic Sands associated with *Ammonites variabilis*, is a very different shell, whose figure is ovately trigonal and moderately convex, with prominent apex, well-marked lunule and depressed concentric rugæ; it does not therefore present a near approximation to our species.

Astarte ungulata has the height and lateral diameter equal; the valves are moderately thick; the size varies from 4 to 10 lines across. It is rare.

Geological Positions and Localities. Professor Phillips figured the interior of a valve from the Oxford Clay of Scarborough. Mr. Leckenby has recorded it in the Kelloway Rock of the same locality; our figure is taken from a Cornbrash specimen of the same coast now in the collection of Mr. Leckenby, and formerly in that of Mr. Bean, who identified the species with that originally figured in the 'Geology of Yorkshire.'

Astarte orbicularis, *Sow.* Tab. XL, fig. 33.

Astarte orbicularis, *Sow.* Min. Con., v, p. 65, tab. 444.
— — *Morris.* Catal., p. 187.
— — *D'Orb.* Prod. de Paléont., i, p. 308.

Testa parva suborbiculari, convexa, umbonibus medianis elevatis, lunula magna, valvis costulis concentricis numerosis, depressis, interstiis latioribus, subæqualibus.

Shell small, nearly orbicular, convex; umbones mesial and produced; lunule distinctly marked, rounded, the surface with numerous (about twenty) depressed, narrow, concentric little ribs, separated by somewhat wider and nearly equal spaces, upon the posterior side the ribs are slightly undulated.

The little ribs are strongly marked upon the sides, but much less so upon the middle of the valve, and are scarcely to be distinguished upon the umbones; they are so delicate that the surface appears plain without the aid of a magnifier; this latter feature will serve to distinguish it from other small species, as *A. minima*, Phil., *A. pisiformis*, Sow., *A. Parkinsoni*, Quenst. Of other small examples of the genus, *A. pisum*, Kock and Dunker, and *A. Pontonis*, Lyc., are much less orbicular, and have more prominent costæ; *A. mediolævis*, Buv., has the ornamentation of a similar character, but the figure is ovately trigonal, and therefore sufficiently distinct.

Geological Positions and Localities. The upper beds of the Great Oolite near Bath, where it appears to be not uncommon; also upon the same horizon at Ancliff, Wilts. Luc (Calvados).

Astarte politula, *Bean.* Tab. XXXV, fig. 16.

Astarte politula, *Bean.* Mag. Nat. Hist., 1839.

Testa suborbiculari, convexo-plana, umbonibus antemedianis parvis, acutis, incurvis, margine cardinali curvato, fossa ligamenti, angusto, elongato, margine antico subrecto lunula lanceolata, leviter excavato; valvis striis regularibus tenuissimis concentricis, inferiore irregulariter plicatis.

Shell suborbicular, rather depressed; umbones anterior to the middle of the valves, small, acute, incurved; hinge-border slightly curved; ligamental groove narrow and lengthened; anterior border nearly straight; lunule lanceolate and slightly excavated, its margins subacute; the surface of the valves with very fine, regular, concentric striations; the lower portion of the surface is destitute of striations, but has several irregular, concentric plications.

The convexity is moderate about the middle of the valves, but the test has not much thickness towards the borders, the outline has a considerable resemblance to *Lucina crassa* but the latter is much thicker towards the borders of the valves, and has a different kind of surface. The hinge has not been exposed.

Geological Position and Locality. The Cornbrash of Scarborough; in the collection of Mr. Leckenby.

Astarte Leckenbyi, *Wright.* Tab. XLII, fig. 3.

Testa crassa, transversa, ovata, subdepressa, umbonibus parvis, prominulis antero-medianis; latere antico brevi, margine rotundo, lunula subnulla; latere postico producto, margine superiori subrecto, elongato, oblique declivi; basi arcuato curvato; superficie rugis crebris concentricis et striis subtilibus ornatis.

Shell thick, transverse, ovate, rather depressed; umbones small, prominent, placed at the commencement of the anterior third of the shell; anterior side short, its margin rounded with scarcely any lunule; posterior side produced and compressed, its superior margin nearly straight, lengthened, sloping obliquely; the base is elliptically curved; the surface has prominent, concentric, closely arranged, rounded rugæ near to the umbones, which afterwards degenerate into depressed, irregular plications; there are also fine, concentric striations.

A large species, remarkable for the depression of the valves and for the great length and straightness of the superior border, whose measurement is equal to the height or to two thirds of the entire length of the shell; the rugæ are so closely arranged near to the apex that upwards of thirty may be counted upon one fourth the height of the shell.

From *Astarte elegans*, Sow., it is distinguished by the more lengthened, depressed figure, and by the absence of a smooth, excavated lunule; it is much less orbicular and convex than *A. detrita*, Goldf.; the depressed figure, lengthened, straight, upper margin, and large rugæ, will serve to distinguish it from other large ovate species of the lower Oolites. Specimens in Mr. Leckenby's collection exceed three inches in length. It is not rare, but, in common with other large shells of the Cornbrash, it has usually undergone compression.

Geological Position and Locality. The Cornbrash of Scarborough, in hard, gray limestone.

Astarte robusta, *Lyc.* Tab. XXXV, figs. 6, 6 *a.*

Testa parva suborbiculari, perinflata, umbonibus magnis medianis incurvis, margine posteriore et inferiore rotundo, lunula magna concava marginibus rotundis; valvis costis concentricis, regularibus, angustis, elevatis (16—18) *striisque subtillissimis, concentricis, impressis.*

Shell small, suborbicular, much inflated; umbones large, mesial, incurved; posterior and lower margins rounded; lunule very large, concave, its margins rounded; the surfaces of the valves have narrow, concentric, regular, elevated costæ, 16—18 in number, which are impressed by very delicate concentric striations; the intercostal spaces are upwards of three or four times the breadth of the costa.

Height, lateral diameter, and diameter through both the valves, each about 4 lines.

About thrice the size of a minute Cotteswold Inferior Oolite species which possesses a similar figure, but whose costæ are irregular. *Astarte Bulla*, Goldf., is also globose, but has only half the number of costæ. *A. integra*, Goldf., has less convexity and is more oblique; other small species, figured by Roemer, Buvignier, and by Quenstedt, have less convexity and more obliquity.

Geological Position and Locality. One of the more rare testacea of the Scarborough Cornbrash; in the collection of Mr. Leckenby.

ASTARTE PONTONIS, *Lyc.* Tab. XL, fig. 31.

Testa parva, convexa, ovato-orbiculari, umbonibus submedianis, acuminatis, antrorsum curvatis, margine cardinali elongato, subrecto, oblique declivi, lunula magna, costata; valvis costis concentricis numerosis (20) *elevatis, rotundis, interstiis angustis; latere superiore, area, elongata, planata et lævigata.*

Shell small, convex, ovately orbicular; umbones elevated, pointed, nearly mesial, and curved forwards; hinge-border lengthened, nearly straight, sloping obliquely downwards, forming a narrow, smooth area, separated from the costated part of the shell by an acute angle; the lunule is large, costated, and somewhat excavated; the surfaces of the valves have large, numerous (about 20) concentric, elevated, and rounded costæ, separated by more narrow interstitial spaces; adult shells have a large fold of growth near to the lower border.

A small, convex, neatly ornamented species, allied to *A. minima*, Phil., and *A. pisum*, Kock and Dunker; from the former it is distinguished by the more numerous and more closely arranged costæ, by the more pointed and more curved umbones, by the larger lunule, and by the posterior, straight, smooth, acutely bordered area; the latter feature will also separate it from *A. pisum* and from *A. supracorallina*, D'Orb.

The height and lateral diameter are about 4 lines.

Geological Position and Localities. It is abundant in the White Oolite (Great Oolite?) of Ponton, Lincolnshire.

Astarte Bathonica, *Lyc.* Tab. XL, figs. 23, 23 *a.*

Testa ovato-trigona, crassa gibbosa; umbonibus sub-anticis antrosum curvatis; lunula cordata, excavata, marginibus rotundatis, latere postico obtusangulo formante, superficie costis regularibus, rotundis, crebris, concentricis, marginibus interne denticulatis.

Shell ovately trigonal, thick, gibbose; umbones anterior and curved forwards; lunule excavated, cordate, its margins rounded; the posterior side has an obtuse, oblique angle; the surface has closely arranged, rounded, regular, concentric costæ; the margins of the valves are denticulated internally.

Height, 6 lines; opposite diameter, 5 lines; diameter through the valves, $4\frac{1}{2}$ lines.

A short and very convex, thick, shell, with elevated umbones and slightly truncated posterior border, which is pointed at its inferior extremity, near to which is a large fold of growth.

Geological Position and Locality. Hampton, Cliffs near Bath; collected by W. Walton, Esq., who states that, having found it at the base of the cliffs, some doubt may exist as to its real geological position. The mineral character of the specimen is ferruginous and identical with that of the bed of Great Oolite Corals and of other shells which unquestionably belong to the Great Oolite.

Astarte rustica, *Walton*, MSS. Tab. XXXV, fig. 5; Tab. XL, f. figs. 8, 8 *a.*

Testa parva, crassa, ovato-oblonga, plano-convexa, umbonibus parvis, antemedianis, acutis, margine, cardinali brevi, subhorizontali, antice rotundato, basi subarcuato, marginibus internis dentatis; lateribus costis angustis imprimis regularibus, deinde inæqualibus.

Shell small, ovately oblong, moderately convex, with thickened margins, internaly denticulated; umbones anterior to the middle of the valves, curved forwards, and acute; hinge-border short and horizontal, terminating in an obtuse angle. The anterior border is rounded; the lunule is only slightly excavated; the base line is nearly straight; the surface of the valves has an obscure, posterior, oblique angle; the costæ are narrow, at first regular, afterwards they become irregular and crowded.

Length, 5 lines; height, 4 lines; diameter through the valves, 3 lines.

Much variability exists in the prominence and arrangement of the costæ, which are sometimes very numerous and nearly obsolete, or they are distant and elevated. A little species, allied to *A. Voltzii*, Roem., *A. recondita*, Phil., and the young of *A. rhomboidalis*, Phil.; neither of these species, however, has the test so thickened towards the margins.

Geological Position and Locality. The Forest Marble of Laycock, Somerset; in the cabinet of W. Walton, Esq.

ASTARTE FIMBRIATA, *Walton*, MSS. Tab. XL, figs. 34, 34 *a*.

Testa transversa, ovata, subdepressa, umbonibus antemedianis parvis, margine cardinali elongato, subrecto, obliquo, acuto; lunula magna elliptica; lateribus costulis concentricis acutis, elevatis subdistantibus; ætate progrediente crebrioribus et irregularibus instructis.

Shell transverse, ovate, somewhat depressed; umbones small, depressed, curved forwards; hinge-margin lengthened, nearly straight, its margin acute and rendered fimbriated by the acute, projecting extremities of the costæ, which are elevated, concentric, distantly arranged, and regular in the young shell, but more closely arranged and irregular in specimens of adult growth; the lunule is large, elliptical, its margins acute.

Allied to *A. depressa*, Goldf., compared with which the umbones are less prominent and more oblique, the hinge-border more lengthened, the costæ more elevated and fewer; the convexity of the valves is also greater. The test is thinner than is usual with this genus.

Occasionally a small and ill-preserved specimen has been found in the Great Oolite of Minchinhampton, and mistaken for *A. minima*, Phil.; the costæ in the latter shell are more obtuse and more closely arranged, the general figure being more orbicular.

Geological Positions and Localities. The Forest Marble of Farleigh and the Great Oolite of Bussage, near Bisley Common.

ASTARTE? IGNOTA, *Lyc.* Tab. XL, fig. 10.

Testa subovata, subdepressa, postice truncata, inferne et postice oblique subangulata, umbonibus antemedianis acuminatis, lunula parva, superficie, plicis incrementi numerosis, delicate instructis.

Shell subovate, subdepressed posteriorly, with a truncated extremity to the hinge-border and with an oblique angle proceeding from the umbo to the inferior-posterior border; umbones antero-mesial, pointed, and curved forwards; lunule slightly impressed; the surfaces of the valves with delicate, irregular, numerous plications of growth.

The hinge not having been seen, the genus is rather doubtful; possibly it may be a *Cypricardia*.

Geological Position and Locality. The Forest Marble of Laycock; in the collection of W. Walton, Esq.

Astarte Hilpertensis, *Lyc.* Tab. XXXVI, fig. 10.

Testa crassa, convexa, ovato-trigonata, umbonibus subanticis prominentibus, lunula ovata profunda, margine cardinali curvato, elongato, oblique declivi, marginibus anterioribus, posterioribus et inferioribus ellipticis curvatis; superficie plicis incrementi crebris tenuibus.

Shell thick, convex, ovately trigonal; umbones antero-mesial, elevated, and curved forwards; lunule smooth, ovate, deep; hinge-margin lengthened, curved, sloping obliquely downwards; the anterior, posterior, and lower borders curved elliptically; the surface with delicate, numerous plications of growth.

A large, thick species, somewhat allied to *A. subtrigona*, Munst., but more convex, less angulated, and with a larger lunule.

Geological Position and Locality. The Cornbrash of Hilperton, Wilts, in the collection of W. Walton, Esq.

Astarte Aytonensis, *Bean* MSS. Tab. XL, fig. 13.

Testa ovato-oblonga, valde elongata, compressa, umbonibus depressis antemedianis, lunula concava, margine cardinali subhorizontali elongata, margine inferiore parallelo; lateribus rugis ellipticis, crebris, depressis subregularibus instructis.

Shell ovately oblong, much elongated, compressed; umbones anterior to the middle of the valves flattened; lunule concave; the hinge-margin lengthened and nearly horizontal; lower border conformable; the two extremities elliptically rounded; the surface with closely arranged, depressed, rounded, elliptical, partially irregular rugæ.

The general aspect has some resemblance to the shell figured in Part II, Pl. IX, figs. 18, 19, as a variety of *Astarte excavata*, but still more flattened and more elongated, with more conspicuous, regular, elliptical rugæ. Additional experience now leads me to rank *A. excavata*, var. *compressiuscula*, as a distinct species, and not as a dwarfed variety of the large Inferior Oolite shell; the present form is even more thin and flattened than *compressiuscula*, so much so as scarcely to allow any space for the animal.

Length nearly twice the height; the diameter through the united valves is little more than equivalent to their apparent thickness.

Geological Positions and Localities. The Great Oolite of Hampton Cliffs and of Comb Down, near Bath; collected by W. Walton, Esq. It occurs also in the Calcareous Grit of Ayton, near Scarborough, quite unaltered in any particular; the name from the locality having been adopted by Mr. Bean many years since, and sent to public collections, has therefore been retained.

ASTARTE FLEXICOSTATA, *Lyc.* Tab. XL, fig. 26.

Testa transversa, subtrigona, convexa, umbonibus anticis acutis, elevatis, margine anteriore truncata, abrupte declivi inferne angula formante ; lunula magna lævigata concava, margine acuto; margine inferiore subrecto; margine posteriore imprimis subhorizontali postice oblique declivi; superficie striis concentricis regularibus instructis, in medio evanescentibus.

Shell transverse, subtrigonal, convex; umbones anterior, pointed, and conspicuous; anterior side truncated, descending abruptly, and forming an angle with the lower border at its extremity; the lunule is large, concave, smooth, with an acute margin; the lower border is nearly straight; the posterior margin is nearly horizontal for the half of its length, then slopes obliquely downwards; the shell is moderately convex, with an oblique, obtuse angle, posterior to which the surface is more flattened; it has regular striations, which follow the direction of the lines of growth; they are conspicuous near to the umbones, but disappear upon the middle portion of the dorsal surface.

Height, 5 lines; length, 7 lines; diameter through the united valves, 3½ lines.

Geological Position and Locality. Collected by E. Witchell, Esq., in the white stone (Great Oolite) of Bussage, near to Bisley Common; a single specimen.

GRESSLYA PEREGRINA, *Phil.*, sp. Tab. XXXVI, figs. 2, 2 *a*, *b*.

In addition to the specimen figured in Pl. XV, Part II of the 'Great Oolite Monograph,' it has been deemed advisable to exemplify three other variations of form, by the aid of which the intermediate connecting links may readily be imagined. This Gresslya is very abundant in the Cornbrash, both in Wiltshire and Yorkshire, so that ample opportunities are afforded of studying every variation of form which it presents; these, as will be seen from our figures, are so considerable and so common that it seems impossible fairly to disconnect from them some other examples of Gresslya from the Inferior Oolite, as *Unio abductus*, Phil., *Gresslya latior*, Ag., *G. conformis*, Ag., *G. lunulata*, Ag., *G. erycina*, Ag., *G. concentrica*, Ag., and perhaps also *G. zonata*, Ag. In all these the same kind of surface obtains, and the outer, granulated tegument is precisely identical, belonging to that section of the genus in which the radiating lines and the granules are of the most minute size, and very densely arranged. It has been usual to select for *G. abducta* Inferior Oolite examples with short forms, elevated umbones, tumid anterior sides, and compressed posterior sides; but the shortness of figure is surpassed by some from the Cornbrash, and the inflation of the anterior side varies in amount with every specimen. From these, probably, must be separated *G. latirostris*, Ag., which attains to large dimensions, with a lengthened general form, compressed anterior side, and large longitudinal plications over the whole of the surface; it appears to be comparatively rare, and belongs to the upper stage of the Inferior Oolite.

THRACIA AMYGDALOIDEA, *Lyc.* Tab. XLIII, fig. 4.

Testa convexa, elongata, umbonibus depressis submedianis, latere antico producto, rotundato; postico subcompresso, attenuato, basi curvato, plicis longitudinalibus paucis, leviter instructis.

Shell elongated, convex; umbones postero-mesial, depressed; anterior side produced, its margin curved elliptically; posterior side rather compressed and attenuated, its superior border slightly excavated; the base is nearly straight; the surface has a few faintly marked, longitudinal plications of growth.

Compared with other examples of the genus, the length and the convexity are considerable; the umbones are likewise much depressed, obtuse, and but little conspicuous; the posterior angle is only distinguishable near to the umbones; the posterior extremity is slightly truncated. The height only very slight exceeds half the length.

Geological Position and Locality. Associated with valves of *Myacites calceiformis* in flaggy, argillaceous Oolite, upon the western border of Minchinhampton Common, at the lower boundary line of the Great Oolite; a single specimen.

MYACITES CALCEIFORMIS, *Phil.*, sp. Part II, Tab. XI, fig. 2; et Tab. XLII, figs. 1, 1 *a*.

As this shell possesses considerable variability of figure, another example is given from the Cornbrash of the Yorkshire Coast. In the former description (p. 114, line 8), these words should be erased—"*in the upper beds of the Inferior Oolite.*" An examination of numerous Yorkshire specimens has proved that they were all obtained in the Cornbrash, including the original specimen figured in the 'Geology of Yorkshire,' which was erroneously placed with the Inferior Oolite fossils, and figured with them in pl. xi of that work. The Cornbrash specimens have the test with its granulated tegument well preserved, but usually the fossil has undergone some compression or distortion. The former figure, Plate XI, fig. 2, represented a Minchinhampton specimen from the base of the Great Oolite. An Inferior Oolite shell frequently mistaken for *Myacites calceiformis* occurs only in the form of casts; it is more gibbose, with larger, more elevated umbones, the posterior side being much shorter and more attenuated. As the casts are common, and these distinctive characters are persistent, there can be no doubt that it must be distinguished from the species of Professor Phillips. Authorities generally have followed the 'Geology of Yorkshire,' and placed *Myacites calceiformis* in the Inferior Oolite, and Dr.

Oppel ('Juraformation') has made the Cornbrash shell into a new species, with the name of *Panopea Haueri;* I can, however, with confidence state that there is no evidence that the fossil in question has ever been obtained in Yorkshire lower than the Cornbrash; in Gloucestershire its lowest position is at the base of the Great Oolite.

MYACITES RECURVUM, *Phil.*, sp. Tab. XXXVI, figs. 4, 4 *a*.

AMPHIDESMA RECURVUM, *Phil.* Geol. York., i, pl. 5, fig. 25.
LUTRARIA SINUOSA, *Roemer.* Ool., tab. 19, fig. 24, Nachtr., p. 42.
PLEUROMYA RECURVA, *Ag.* Et. Crét. Myes., p. 234 et p. 246, t. 29, fig. 9.
LYONSIA RECURVA, *D'Orb.?* Prodr., 12 ét., No. 123.
MYACITES RECURVA, *Mor.* Cat. Brit. Foss., 1854, p. 214.
AMPHIDESMA RECURVUM, *Bean.* Mag. of Nat. Hist., 1839.
MYACITES RECURVUM, *Leckenby.* Proc. Geol. Soc., vol. xv.

Testa elongato-trapeziformi plano-convexa concentrice striato-rugosa antice brevissima oblique truncata basi perarcuata posterius producta dorso antice sinuatim depressa, margine cardinali postico sinuato, umbonibus crassis incurvis. (Roemer.)

Shell a lengthened trapeziform, moderately convex, with large, concentric, rugose plications; anterior side very short, obliquely truncated; base curved elliptically; the posterior side produced, compressed, close-fitting; the superior margin somewhat sinuated or concave; the umbones elevated, pointed, and incurved. Usually the anterior side has a furrow, which passes from the umbones downwards perpendicularly or slightly directed forwards to the inferior border, but in some of the more gibbose specimens it cannot be distinguished. The test is delicate; the ornamentation of the surface has the radiating lines of granules so dense and minute, that they can only be distinguished by the aid of a considerable magnifying power. The height is two thirds of the length, the diameter through the valves being equal to half the length. These dimensions apply to the shorter Cornbrash examples, but many of the Kelloway Rock specimens are more elongated. To the latter variety may be attributed the *Lutraria sinuosa*, Roemer; it is necessary, however, to separate altogether the *Lutraria recurva*, Goldf. ('Petref.,' tab. cliii, fig. 15), which has the general figure very different. The example of Agassiz is unusually short and gibbose; and as he has figured a cast, we are precluded from comparing the ornamentation of the surface. D'Orbigny ('Prodrome,' i, p. 359) has separated it under the title of *Panopea subrecurva;* but, considering the varieties of figure which this species assumes, probably it is only a short variety of the species of Professor Phillips.

Myacites recurvum possesses so little of the aspect of a *Gresslya* (Lyonsia, D'Orb.) that we are led to speculate upon the probability that *Lyonsia recurva*, D'Orbigny, is a form erroneously ascribed by that author to the species in question.

Geological Positions and Localities. *Myacites recurvum* is almost peculiar to the

Oxfordian Oolites; for although it occurs in the Cornbrash of Yorkshire and Wiltshire, it is rarely found in a lower position than the Kelloway Rock. Roemer records his *Lutraria sinuosa* in the Lower Coral Rag of Heersthum; Agassiz places his *Pleuromya recurva* in the Terrain à Chailles of Chamsol, in the department of Doubs.

Myacites sinistra, *Agassiz*, sp. Tab. XXXV, figs. 17, 17 *a*.

Arcomya sinistra, *Agassiz*. Ét. Crit. Myes., p. 170, tab. 9, figs. 1—3, et tab. 9′, figs. 10—13.
Panopæa sinistra, *D'Orb.* Prodr., i, p. 273.
— — *Oppel.* Juraformation, p. 480.

Testa ovato-elongata antice attenuata, postice convexa producta, margine hiante, umbonibus subcompressis, depressis, antemedianis, latere antico oblique-declivi, lunula concavo, margine superiori subhorizontali margine inferiore subrecto; valvis lateribus plicis irregularibus crebis longitudinalibus, et sulco superficiali antemediano oblique-declivi. Nucleus glaber.

Shell ovately elongated, with the sides of the valves rather flattened; anterior side attenuated, its margin sloping obliquely downwards; lunule concave; posterior side more convex and lengthened, its superior border nearly horizontal; the posterior extremity is somewhat rounded, with an aperture moderately large; the umbones are depressed, and somewhat compressed laterally; they are placed a little posterior to the anterior third of the shell, and there is a slight sulcation, which proceeds from them obliquely forwards and downwards towards the lower border; the inferior margin is lengthened and nearly straight; the surface of the test has numerous irregular and rather delicate longitudinal plications; the granules over the greater portion of the valves are so minute and crowded that they cannot be traced to form connecting lines, but towards the sides they are larger, more distantly arranged, and distinctly linear; the test upon the anterior side is of moderate thickness, posteriorly it is much thinner; the nucleus is smooth, and exhibits the adductor and pallial scars.

Length, 2 inches; height, 1 inch; diameter through both the valves, ⅞ inch; but our specimen is imperfect, and appears to have lost about 2 lines in length at the posterior extremity.

The more depressed umbones, the anterior attenuation, and the nearly horizontal figure of the superior border, will serve to distinguish it from all the varieties of *Pleuromya elongata*, Ag., to which it bears some resemblance.

The *Arcomya sinistra* of Quenstedt, 'Der Jura,' p. 451, tab. lxii, fig. 2, from the higher stage of the Inferior Oolite, occurs also in the same position in the vicinity of Cheltenham; it is, however, distinct from *Myacites sinistra*. Some varieties of *Myacites decurtatum* approach to it in the general figure, but are readily distinguishable when the granulated surface can be examined and compared, the minute, crowded pattern upon *M. sinistra*, with the widely separated lines of granules upon *M. decurtatum*.

Geological Positions and Localities. The Cornbrash of Scarborough; in the collection of Mr. Leckenby. In Switzerland M. Agassiz records it from the same geological position (calcaire roux-sableux) at Goldenthal, Soleure; also in the Bernese Jura.

MYACITES MODICA, *Bean*, sp. Tab. XLIII, figs. 1, 1 *a*.

MYA MODICA, *Bean*. Mag. Nat. Hist., 1839.

Testa-ovato elongata subdepressa, umbonibus subdepressis antemedianis, margine antico producto, rotundo, postico oblique declivi subrecto, margine inferiore elliptico curvato, area ligamenti lanceolata lata, subdepressa, marginibus acutis, valvis lateribus concentrice delicate plicatis; lineis radiantibus granulatis, subtillissimis dense instructis.

Shell ovately elongated, rather depressed; umbones antero-mesial, rather depressed; anterior margin produced, rounded; posterior margin more lengthened, nearly straight, sloping downwards obliquely, lower border curved elliptically; the granulated test consists of extremely delicate, very densely arranged, radiating lines, visible only under a magnifier; the concentric plications are numerous and faintly traced, so that the surface is smooth; the valves are close-fitting, or have no perceptible aperture at either of the extremities.

Length, 2¼ inches; height, 1⅓ inch; diameter through both the valves, ⅞ inch.

The general figure and aspect of this species renders it easy to distinguish from other examples of the genus.

Geological Position and Locality. The Cornbrash of Gristhorpe Cliffs, in which it has occurred very rarely; Mr. Leckenby's collection.

ANATINA (CERCOMYA) SILIQUA, *Ag*. Tab. XXXV, fig. 15.

SANGUINOLARIA UNDULATA, *Phil.* Geol. York., i, pl. 5, fig. 1, non Sow.
CERCOMYA SILIQUA, *Ag.* Ét. Crit. Myes., p. 148, tab. 11 *a*, figs. 9—13.
— ANTICA, *Ag.*? Ib., p. 147, tab. 11, figs. 16—18; tab. 11*a*, figs. 14—16.
ANATINA BELLONA, *D'Orb.* Prod., i, p. 336, 12 ét., No. 132.
— UNDATA, *Id.* Ib., p. 361, 13 ét., No. 221.
SANGUINOLARIA UNDULATA, *Quenstedt.* Der Jura, p. 508, t. 68, fig. 9.
ANATINA UNDULATA, *Leckenby.* Proc. Geol. Soc., vol. xv, 1858.

Testa transverse elongata inæquilatera umbonibus subanticis parvis acutis, postice rostrata, attenuata, area lata, plicis duobus longitudinalibus; latere antico subcompresso, elliptico curvato, plicisque regularibus et longitudinalibus.

Shell transversely elongated, very inæquilateral; umbones placed anterior to the middle of the valves, small, depressed, and anterior; posterior side rostrated or attenuated, and much elongated; area large and wide, with two longitudinal ridges, in addition to a distinct marginal ridge which separates the area from the other portion of the shell; anterior side rather compressed, its border is curved elliptically; the anterior portion of the sides of the valves have regular, longitudinal ridges and furrows, which disappear posterior to the umbones; the oblique sulcation which proceeds downwards from the umbones in all examples of Cercomya is only faintly impressed.

The specimen figured has the general form of the shell unusually well preserved, but the test has disappeared; the very inequilateral figure, with the attenuation and elongation of the posterior side, will readily distinguish it from *Anatina undulata*, Sow., as also from most other examples of the genus.

Height, one third the length; diameter through both the valves, one fourth the length.

Geological Positions and Localities. It occurs rarely in the Cornbrash of Scarborough. Professor Phillips has recorded it in the Oxford Clay, and Mr. Leckenby in the Kelloway Rock and Calcareous Grit of Yorkshire. M. Quenstedt quotes it from the Cornbrash of Wurtemburg; M. Agassiz from the Oxfordian Strata of the Vadois Jura and the Jura of Soleure.

PHOLADOMYA OVULUM, *Ag.* Tab. XXXV, figs. 18, 18 *a*.

PHOLADOMYA OVULUM, *Ag.* Ét. Crit. Myes., p. 119, tab. 3, figs. 7—9; tab. 3 *b*, figs. 1—6.
— — *D'Orb.* Prodr., 11 ét., No. 168, vol. 1.
— — *Morris.* Catal. Brit. Foss., 1854, p. 221.
— — *Oppel.* Juraformation, p. 481.

Testa ovato-elongata, antice breviore, rotundata, cordata, posterius producta, attenuata, margine inferiore arcuato curvato, superiore subhorizontali, concavo, umbonibis crassis subanticis prominulis; valvis concentrice plicatis, plicis longitudinalibus numerosis inæqualibus mediocriter tenuibus; costellis radiantibus obliquis æqualibus angustis, inferne evanescentibus, apertura postico et antico angusto.

Shell ovately elongated; the anterior side short, rounded, cordiform; the posterior side produced and attenuated; the inferior margin is curved elliptically; the superior margin is moderately lengthened and concave; the umbones are elevated and tumid; the sides of the valves are convex, with closely arranged but not prominent longitudinal plications; the radiating costæ are very narrow or linear, disposed obliquely, about twelve in number;

they are slightly impressed by the decussating plications, and disappear before reaching the lower border; the apertures, both posterior and antero-inferior, are narrow, and not much lengthened; the post-ligamental area is wide, and bounded by a distinct elevation upon each side.

The test is thin, and is sometimes preserved, the characters of the surface being very well shown upon the casts; in many specimens the radiating lines, or little costæ, are so faintly marked that they are only visible near to the umbones. The very delicate, radiating little ribs and the nearly equally faintly marked longitudinal plications will usually serve to distinguish it from allied forms of the genus when combined with the elongated figure. In the Pholodomyæ the relative measurements of the parts are little to be depended upon; but in the Cornbrash specimen figured, the diameter, the height, and the length, are as 1—1½—2. Occasionally the length has a greater proportion.

Geological Positions and Localities. It is somewhat rare in the Cornbrash of the coast of Yorkshire, but it is common in the Inferior Oolite of the Cotteswold Hills, its position being the stratum with Conchifera immediately underlying the bed with *Gryphæa sublobata.*

PHOLADOMYA PHILLIPSII, *Phil.*, sp. Tab. XLII, figs. 2, 2 *a*.

PHOLADOMYA MURCHISONI, *Phil.* Geol. York., i. pl. 7, fig. 9, non Sow.
— PHILLIPSII, *Morris.* Cat. Brit. Foss., p. 221.

Testa ovato-cordata, inflatra, umbonibus magnis elevatis, antice brevissima truncata, postice producta, valde hiante; lateribus rugis irregularibus numerosis, leviter impressis, costisque (7—8) *perpendiculariter, angustis; costa secunda majora.*

Shell ovately cordate, much inflated; umbones large, anterior, elevated, but obtuse; anterior side short and truncated; posterior side produced, its superior border concave, with a lengthened, large aperture, which extends upwards even to the ligament; the sides of the valves have very numerous, irregular, longitudinal rugæ, which are not very prominent, and only slightly indent the narrow, perpendicular costæ, of which there are seven or eight; the second costa is much larger than the others, and is more remotely placed, imparting a degree of angularity to the anterior side of the shell; the other costæ are symmetrical, and descend almost perpendicularly to the lower border, leaving a considerable space upon the posterior side of the valves destitute of costæ. The young shell is much less inflated, and more produced upon the posterior side, the aperture at that part being, in proportion, more narrow; the second costa has very little more prominence than the others, so that the anterior side has less angularity and its border is more rounded than in the adult form. In old specimens the height and convexity of the valves are nearly equal, the length being a little more considerable; in young shells, not exceeding an inch and a half in length, the convexity is one third less.

It has only been after long consideration, and an ample comparison of specimens of various dimensions, that I have seen fit to adopt the view taken by Professor Morris in his 'Catalogue,' and separate this shell both from *Pholadomya deltoidea* and from *Pholadomya Heraulti*, of the Inferior Oolite. Compared with the latter form, it will be found that *P. Phillipsii* has the anterior side more truncated, and the posterior side gapes with a larger aperture; this latter feature is, in fact, distinguishable in shells of all dimensions; the longitudinal rugæ are more irregular and much less conspicuous, so that they only slightly indent the costæ, these latter being less oblique than in *P. Heraulti*. The superior largeness and regularity of the rugæ, together with the deep indentations of the costæ, is the feature which, at the first glance, impresses the spectator upon inspecting *P. Heraulti*; the costæ are usually somewhat more numerous, there being two anterior to the large costæ and an additional one posterior to it, so that, together with their greater obliquity, only a small portion of the posterior side of the shell is destitute of costæ.

Compared with *P. deltoidea*, Sow., the figure of the latter is more inflated, the costæ larger and less indented, it also is without the angularity which is imparted by the second large costa of *P. Phillipsii*.

Geological Position and Locality. *Pholadomya Phillipsii* is abundant in the Cornbrash of Scarborough, Gristhorpe, &c., and usually has the test preserved.

PHOLADOMYA DELTOIDEA, *Sow.* Tab. XLII, figs. 4, 4 *a*.

CARDITA DELTOIDEA, *Sow.* Min. Con., t. 197, fig. 4.
PHOLADOMYA MURCHISONI, *Sow.* Ib., t. 545, the shorter figure only.
— BUCARDIUM, *Ag.* Ét. Crit. Myes., p. 77, pl. 5, figs. 3—7; pl. 5 *a*, fig. 8.
— — *Chapuis* and *Dewalque*. Fos. Ter. Sec. de Luxembourg, p. 124, pl. 18, fig. 1.
— — *Damon*. Geol. Weymouth, p. 17, fig. 6.
— SOLITARIA, *Mor.* and *Lyc.* Gr. Ool. Moll., part 2, p. 124, tab. xii, fig. 2, et tab. 11, fig. 1.

This species, so abundant in the Great Oolite, Fuller's Earth, and Cornbrash of the south of England, varies greatly in its general figure, even in the same bed and locality; and as its synonyms may now be considered as clearly ascertained, I have deemed it desirable to figure a specimen from the Cornbrash of Wiltshire, in which the costæ are irregularly arranged, and the general figure is more lengthened than in the two specimens formerly figured in the second part of the 'Monograph of the Great Oolite Mollusca,' under the name of *P. solitaria*. Of these latter, the index facing Tab. XII, fig. 2, by a typographical error, was printed *P. oblita*, a shell which is given at fig. 5 upon the same plate. Even the two Great Oolite specimens have the anterior side less truncated, the umbones more obtuse, and the general figure less inflated, than obtains in the greater number of those from the Minchinhampton district; and, upon the other hand, all of them are less lengthened upon the posterior side than is seen in the figures given by Agassiz and by Messrs. Chapuis and Dewalque.

Pholadomya deltoidea is remarkable for the large, prominent, and slightly indented costæ, usually seven in number, of which the two posterior ones are much less conspicuous, and are usually evanescent towards the lower border.

The frequent truncation of the anterior side in *Pholadomya*, and the general distortion of the shell which usually accompanies it, is a source of frequent difficulty in the discrimination of species, and is seen commonly and even usually in *P. deltoidea*, when specimens are collected without selection. The shell in its normal position rested upon the compressed anterior side; the general distortion of figure consequent upon it commenced at a very early period in the growth of the mollusc, continued throughout its existence, and did not prevent it from attaining to the usual dimensions of the species; it occurs equally in all the other forms assumed by the genus. Where the flattening of the anterior side is considerable the umbones become more pointed and prominent, the radiating elevations or ribs are directed more obliquely backwards; in other instances they become more closely arranged, or they are waved and irregular. The distortion is not limited to specimens connected with any particular kind of lithological condition, as it occurs in compact, thin-bedded limestones, in thick beds of soft, sandy marl, or in thick-bedded Oolitic limestone; it is also common to find both compressed and uncompressed examples in contiguity.

PHOLADOMYA LYRATA, *Sow.* Tab. XLIII, figs. 3, 3 *a*.

CARDITA? LIRATA, *Sow.* Min. Con., t. 197, fig. 3.
PHOLADOMYA LYRATA, *Sow.* Ibid., p. 220.
— — *Oppel.* Juraformation, p. 482.

Testa obovato-trigona, ventricosa, umbonibus elevatis antero-medianis, latere antico truncato, postico oblique declivi, costis 9—10, *tertia majora, carinam efformante, costis aliis approximatis, plicis magnis concentricis regularibus indentatis; apertura postica angusta, elongata.*

The figure is nearly that of a cone, compressed laterally; the umbones are elevated, pointed, and placed a little anterior to the middle of the valves; the steepness and straightness of the posterior slope, together with the nearly straight lower border, imparts a distinctive character to the shell, irrespective of the large, carinated third costa, which is so much more conspicuous than the others that it forms a kind of keel or angle upon the anterior side; it descends to the lower border without curvature, but is directed slightly forwards; the six or seven costæ posterior to it are much smaller, they diminish regularly in prominence, are closely arranged, and are deeply indented by the regular, large, concentric plications; the anterior side gapes slightly, and has two inconspicuous, indented costæ; the posterior aperture is narrow and lengthened.

The sub-conical figure, pointed posterior side, and large, carinated rib, will serve to distinguish it from *P. Heraulti*, Ag., to which it is nearly allied; the more angulated figure, and more numerous costæ, from *P. carinata*, Ag. Some examples of Pholadomya from the Inferior Oolite are not distinguishable from *P. lyrata;* but between these and *P. Heraulti* are others, which apparently serve to connect the two forms, so that it is difficult to separate them altogether from *P. lyrata*, although undoubtedly they must be merged with *P. Heraulti;* these connecting links are also quite irrespective of any changes that may be due to the stage of growth in either of the two species.

Geological Positions and Localities. P. lyrata is common in the Cornbrash of Wiltshire and Dorsetshire. Dr. Oppel records it in the same rock at Marquise, near Boulogne, and Egg, near Aran. D'Orbigny ('Prodrome,' i, p. 252) quotes it from the Upper Lias, near Bath, which is an error copied from the 'Mineral Conchology of Great Britain.'

HOMOMYA GIBBOSA, *Sow.*, sp. Part II, Tab. XII. fig. 14; Tab. XLIII, figs. 2, 2 *a*.

Described at page 138, Part II, under the name of *Myacites gibbosus.* As this shell occurs abundantly both in the Cornbrash and the Inferior Oolite of the southern counties of England, a full-sized average example is here figured; occasionally, indeed, the species acquired much larger dimensions, as in the Cornbrash of Wiltshire, but it is then invariably more or less distorted and imperfect; it is also more gibbose than the smaller examples. Since the publication of the former portions of this Monograph more extended information respecting this and other allied species comprised in the proposed genus *Homomya* of Agassiz has led to the conclusion that they cannot be assigned to the genus *Myacites*, of which they possess neither the external granulated tegument nor the peculiar characters of the hinge.

When the surface of *Myacites* has been denuded of the granulated tegument it is smooth, with irregular, longitudinal laminæ, whereas *Pholadomya* and *Homomya* have a wrinkled or corrugated surface.

The genus Homomya was intended by Agassiz to include shells whose forms resemble those of the more lengthened Pholadomyas, but which are destitute of radiating costæ, and have usually a thicker test, the hinge being identical with that of Pholadomya, usually, indeed, more massive; but although the sides of the valves are destitute of costæ, it occasionally happens that a few delicate, radiating lines, more or less obscurely marked, are visible upon the umbones, but vanish before they reach the middle of the valves. Examples of this are supplied by the large Liassic *Homomya ventricosa*, Ag., by *Homomya Vezelayi*, D'Arch., and by *Homomya crassiuscula*, Mor. and Lyc. The hinge of the latter shell exhibits its perfect identity with that of *Pholadomya*. It is therefore evident that *Homomya* cannot claim a generic separation; but that, viewed as a subgenus or section of *Pholadomya*, the name may conveniently be retained. *Myacites Vezelayi*, page 111, and *Myacites crassiusculus*, page 112, should therefore also be removed to *Homomya*.

HOMOMYA CRASSIUSCULA, *Mor.* and *Lyc.* Tab. XLIII, figs. 5, 5 *a*.

A small example from the Great (?) Oolite of Lincolnshire was figured, Part II, Tab. XI, fig. 3. As the species occurs of full dimensions in the Cornbrash of Scarborough, a specimen, with the test preserved, is here given.

ADDENDA.

A PORTION of the text of this Supplement passed through the hands of the printer long prior to the execution of the plates; and during this lengthened interval many additional testacea were placed at the disposal of the author, including a considerable series from the Forest Marble of the counties of Wilts, Somerset, and Dorset, which had recently been disengaged from the investing matrix by the exertions of W. Walton, Esq., of Bath, obtained by that gentleman, and by the late John Kilvert, Esq., of the same place. This fine collection has yielded many new forms, and also some superior examples of others that had previously been figured from specimens less suitable for the purpose; advantage has been taken of the opportunity thus afforded to give additional illustrations. The descriptions of the more recently acquired fossils could not, therefore, for the most part, be placed in their proper order, and necessarily form *Addenda* to the Supplement.

CERITHIUM (?) HEMICINCTUM, *Lyc.* Tab. XLI, fig. 17.

Testa parva, elongata, anfractibus (7), *valde convexis, postice subplanis, lævigatis, antice tricinctis, convexis, anfractu ultimo basi concentrice striato. Apertura et canali ignota.*

Shell small, elongated; volutions (7) very convex, their posterior portions oblique, flattened and smooth, their anterior portions with three prominent encircling costæ, the sutures are deeply constricted; the last volution has the base concentrically sulcated; the outer lip and the base are imperfect; the genus, therefore, is somewhat uncertain; there are some traces of an umbilical opening at the base of the columella.

Geological Position and Locality. The Forest Marble of Laycock; in the collection of W. Walton, Esq.

Cerithium (?) neglectum, *Lyc.* Tab. XLIV, fig. 21.

Testa parva, subulaba, anfractibus (*circa* 7) *subplanis, longitudinaliter costatis, costis* (5), *magnis, depressis, subobliquis, a sinistro ad dextrum versus, apertura parva, canala* (?),

Shell small, subulate; volutions (about seven) flattened, with five longitudinal large, depressed, and smooth costæ, which are directed somewhat obliquely from left to right, and are slightly interrupted by the sutures; the aperture is small and depressed, the canal is imperfect.

The extremities of the costæ do not always exactly accord with those of the next volution, which gives some irregularity to the appearance of the volutions; no traces of encircling striations are visible.

The spire is not angulated as in *C. pentagonum*, the subulate figure and plain surface distinguishes it from *C. sexcostatum*.

Geological Position and Locality. The Great Oolite of Bussage; collected by E. Witchell, Esq.

Cerithium costigerum, *Piette.* Tab. XLI, figs. 11, 11 *a*, *b*.

Testa inflata, subcylindrica, anfractibus (7—9), *costis* (12) *rectis, angustis, elevatis, postice acuminatis, lineisque transversalibus, instructis; apertura parva, canali recto, elongato.*

Shell somewhat inflated and subcylindrical, volutions (7 to 9) with the sides perpendicular, costæ (12) perpendicular, narrow, and much elevated, terminating posteriorly each in a projecting point, anteriorly they bend inwards slightly to the suture, there are also regular encircling lines; the base is smooth, the aperture is small, the canal lengthened and straight.

There is much variability in the elevation of the spire, and, consequently, in the height of the volutions; a specimen more than usually lengthened has the costæ somewhat oblique.

Geological Positions and Localities. The Forest Marble of Laycock; in the collection of W. Walton, Esq. It is recorded by M. Piette in the Great Oolite Limestones of Eparcy and Rumigny.

Cerithium (?) Waltoni, *Lyc.* Tab. XLI, fig. 16.

Testa parva turriculata anfractibus numerosis angustis, inflatis, saturis bene impressis, costis rectis angustis, elevatis (*circa* 11) *in ambitu lineis regularibus cingendis; apertura et canali ignota.*

Shell small, turreted, volutions numerous (8—9), narrow, inflated, the sutures deeply impressed; costæ (about 11 in the circumference) perpendicular and narrow, crossed by a few regular encircling lines. The aperture and canal are imperfect.

Geological Position and Locality. The Forest Marble of Laycock; in the collection of W. Walton, Esq.

CERITHIUM (?) POCULUM, *Lyc.* Tab. XLIV, fig. 24.

Testa parva, subcylindrica, anfractibus (9) *lævigatis, postice expansis et profunda canaliculatis, antice contractis; apertura parva, canali contracto et contorto.*

Shell small, subulate, subcylindrical, volutions (about 9) smooth, expanded posteriorly and deeply channelled, contracted anteriorly, the aperture is small, the canal is produced, narrow, and twisted.

The genus is somewhat doubtful, additional specimens may prove it to be a *Nerinæa.*

Geological Position and Locality. The Great Oolite of Bussage, near Bisley Common; collected by E. Witchell, Esq.

CERITHIUM EXSCALPTUM, *Lyc.* Tab. XLIV, fig. 23.

Testa parva, subulo-elongata, anfractibus (10) *angustis, sub-planis, transverse tenuissime striatis, anfractu ultimo rotundo, canali brevi, sub-recto.*

Shell small, subulately turreted, pointed, volutions (10) slightly convex, narrow (two and a half times as wide as high), with numerous very delicate encircling striations, the last volution has the base rounded, the canal is short and nearly slight.

Obtained by crushing the white stone for the Great Oolite for minute Gasteropoda.

Geological Position and Locality. The Great Oolite of Bussage; collected by E. Witchell, Esq.

KILVERTIA, *Gen. Nov.*

Testa elongata, sub-cylindrica, anfractibus numerosis, perpendiculariter costatis tuberculatis aut spinosis; anfractu ultimo cylindrico, basi sub-contracto; apertura integra, rotundata aut ovali, labris protractis, tenuiter incrassatis, non nunquam sub-undulatis, columella solida.

Shell elongated, sub-cylindrical, sometimes somewhat pupæform; volutions numerous, perpendicularly costated, tuberculated or spined; the last volution cylindrical, sometimes contracted at the base; aperture entire, orbicular or ovate, the lips elevated, produced and slightly thickened, sometimes undulated, columella solid.

Allied to Cerithium, Potamides, Turritella, Omphalia, Rissoa, and Aclis; from the two former it is separated by the absence of an anterior and posterior canal, the thickened and produced margins of the aperture distinguish it from Turritella, and from the Omphalia of Zekeli, from Omphalia more especially by the absence of a sinus or fissure of the outer lip, from Rissoa by the many-whirled figure and produced lips, from Aclis by the costated or spined volutions, cylindrical last volution, and produced aperture.

The Great Oolite species obtained in the Minchinhampton district are always small and sometimes minute, these are *Cerithium* (?) *spiculum*, Lyc., p. 9; *C.* (?) *strangulatum* D'Arch., p. 8; *C.* (?) *pulchrum*, Lyc., p. 10, of which latter species very fine and large examples occur also in the Forest Marble clays of Laycock, accompanied by *Kilvertia formosa*, Lyc. Other examples, known only in foreign localities, are *Rissoa* (?) *elegantula*, Piette, from the Great Oolite of Eparcy; *Cerithium angistoma*, *C. quinquangulare* and *C. pupoides*, Hebert and Deslongchamps, from the Kelloway Rock of Montreul-Bellay; *Scalaria* (?) *minuta* and *Cerithium pygmeum*, Buvignier, from the Calcaire à Astartes of the department of the Moselle. In selecting a name for this proposed genus, I have much pleasure in adopting the suggestion of Mr. Walton, and dedicate it to the memory of the late John Kilvert, Esq., of Bath, whose researches in the Palæontology of the Jurassic rocks of the southern counties resulted in the acquisition of a fine and instructive collection of the Mollusca.

KILVERTIA PULCHRA, *Lyc.* Tab. XLIV, fig, 4; Tab. XLI, figs. 12, 12 *a*.

CERITHIUM? PULCHRUM, p. 10, of this Supplement.

The fine collection of Forest Marble shells forwarded by the kindness of Mr. Walton, contains many specimens of this Kilvertia which exhibit much variability in their ornamentation, and are upwards of three times the linear dimensions of the Minchinhampton examples; the Laycock shells having been obtained by washing layers of clay and shale; there is an entire absence of that abrasion of the surface to which oolitic fossils have so frequently been subjected; additional figures of this fine species will be found Tab. XLI, figs. 12, 12 *a*. The figure of the aperture in shells of the same size also presents some variability, the typical suborbicular figure becomes sub-quadrate, and in other instances is somewhat pointed at the two extremities, but in the young condition apparently the aperture is always orbicular.

KILVERTIA FORMOSA, *Lyc.* Tab. XLIV, fig. 5.

Testa parva subulo-pupæformi, anfractibus (6 ?) *latis, planatis, suturis bene distinctis, costis longitudinalibus rectis* (*circa* 7 *in ambitu*) *rotundis, depressis, inferne evanescentibus; lineis transversis* (*circa* 7) *regularibus, elevatis; apertura parva suborbiculari, labris integris, simplicibus.*

Shell small, elongated, pupæform or lessening at both the extremities, volutions (6 ?) wide, flattened or very slightly convex, the sutures well impressed, aperture small, suborbicular; the lips continuous without undulation; longitudinal costæ (about 7) straight, rounded, and but slightly elevated, indistinct upon the latter volutions, knotted where they are crossed by encircling lines, of which each volution has about seven, regular and conspicuous; the costæ are not continuous, neither do their extremities exactly correspond at the sutures of the successive volutions, they are more prominent upon the upper half of each volution; the apex is imperfect, the first volution having disappeared.

Allied to *Kilvertia strangulata* = *Cerithium strangulatum*, D'Arch., from which it is distinguished by the smaller dimensions, the greater elongation of the spire, and by the costæ, which are much smaller, more depressed, and do not form continuous elevations.

Geological Position and Locality. Collected by E. Witchell, Esq., in the white (Great) Oolite of Bussage, near Bisley Common.

AMBERLEYA CAPITANEA, *Goldf.*, sp. Tab. XLI, fig. 1.

Part I, p. 65, contains a correct description of this species (*Turbo capitaneus*, Goldf.), which is not uncommon in the Supra-liassic sands and the Inferior Oolite of the southern counties; Mr. Walton has also forwarded two small examples obtained in the Forest Marble of Laycock, and of Pound Pill. The shell figured Tab. IX, Part I, fig. 33, was referred doubtfully to this species, of which it was supposed to be a badly preserved example; subsequent examinations of other specimens from the same locality have proved that this view was erroneous, and that it is a distinct species; a description of this latter shell will be found in this Supplement (p. 19) under the title of *Amberleya Jurassi.*

AMBERLEYA MONILIFERA, *Lyc.* Tab. XLI, fig. 10.

Testa parva, ovato-elongata, spira alta, acuta, anfractibus (4—5) *in medio carinatis, tabulo-nodiferis, postice et antice concavis, ejusdem carina parva, nodifera; anfractu ultimo basi sulcis quinis, concentricis, apertura antice subcontracto.*

Shell small, ovately elongated, spire elevated, acute, consisting of four or five volutions, which have a prominent encircling nodiferous carina in their middle portion, their posterior and anterior surfaces being concave, each having a small noderous carina; the last volution has at its base fine encircling sulcations; the aperture has the anterior extremity rather pointed.

. The tubercles upon the mesial carina are large, projecting slightly forwards, very closely arranged and tubular, about eighteen in a volution, the anterior and posterior carinæ have similar tubercles, but much smaller. The height of the shell is one third greater than the opposite measurement.

Geological Position and Locality. The Forest Marble of Laycock; in the collection of W. Walton, Esq.

AMBERLEYA TRICINCTA, *Lyc.* Tab. XLI, fig. 14.

Testa ovato-elongata, anfractibus (8—9) *turbinatis, inferne angulatis, cingillis, tribus, lineis perpendicularibus decussatis, anfractu altimo, lineis magnis concentricis; apertura pyriformi.*

Shell ovately elongated, volutions (8—9 turbinated, angulated towards their lower portions, and flattened or slightly convex above the angle, the sutures are strongly marked, encircling lines three, of which one is above and another beneath the angle; these are decussated by other lines perpendicular and smaller, forming tubercles more or less distinct where they cross the angle, the decussating lines are distantly and sometimes irregularly arranged; the last volution has large, regular, concentric elevations; the aperture is pyriform.

An elegantly turbinated more or less lengthened shell, with convex volutions and a delicately ornamented surface; about a dozen specimens have been compared, which do not vary much in size; the length of the aperture is about two fifths of the entire shell. All the examples are more or less imperfect at the base.

Geological Position and Locality. The Forest Marble of Laycock; in the collection of W. Walton, Esq.

NATICA TEXATA, *Lyc.* Tab. XLV, figs. 30, 30 *a.*

Testa ovata, depressiuscula, crassa, spira anfractibus (3) *patens, vix elevatis, convexis; anfractu ultimo inflato, basi umbilicato, apertura subreniformi, labro interno crasso; superficie striis vel lineis texatis delicatissimis ornata.*

Shell ovate, depressed, thick, spire consisting of three depressed but exposed and rounded volutions, the last volution much inflated, the base umbilicated, the aperture somewhat reniform, the inner lip thick and conspicuous; the surface with very delicate encircling lines or striations, which are rendered granular by others decussating them.

Allied to *Natica Montreuilensis*, Heb. and Desl., from the Kelloway Rock of Montreul-Bellay, which species, however, is less depressed and the aperture more lengthened.

The ornamentation of the surface in our shell is partially preserved, and can only be perceived by the aid of magnifying power.

Geological Position and Locality. The Forest Marble of Laycock; in the collection of W. Walton, Esq.

NATICA ARATA. Tab. XLV, fig. 2.

Testa parva, crassa, inflata, spira exserta, anfractibus (4) *convexis, ultimo, permagno, transverse striato, suturis valde impressis, apertura ovata, umbilico nullo.*

Shell small, thick, inflated, spire produced, volutions (4) convex, the last volution very large and globose, with delicate encircling striations, the sutures deeply impressed, the aperture is ovate; there is no umbilicus.

Geological Position and Locality. The Great Oolite of Bussage; collected by E. Witchell, Esq.

NATICA (EUSPIRA) ALTA, *Lyc.* Tab. XLV, figs. 22, 22 *a.*

Testa parva, lævigata, subglobosa, spira elongata, apice acuto, anfractibus (4) *convexis, latis, suturis valde impressis, anfructu ultimo permagno, subgloboso, apertura ovata, obliqua, subumbilicata.*

Shell small, smooth, spire elevated, its apex pointed, volutions (4) convex, moderately wide, the sutures strongly marked, slightly constricted, the last volution very large, subglobose, the aperture ovate, oblique, the inner lip prominent, the base with an umbilical groove. The height of the aperture is slightly greater than that of the other portion of the shell. Perhaps this is the young condition of a much larger species.

Geological Position and Locality. The Forest Marble of Laycock; in the collection of W. Walton, Esq.

NATICA INSIGNIS, *Lyc.* Tab. XLV, fig. 21.

Testa parva inflata, spira elevata, acuta, anfractibus (7) *convexiusculis, angustis, suturis bene impressis, anfractu ultimo permagno, subgloboso, apertura ovali, umbilico nullo.*

Shell small, inflated, spire much elevated, its apex acute, volutions (7) moderately convex, narrow, the latter two volutions increasing rapidly, and becoming much inflated, the last volution is very large, subglobose, the aperture rather depressed, ovate, with no distinct umbilicus, or with a slight groove.

The unusual number of the volutions and the sudden inflation of the last volution renders its discrimination easy.

The height is about equal to the transverse diameter of the last volution.

Geological Position and Locality. Collected by E. Witchell, Esq., in the Great Oolite of Bussage, near Bisley Common; it has also occurred rarely in the Cornbrash of Scarborough.

RISSOINA SUBULATA, *Lyc.* Tab. XLI, fig. 9.

Testa elongata, subcylindrica, anfractibus (9) *convexis, altis, longitudinaliter oblique costellatis, costellis, crebris* (*circa* 30 *in ambitu*), *apertura ovato-obliqua, parva.*

Shell elongated, subcylindrical, volutions (9) convex, high, longitudinally obliquely costellated, costellæ closely arranged (about 30) in a volution; aperture ovate, oblique, small.

A slender, subulate, delicately ornamented shell; the height of the volutions is equal to three fourths of their opposite diameter.

Geological Position and Locality. The Forest Marble of Laycock; in the collection of W. Walton, Esq.

RISSOINA (?) TUMIDULA, *Lyc.* Tab. XLIV, fig. 13.

Testa ovato-tumidula lævigata, spira elevata, anfractibus (5) *convexis, latis, suturis bene distinctis, apertura ovata, antice angulata, labro externo crasso.*

Shell ovate, inflated, smooth; spire short, but elevated; volutions (5) convex, wide, their sutures deeply impressed; aperture ovate; the outer lip thick, forming an angle at its junction with the base of the columella. There is no distinct notch.

A short, inflated species, resembling in the figure of the aperture *R. lævis*, Sow., both seeming to constitute aberrant examples of Rissoina, and approximating to Rissoa.

Geological Position and Locality. Collected by E. Witchell, Esq., in the Great Oolite of Bussage, near to Bisley Common, Gloucestershire.

NERITA CLAVATULA, *Lyc.* Tab. XLV, fig. 3.

Testa hemispherica, spira parva, subdepressa, anfractu ultimo permagno, inflato, tuberculis parvis, remotiusculis, per series quinis, regularibus, et lineis radiantibus, tenuibus, decussatis; basi carina una, lævigata.

Shell hemispherical; spire small, obtuse, and rather depressed; the last volution very large, inflated, with small depressed tubercles, rather remote, and arranged in fine encircling rows, the rows of tubercles are connected by delicate radiating lines, one of which is united to each tubercle; the base has a single, smooth, encircling keel; the aperture and inner lip are similar to those of *Nerita minuta.*

A pretty little and rare species, with the tubercles rather distantly arranged in each row, they are somewhat lozenge-shaped or pointed posteriorly, about fourteen occupying an entire volution.

Geological Position and Locality. The Great Oolite of Bussage, adjoining Bisley Common, in the bed of white stone; collected by E. Witchell, Esq.

TROCHUS BURTONENSIS, *Lyc.* Tab. XLV, fig. 16.

Testa conica, lævigata, spira elevata, anfractibus (6), *postice planatis antice concavis et obtuse angulatis, anfractu ultimo basi leviter convexa, imperforata, apertura subrotunda, columella basi dente callosa.*

Shell conical, smooth; spire elevated; volutions (6), their posterior portions flattened, the anterior portions concave, bounded by an obtuse carina, the last volution has the base slightly convex, imperforate, but with an umbilical depression; the aperture is rounded; the base of the columella has a thickened dental process. Small specimens have the spire less elevated, and the bounding carina much less prominent.

Geological Position and Locality. The Forest Marble of Burton Bradstock; in the collection of W. Walton, Esq.

TURBO DEPAUPERATUS, *Lyc.* Tab. XLV, fig. 13.

PLEUROTOMARIA PAGODUS, var. DEPAUPERATA, Gr. Ool. Mon., Pal. Soc., 1850, part 1, pl. 10, fig. 9, p. 77.

The shell figured in the first part of this Monograph as a doubtful variety of *Pleurotomaria pagodus,* Desl., has, by the aid of other specimens, been clearly shown to be a different shell, which does not belong to the genus Pleurotomaria. Very few examples have hitherto been obtained, all of which are more or less imperfect, have suffered compression, or have been indifferently preserved; however, by comparing one with another, the distinctive characters have been fully ascertained.

A Forest Marble specimen, slightly compressed, is now figured; compared with the original of the former figure the spire is less elevated, the ornamentation of the surface and of the base are better preserved.

The description formerly given applies to the species of Deslongchamps, the following to *Turbo depauperatus.*

Testa turbinata, spira elevata, apice obtuso, anfractibus (5) *convexis, imprimis inornatis, anfractu ultimo et penultimo in medio angulato, costis subnodulosis cingendis, angulo tuberculis regularibus depressis coronatis; basi striis concentricis et radiantibus decussatis, umbilico patens, angulato, concentrice striato; apertura depressa, sublunulata.*

Shell turbinated; spire elevated, its apex obtuse; volutions (5), of which the first three are rounded and without ornamentation, the two latter enlarge rapidly, are angulated in their middle, and coronated with a row of regular depressed encircling tubercles, above and beneath the angle are also three or four rows of nodulous encircling costæ, of which those beneath the angle are the most prominent; the base is slightly convex, concentrically and radiately striated; there is an open umbilicus encircled by an angle, and concentrically striated; the aperture is depressed and sublunulate.

The last volution has the surface above the angle much flattened, and rendered rugose by the nodulous elevations; the encircling costæ are closely arranged, somewhat irregular, and become smaller towards the base of the last volution. In the specimen figured the outer lip is imperfect.

Geological Positions and Localities. The Forest Marble of Laycock and Pound Pill; in the collection of W. Walton, Esq.

TURBO BURTONENSIS, *Lyc.* Tab. XLV, fig. 15.

Testa turbinata, spira elevata, anfractibus (4) *convexis, cingillis tuberculosis tribus magnis instructis; ultimo anfractu basi cingillis* (3 *aut* 4); *apertura ovata, umbilico nullo.*

Shell turbinated; spire elevated; volutions (4) convex, each encircled by three rows of closely arranged large tubercles; the last volution has at the base three or four concentric rows of smaller tubercles; the aperture is ovate; there is no umbilicus.

The upper part of each volution is somewhat flattened, upon which is one row of tubercles, the other two rows are more closely arranged; the tubercles are large and obtusely rounded. The basal transverse diameter is one fourth greater than the height. It is allied to *Turbo muricatus*, Sow., but with a shorter spire, more constricted sutures, and the tubercles much larger.

Geological Position and Locality. The Forest Marble of Burton Bradstock; in the collection of W. Walton, Esq.

TURBO SUBTEXATUS, *Lyc.* Tab. XLI, figs. 15, 15 *a.*

Testa parva, inflata, spira elevata, anfractibus valde convexis, postice subhorizontalibus, antice convexis, suturis profunde impressis, anfractu ultimo permagno, apertura ovali, umbilico nullo; superficie lineis concentricis et longitudinalibus tenuissimis, aut punctis vix notatis.

Shell small, inflated; spire elevated; volutions (4) very convex, their posterior portions nearly horizontal, their anterior portions convex, with the sutures deeply impressed; the last volution very large and ovate; the aperture oval, no umbilical depression; the surface, with lines encircling and perpendicular, very densely and irregularly arranged, having sometimes an imperfectly punctated aspect.

It is allied to *Turbo gibbosus*, D'Orb., but the latter is shorter and more inflated.

Geological Position and Locality. The Forest Marble of Farleigh; in the collection of W. Walton, Esq.

MONODONTA COMMA, *Lyc.* Tab. XLV, figs. 24, 24 *a.*

Testa ovato-discoidea, anfractibus (4), *elevatis, subplanis, suturis distinctis, anfractu ultimo magno, apertura elliptica, umbilico parvo, dente basili magno obtuso; superficie striis concentricis tenuissimis, regularibus.*

Shell ovate, discoidal; spire elevated; volutions (4) rather flattened, apex obtuse; the sutures distinct; the last volution large, rather depressed, aperture elliptical; umbilicus small; basal tooth large, obtuse; the surface has very delicate, closely arranged, regular encircling striations.

The general figure nearly approaches to *Monodonta* (*Crossostoma*) *heliciforme*, but the latter shell is without ornamentation, and has a smaller and more depressed basal tooth and sulcus.

Geological Position and Locality. The Forest Marble of Farleigh; in the collection of W. Walton, Esq.

MONODONTA WALTONI, *Lyc.* Tab. XLV, figs. 31, 31 *a, b.*

Testa crassa, ovoidea, tenuissime concentrice striata, spira brevi depressa, suturis distinctis, anfractibus (5) *angustis, subconvexis, anfractu ultimo permagno; basi obliquo subumbilicato, dente et sulco magno obtuso; apertura ovata.*

Shell thick, ovoidal, delicately concentrically striated; spire short, depressed; volutions (5) narrow, slightly convex, their sutures distinct, the last volution very large, base oblique, and slightly umbilicated; the basal tooth and sulcus prominent; aperture ovate, outer lip thick.

A pretty little delicately ornamented species, of twelve examples the smallest is scarcely larger than the head of a pin, and has a distinct umbilicus; the largest has a diameter of four lines.

Geological Position and Locality. The Forest Marble of Farleigh; in the cabinet of W. Walton, Esq.

Monodonta arata, *Lyc.* Tab. XLV, fig. 19.

Testa trochiformi, spira elevata, anfractibus (6) *latis, concavis, postice et antice carina, striata, obtusa, suturis valde impressis, anfractibus semel concentrice tenuissime lineatis et decussatim oblique striatis; basi lineis concentricis majoribus et minoribus alternatis; sulco columellari magno et dente obtuso.*

Shell trochiform; spire elevated; volutions (6) wide, concave, having a striated obtuse keel upon their posterior and anterior borders; there are also very delicate encircling lines, which are indented by oblique decussating striations; the base is concentrically lineated, the lines being alternately large and small; there is also a conspicuous columellar groove and obtuse tooth; the aperture is nearly circular.

Height and basal diameter nearly equal.

Geological Position and Locality. The Forest Marble of Laycock; in the collection of W. Walton, Esq.

Monodonta tegulata, *Lyc.* Tab. XLV, figs. 17, 18.

Testa sub-trochiformi, spira elata, anfractibus (4), *latis, in medio angulatis, carinis, tribus cingendis, superne oblique planatis, inferne concavis, anfractibus semel concentrice lineatis, lineis granosis, striis tenuissimis decussatis; basi concentrice lineatis, sulco magno umbilicali et sulco et dente obtuso instructo.*

Shell sub-trochiform; spire elevated, consisting of four wide and carinated volutions, angulated in their middle portions by a prominent encircling keel, a keel being also placed at the anterior and posterior border of each volution; between the carinæ are numerous regular encircling lines, rendered granulated by decussating very fine oblique striations; the base is concentrically lineated, and has a large umbilical groove bounded by a prominent keel; the columellar sulcus and tooth are also conspicuous; the aperture is subcircular, its outer border impressed by the carinæ.

The diameter at the base is one third greater than the height. A pretty species, with strongly sculptured ornamentation. The volutions are obliquely flattened above and concave beneath the median carina.

Geological Position and Locality. The Forest Marble of Laycock; in the collection of W. Walton, Esq.

Genus—Onustus, *Humphrey.*

Shell conical, with several volutions, which are flattened or are rendered somewhat concave by an expansion of their lower borders, which overhang and conceal the suture; the lower border of the last volution is produced horizontally to support a membranous expansion; the surface has striations, or radiately undulating lines, which are somewhat irregular. The base is concave towards the outer border, and convex towards the centre; the umbilical orifice is sometimes large, but in other instances small, and becomes nearly concealed by advance of growth; the aperture is depressed and ovate. Some Tertiary and Recent species have the spire encrusted with fragments of shells or stones, which obscure the ornamentation.

Xenophora, Fischer, and *Phorus*, Montfort, are synonyms of this genus.

Onustus Burtonensis, *Lyc.* Tab. XLV, figs. 7, 7 *a*, *b*.

Testa subconica, spira elevata, obtusa, anfractibus (4-5), *angustis subconcavis, longitudinaliter costatis, costis* (*circa* 24—26) *inferne alternatim in spinis producta; basi subconcavo, concentrice et radiatim striato, umbilico amplo.*

Shell subconical, wider than high; spire moderately elevated obtuse; volutions four or five, narrow, slightly concave, with about twenty-four to twenty-six longitudinal rounded and elevated costæ; the base of every alternate costa forms, with the lower expanded margin of each volution, a projecting process, which renders the lower margins of the volutions undulated; the base is expanded, slightly concave, concentrically and radiately striated; the umbilicus is large.

A pretty species, possessing the generic features strongly defined, more especially the expansions at the lower border of each volution, which impart a pagoda-like aspect to the spire. Only two other British Jurassic species are known, viz., *Trochus pyramidatus*, Phil., = *Trochus lamellosus* D'Orb., a more depressed species, which occurs in the Supra-Liassic sands, and in the Inferior Oolite of Gloucestershire and of Yorkshire; the other is the *Trochus ornatissimus*, D'Orb., with a very elevated spire, and inordinately expanded at the lower border; it occurs in the Inferior Oolite of the Cotteswolds, and in the White Oolite of Ponton, Lincolnshire. Our species is most nearly allied to *Trochus ornatissimus*, but with a shorter spire, fewer volutions, and with prominent overwrapping expansions at the lower border of each volution. Other foreign Jurassic species are *Trochus heliacus*, D'Orb., *T. Tytirus*, D'Orb., *Solarium callaudianum*, D'Orb., *Onustus exul*, Eug. Desl., and *Onustus liasinus*, E. Desl. None of these species exhibit those agglutinations of shells and stones which are so characteristic of the Tertiary and Recent examples of Onustus.

Geological Position and Locality. The Forest Marble of Burton Bradstock; in the collection of W. Walton, Esq.

PHASIANELLA VARIATA, *Lyc.* Tab. XLV, figs. 28, 28 *a*, *b*.

Testa ovato-elongata, spira acuta, anfractibus (6-7), *subconvexis, latiusculis, suturis valde impressis, ultimo anfractu amplo, apertura obliqua, ovato-elongata.*

Shell variable in figure, ovately elongated; spire lengthened, with the apex acute; volutions six to seven, wide, more or less convex; the sutures strongly impressed; the last volutions conformable, the aperture oblique, ovate, narrow, but always less than half the height of the shell.

The variability in the convexity of the volutions and their height is considerable. The general aspect resembles *P. elegans*, Mor. and Lyc., in which the spire is always less pointed and less slender, the last volution being also longer.

Geological Position and Locality. The Forest Marble of Laycock; in the collection of W. Walton, Esq.

SOLARIUM TURBINIFORMIS, *Lyc.* Tab. XLV, figs. 23, 23 *a*, *b*.

Testa turbinata, spira dextra, elevata, obtusa, anfractibus (4), *tuberculis numerosis, coronatis; basi convexa, umbilico magno, margine, nodis* (*circa* 9) *cingendo, superficie lineis transversalibus et longitudinalibus decussatis; apertura suborbiculari.*

Shell turbinated, spire dextral, elevated, volutions four, their borders coronated with a circle of tubercles, about eighteen in a volution; the base is convex, with a large and deep umbilical cavity, bordered by large nodose elevations, about nine in the volution; the aperture is suborbicular; the entire surface has encircling lines, with more narrow interstitial spaces decussated and rendered granular by densely arranged transverse striations.

Allied to *Straparollus altus*, D'Orb.; the latter species, however, has the last volution more elevated and the sides much more flattened, which impart a subquadrate figure to the aperture; the nodose elevations encircling the umbilicus are also fewer and larger.

Geological Position and Locality. The Great Oolite of Hampton Cliffs; in the collection of W. Walton, Esq.

SOLARIUM WALTONI, *Lyc.* Tab. XLV, figs. 26, 26 *a*, *b*, *c*.

Testa discoidea, latere superiori et inferiori concavo, dorso angusto, convexo, tuberculis per series duobus instructis; latere superiori anfractibus subconcavis, varicibus obscuris transversalibus instructis; latere inferiore anfractibus planatis; lineis transversalibus et longitudinalibus cancellatis; apertura subquadrata.

Shell discoidal, the superior and inferior sides concave, the back narrow, rounded, encircled upon its upper part by two rows of tubercles, of which there are about nineteen in a volution; the upper surface has the volutions slightly concave, and traversed transversely by obscure varices, proceeding from the tubercles; the lower side is but little more concave than the other; the volutions are flattened. The entire surface of the shell has delicate transverse and encircling lines, forming a regularly reticulated surface; the aperture is subquadrate.

A beautiful and remarkably discoidal species.

Geological Position and Locality. The Great Oolite of Hampton Cliffs; in the collection of W. Walton, Esq.

Pleurotomaria Bathonica, *Lyc.* Tab. XLV, fig. 10.

Testa trochiformi, conoidea, spira apice obtuso, anfractibus convexis lineis transversis et perpendicularibus, sub-æqualibus, cancellatis; ultimo anfractu superne tuberculato-nodosis; sinu magno, fascia sinus, plana, transversim lineata, in baso anfractuum sita; ultimo anfractu basi plano, concentrice lineato; umbilico subnullo, apertura subquadrata.

Shell trochiform, conoidal; spire obtuse; volutions convex, with cancellated transverse and perpendicular lines; the last volution with a row upon the upper part of nodose tubercles; the sinus is large, the fascia of the sinus is flattened and transversely lineated; the base is flattened, and concentrically lineated; the aperture is subquadrate; there is no umbilicus.

The encircling lines, of which there are three or four above the fascia of the sinus, are more prominent than the perpendicular lines. The height is one third less than the basal diameter.

Geological Position and Locality. The Forest Marble of the Box Tunnel, near Bath; in the collection of W. Walton, Esq.

Pleurotomaria Burtonensis, *Lyc.* Tab. XLV, fig. 8.

Testa trochiformi, conoidea, anfractibus (5—6), *superne inflatis, nodoso-undulatis, inferne subplanis; superficie lineis transversalibus et perpendicularibus, æqualibus, dense cancellatis, anfractu ultimo basi concentrice et radiatim lineatis, subconvexo, umbilico subnullo; sinu magno, in medio anfractuum situ; fascia sinus delicate cancellatis.*

Shell trochiform, conoidal; volutions (5—6), very convex in their upper parts, and nodosely undulated; their lower portions rather flattened; the surface, with encircling and perpendicular equal lines, forming a delicately cancellated surface; the last volution has the base wide, somewhat convex, with regular concentric and radiating lines, the latter being the less conspicuous; there is scarcely any umbilical depression; the sinus is large, placed in the middle of the volutions; the fascia of the sinus is delicately cancellated; the nodose elevations upon the upper half of each volution are regular, numerous, and not very strongly defined in the greater number of the specimens.

The height is equal to two thirds of the basal diameter. Of the seven specimens examined, the largest has a basal diameter of about an inch.

Geological Position and Locality. The Forest Marble of Burton Bradstock; in the collection of W. Walton, Esq.

PLEUROTOMARIA RECONDITA, *Lyc.* Tab. XLV, fig. 7.

Testa trochiformi, discoidea, anfractibus* (4) *subplanis, inferne obtuse carinatis; fascia sinus lata, transverse delicate striata, in medio anfractum situ; anfractibus cingillis angustis* (3—4) *supra et infra sinus instructo, striis obliquis tenuissimis, impressis; carina marginali lævi; basi lato, concavo, umbilicato, delicate concentrice striato.

Shell trochiform, discoidal; volutions (4) flattened, but rendered concave in the lower portions by a prominent, obtuse, smooth, marginal carina; the fascia of the sinus is mesial, wide, with very delicate transverse striations; above aud beneath the sinus are three or four narrow encircling little costæ, which are impressed by delicate oblique striations; the base is wide, concave, with a distinct umbilicus, with fine concentric striations; the outer lip and sinus have not been obtained perfect.

The height is equal to about three fifths of the basal diameter.

A small species, remarkable for the great breadth of the mesial band, and the prominence of the infero-marginal smooth carina.

Geological Position and Locality. The Great Oolite of Bussage, near Bisley Common, and of Minchinhampton Common; it is rare.

ACTEONINA LUIDII, p. 27. Tab. XXXI, fig. 16, and Tab. XLI, fig. 18.

A fine series of examples kindly communicated by Mr. Walton, and collected by him in the Forest Marble of Laycock, has enabled the artist to illustrate the more striking varieties of figure. The differences in the elevation of the spire are so considerable that any measurement of the spiral angle is useless; the sides of the volutions are always flattened, with a mesial angle; in short spired examples the space anterior to the angle is nearly concealed, and the space posterior to it is nearly horizontal.

Another remarkable instance of variability in the elevation of the spire in the same genus is seen in *A. olivæformis*, Tab. XLI, figs. 4, 4 *a*, which may be compared with that given in Tab. VIII, fig. 14, part 1.

ACTEONINA SUESSEA, *Lyc.* Tab. XLV, fig. 29.

Testa ovato-elongata, spira elevata, apice acuminata anfractibus (7) *angustis, subangulatis, superne concavis anfractu ultimo basi attenuato; apertura obliqua subreniformi, labro interno incrassato.*

Shell ovately elongated; spire elevated; apex pointed; volutions (7) narrow, convex, subangulated, their upper surfaces concave, their upper borders strongly impressed with a slightly tumid band; the last volution attenuated towards the base; the aperture oblique, and somewhat reniform; the inner lip conspicuous and thickened; the lines of growth are very conspicuous upon the spire.

Geological Position and Localities. The Forest Marble at Farleigh, Laycock, and Pound Pill; in the collection of W. Walton, Esq.

ACTEONINA FASCIATA, *Lyc.* Tab. XLIV, fig. 15.

Testa parva, ovato-elongata aut sub-cylindrica, spira magna elevata, anfractibus (7) *angustis, superne convexis, inferne planatis, ultimo anfractu, valde elongato, apertura basi elliptico curvato, postice angusto; superficie lineis plicisque perpendicularibus crebris et irregularibus notatis.*

Shell small, ovately elongated or subcylindrical, the two extremities being somewhat pointed; spire large, lengthened, consisting of seven narrow volutions, which have their upper portions inflated and their sides flattened; the last volution is much elongated and sub-cylindrical; the aperture has its anterior extremity curved elliptically, its posterior position narrow and lengthened; the surface of the shell, with perpendicular, crowded, irregular plications and lines.

The test is delicate, and all the specimens are more or less broken. Length of the largest specimen, 6 lines; breadth, 2½ lines; length of the aperture, 4 lines.

Geological Position and Locality. The Forest Marble of Laycock; in the collection of W. Walton, Esq.

ACTEONINA WILTONENSIS, *Lyc.* Tab. XLV, fig. 25.

Testa parva, sub-fusiformi, ovato-elongata, spira elata, anfractibus (5—6) *sub-convexis, anfractu ultimo ovato, apertura elliptica, basi angusto; superficie lineis perpendicularibus, tenuissimis, crebris notatis.*

Shell small, sub-fusiform or ovately elongated, spire elevated, volutions 5 or 6, rather convex; the last volution ovate; aperture elliptical, its base narrow; the surface, with very delicate, closely arranged, perpendicular lines, which render the surface slightly rough.

As the outer lip is much broken in both the specimens examined, the figure of the anterior extremity of the aperture is rather doubtful, and the general figure of the shell is more fusiform than is usual in this genus; the columella is rounded, and quite destitute of any plication.

Geological Position and Locality. The Forest Marble of Laycock; in the collection of W. Walton, Esq.

OSTREA WILTONENSIS, *Lyc.* Tab. XXXIV, figs. 1, 1 *a.*

Testa, valva libera planata, crassa, solida, ovato-triangulari, brevi, apice erecto, obtuso; sulco cardinis lato, superficiali. Valva affixa ignota.

Shell with the free valve flattened, but solid and thick; its borders are raised internally, rendering the inner surface somewhat concave; the figure is ovately triangular, but short, with the apex erect and obtuse; the hinge sulcus is wide and superficial. The affixed valve is unknown.

Several large specimens of this ponderous but flattened oyster have been obtained by Mr. Walton, including the monstrosity, Tab. XXXIV, fig. 1 *a.* The height is greater than the opposite measurement; it has some resemblance to *O. deltoidea,* but less flattened, not transverse, and with the umbones not oblique; and as the specimens are constant in their general characters, there can be no doubt of its distinctness from that species.

Geological Position and Locality.—The Forest Marble of Pound Pill.

OSTREA (EXOGYRA) LINGULATA, *Walton* MSS. Tab. XXXII, figs. 2, 2 *a,* 2 *b.*

Testa valva inferiore sublævi, excavata, elongata, postice carinata, margine anteriore subrecto, cardine brevi, antrorsum curvato. Valva libera planata, elongata, linguæformi, umboni compresso, arcuato; facie interno sulco longitudinali oblique instructo.

Shell, with the affixed valve excavated, elongated, smooth, with a posterior external, longitudinal angle; hinge margin short, and curved forwards; anterior border straight, posterior border curved elliptically. Free valve flattened, smooth, lengthened, and tongue-shaped, tapering towards both the extremities; the umbo is depressed, and much curved; the inner surface with a lengthened posterior sulcation. The length is usually about twice the opposite diameter.

A species allied to *Exogyra carinata.* Roemer Nordd, Ool., p. 66, pl. 3, fig. 15. This latter, however, appears to have the affixed valve more flattened and lunulate.

Geological Positions and Localities. This oyster appears to be abundant in the Upper Bathonian Clays of Wiltshire. Mr. Walton has collected it in the Forest Marble of Pound Pill, Farleigh, and Hinton, also in the Cornbrash of Hilperton.

Genus—Harpax—Parkinson, 1811. Deslongchamps, 1858.

Shell irregular, inequivalve, attached by the umbo of the larger or right valve; surface radiately ribbed or smooth, usually with concentric, irregular, lamellose plications, imbricated or tuberculated; borders of the valves close fitting and irregular.

Hinge in the attached valve consisting of a large, flattened, triangular plate, traversed by a central perpendicular or oblique furrow to receive the ligament, with somewhat elevated borders, exterior to which are slightly marked diverging sulcations to receive the elevated borders of the ligamental groove in the other valve; the outer borders of the plate form lengthened and elevated dental processes.

Hinge in the left or free valve with a triangular plate traversed mesially by the ligamental groove, the borders to which are elevated and but slightly diverging; exterior to these are strongly impressed grooves to receive the dental processes of the other valve; the dental processes forming the diverging borders of the plate are but little produced.

The hinge plate in each valve has transverse striations of growth.

The adductor scar is round, placed posterior to the middle of the valve, and strongly marked; the pallial sinus is simple.

The genus *Harpax* having originally been imperfectly described by Parkinson, and founded upon a single small species, remained but little noticed and accepted by few authors until the year 1858, when it was re-established and amply illustrated in a copious work* on the 'Fossil Plicatulas and allied Genera,' by that eminent and veteran palæontologist M. Eudes, E. Deslongchamps, who to the long list of memoirs in which he has so ably developed and illustrated the Jurassic fossils of Normandy, has added the present, which probably surpasses all the former in the critical acumen and lengthened researches which it has necessitated. Of the fifteen species of *Harpax* known to M. Deslongchamps all are Liassic, with one exception (*H. scapha*), from the ferruginous (Inferior?) Oolite of Longwy; the following fine species is therefore the first example of the genus in the oolites of this country.

* Essai sur les Plicatules fossiles et quelque autre genres voisins ou démembrés de ces coquilles, par M. J. A. Eudes Deslongchamps. Extract du XIe volume des 'Memoires de la Société Linnéenne de Normandie,' Caen, 1858.

HARPAX WALTONI, *Lyc.* Tab. XXXII, figs. 1, 1 *a*, 1 *b*.

Testa (valva dextra) magna, crassa, ovata, convexa, sub-auriculata, late adherente, radiatim costatis, lamellis incrementi crebris, crassis nodiferis et imbricatis, facie interno, tabula cardinali magno dentibus et foveis longissimis insigni. Valva sinistra depressa, crassa, lamellis ut in valva altera, tabula cardinali dentibus prominentibus, longissimis, obliquis, sulcis conformibus.

Shell of large dimensions, the right valve with a very large surface of attachment, sub-auriculated, thick, ovate, convex, the surface radiately costated, with thickened, crowded, imbricated and elevated lamellæ of growth; the triangular hinge plate is very large, oblique, transversely striated; the diverging outer grooves which receive the dental processes of the other valve are large, deeply impressed, and exhibit in their course three deeper portions or pits adapted to the successive positions occupied by the anterior projecting or bossed extremities of the dental processes in the free valve; the adductor scar is very large and posterior.

The left or free valve is thick, but less convex than the other; the hinge area occupies upwards of two fifths of the length of the valve; the ligamental groove is narrow and deeply marked, but the other furrows are superficial; the outer diverging dental processes are lengthened and conspicuous, terminating anteriorly in projecting bosses; the adductor scar is prominent and sub-central. In the specimen figured with the valves in contact, the right valve has adhered to a smaller specimen of the same species, whose exposed inner surface exhibits the usual characters of the *left* valve.

Our species is allied to *Harpax calvus* and *H. senescens*, Desl., from the Middle Lias of Calvados, but has more prominent rugose lamellæ, and a larger hinge area in both the valves. In the left valve the anterior termination of the dental processes in bosses with corresponding pits in the furrows of the other valve, has no counterpart in the figures or descriptions of M. Deslongchamps, but as they do not appear to be equally persistent in all specimens their importance can only be small.

Geological Positions and Localities. The Forest Marble of Farleigh Wick, Somerset; collected by W. Walton, Esq., whose labours have been rewarded by the acquisition of several good specimens. The interiors of the valves of this species have also been observed in the Great Oolite of Minchinhampton; in these instances, however, their external surfaces could not be disengaged.

GERVILLIA WALTONI, *Lyc.* Tab. XXXII, figs. 4, 4 *a*, *b*.

Testa fragili, ovato-oblonga, valva sinistra antice convexa, postice explanata in alam brevem producta, umboni prominente, apice acuto, subterminali, ala antica brevi, margine cardinali obliquo, area cardinis longitudinaliter striatis, sulcis transversis magnis (4), *dentibus obliquis internis paucis inconspicuis; superficie plicis incrementi delicate instructis. Valva altera mediocri convexa.*

Shell fragile, ovately oblong; left valve anteriorly very convex, moderately thick, and steep; posterior side expanded, attenuated, and produced into a short wing; umbo prominent, acute, subterminal, the anterior wing being short; the hinge margin is oblique, of moderate length; the hinge area has two or three prominent longitudinal striations; the cardinal transverse sulci, four in number, are large and irregular; the internal oblique teeth are few and inconspicuous; the surface with numerous delicate plications of growth. The other valve is of nearly equal convexity and more strongly plicated.

A well marked convex species, with the hinge border moderately oblique, and the whole of the posterior side expanded and delicate.

Geological Position and Locality. The Forest Marble of Farleigh and Pound Pill; in the collection of W. Walton, Esq.

Gervillia ornata, *Lyc.* Tab. XXXVI, fig. 7.

Testa parva, ovato obliqua; valva sinistra convexa, umboni prominente, ala antica producta; postica obliqua, brevissima; superficie striis tenuissimis concentricis, regularibus, lineisque radiantibus decussatis. Valva altera ignota.

Shell small, ovately oblique; the left valve inflated, the umbo prominent and situated nearly in the middle of the hinge line, which slopes from it obliquely in upon each side; the anterior wing is produced and rounded, the posterior wing is very short; the surface of the valve has very delicate, regular, concentric striations, which are decussated by elevated lines which diverge from the umbo. The other valve is unknown.

A short, oblique, and very convex Gervillia; the radiating lines upon the middle of the valve are slightly undulating and conspicuous, but gradually disappear towards the sides. The general figure is allied to *G. ovata*, Sow., but the latter is less convex, and its surface is destitute of ornamentation.

Length, 5 lines; breadth, 3 lines. From the position of the shell in our figure the short posterior wing is not seen, and the convexity is scarcely sufficiently conspicuous.

Geological Position and Locality. The Great Oolite of Bussage, adjoining Bisley Common; collected by E. Witchell, Esq.

Gervillia bicostata, *Lyc.* Tab. XL, fig. 21.

Testa per-obliqua, convexa, ala antica brevi, altera longiora, emarginata, dorso, costis obliquis elevatis (2) *distantibus, plicis incrementi magnis decussatis. Valva dextra ignota.*

Shell small, very oblique, convex; the anterior wing short, thick, and gibbose; posterior wing more lengthened, emarginated posteriorly; the middle of the valve with two elevated, oblique, longitudinal, distantly arranged costæ, which are crossed by large irregular folds of growth; the right valve has not been obtained.

Our sole specimen has the posterior extremity imperfect.

Geological Position and Locality. The Great Oolite of Bussage, near Bisley Common; collected by E. Witchell, Esq.

Perna Mytiloides, *Lam.* Tab. XXXII, fig. 3.

Perna Mytiloides, *Lamark.* An. sans Vert., 6 Bd., p. 142.
— — *Zieten.* Pet., p. 71, pl. 54, fig. 2.
— — *Goldf.* Pet., p. 104, t. 107, fig. 12.
— — *D'Orb.* Prodrome de Paléont., 1, p. 311, No. 211.
— — *Morris.* Catal., 1854, p. 179.
— — *Oppel.* Jura formation, p. 607, No. 79.
— — *Quenstedt.* Der Jura, p. 383, tab. 52, fig. 8.
— — *Damon.* Geol. Weymouth, Suppl., pl. 2, fig. 5.

Testa ovata-sigmoidea, convexo-plana in alam brevem producta, umbonibus acutis prominentibus, margine cardinali obliquo, foveolis (8-12) *plano-concavis.*

Shell thick, ovately sigmoidal, with a moderate convexity, slightly produced posteriorly into a short imperfect wing; the hinge margin is wide, oblique with transverse pits from eight to twelve in number, and only slightly impressed; the anterior border of the valves is much thickened and excavated.

Geological Positions and Localities. The Forest Marble of Farleigh; in the cabinet of W. Walton, Esq. Unfortunately none of the Forest Marble specimens are altogether perfect. The Geological range of this Perna must be very considerable, if there is no mistake in the identification of the species. Professor Quenstedt records it in the Inferior Oolite of Wurtemburg; Goldfuss, in the Oxford Clay and Upper Oolite of Baireuth and Wurtemburg; D'Orbigny quotes it from Villiers, Trouville, Lyon, Chaumont, Pizieux, Marolles (Sarthe), and other localities in the same department, all in his 'Etage Callovien.'

Mr. Damon has figured it from the Oxford Clay of Weymouth; and it has been recorded in the Kimmeridge Clay of the latter place; and the Portland Oolite of Swindon, by Professor Morris.

Perna obliqua, *Walton* MSS. Tab. XXXIV, fig. 22 *a.*

Testa subæquivalvi convexo-plana, crassa, umbonibus acutis, prominentibus, margine anteriore recto, margine cardinali recto, oblique declivi, valvis lamellis irregularibus concentricis instructis. Area cardinis angusta, elongata, foveolis (8) *latis, subconcavis.*

Shell subequilateral, moderately convex, slightly arched longitudinally in the left valve; test thick, umbones acute and prominent; anterior border straight; hinge-border moderately lengthened, straight, sloping obliquely downwards. Hinge-area narrow, elongated, pits (8) wide, and only slightly concave; lamellæ of growth large and irregular.

Length, about twice as great as the transverse measurement; diameter through the valves, one third of the length.

Geological Position and Locality. The Forest Marble of Gastard; in the cabinet of W. Walton, Esq.

PECTEN SUBSPINOSUS, *Schloth.* Tab. XL, fig. 14.

PECTEN SUBSPINOSUS, *Schloth.* Petref., p 223.
— — *Goldfuss.* Petref., t. 90, fig. 4.
— — *Quenst.* Der Jura, p. 500, pl. 67, figs. 3, 4; and pl. 92, figs. 5, 6.

Testa ovato-orbiculari fornicata æquivalvi, costis (12) *æqualibus elatis subacutis in dorso spinosis, sulcis conformibus transversim lineatis, auriculis inæqualibus costatis lineisque decussantibus striatis.* (Goldfuss.)

Shell ovately orbicular, equivalve; costæ (12) large, elevated, subacute, each having upon its ridge a few short spines; the interstitial sulcations are narrow, with delicate, transverse lines; the auricles are unequal, the anterior auricle of the right valve being the larger; they have radiating and decussating lines. The valves have but little convexity; the radiating costæ form one third of a circle.

Height, 7 lines; transverse diameter, 9 lines.

Geological Positions and Localities. The Forest Marble of Locus and Farleigh, Somerset; in the collection of W. Walton, Esq. The foreign localities cited by Professor Quenstedt are Bopfingen and Waldenburg, in the Parkinsoni Oolite and the Bradford Clay; also Nattheim, in the Coralline Oolite.

MACRODON HIRSONENSIS, var. RUGOSA. Tab. XXXVI, fig. 9.

The Forest Marble of Wilts and Somerset has this species in the form of a variety which is distinguished from the shell of the Inferior and Great Oolite by the following features:—It has greater convexity, a wider hinge-area; the posterior side is more depressed, and is not uncommonly traversed by two or three radiating furrows, and is in some instances separated from the other portion of the surface by a distinct keel. The folds of growth upon the sides of the valves are also remarkably, conspicuous, rendering the surface rugose, and the basal sinuation is very strongly defined; in some of the more aberrant forms the posterior side is so much shortened that the umbones are nearly mesial; they are then much elevated, and an oblique keel descends to the infero-posterior extremity. Our illustration faithfully represents this variety, numerous specimens of which have been placed at our disposal by the kindness of Mr. Walton.

CARDIUM GLOBOSUM, *Bean*. Tab. XXXVIII, figs. 2, 2 *a*, 2 *b*.

CARDIUM GLOBOSUM, *Bean*, in Mag. of Nat. Hist., 1839, p. 60, fig. 18.

Testa suborbiculari, æquilatera, convexa, marginibus ellipticis curvatis; superficie striis concentricis, tenuissimis, crebris instructis.

Shell suborbicular, equilateral, convex; the umbones moderately produced, acuminated, and incurved; the margins of the valves are elliptically curved; the surface has very delicate, regular, closely arranged, concentric striations.

The length and breadth are equal; the diameter through the valves is two fifths less. Our illustration is taken from the original specimen figured by Mr. Bean; its outline should be somewhat more orbicular. The striated surface readily distinguishes it from *Cardium cognatum*, Phil., which in other respects it resembles.

Geological Position and Locality. The Cornbrash of Scarborough; in the collection of Mr. Leckenby.

LITHODOMUS PORTERI, *Lyc.* Tab. XL, fig. 29.

Testa parva ovato-oblonga, convexa, angusta, umbonibus obliquis, subterminalibus; margine anteriore recto, posteriore elliptico curvato, costis longitudinalibus numerosis, tenuibus lineis concentricis decussatis.

Shell small, ovately oblong, narrow, convex; umbones oblique, subterminal; anterior border straight, its sides steep; posterior margin curved elliptically; longitudinal costæ numerous, delicate, closely arranged, sometimes bifurcating towards the lower border, and decussated by closely arranged, concentric lines.

The ornamentation is most prominent towards the middle of the valves, and is very faintly traced upon the anterior side. It is allied to *Lithodomus parasiticus*, Desl., Mor., and Lyc. ('Gr. Ool. Mon.,' "Biv.," p. 41, Tab. IV, fig. 19), but has greater convexity, and is more narrow and cylindrical; the numerous costæ and decussating lines are also distinctive features.

Geological Position and Locality. Collected by W. Walton, Esq., in the Great Oolite of Hampton Cliffs, near Bath.

Dedicated to Henry Porter, Esq., M.D., who has investigated the geology in the neighbourhood of Peterborough.

NOTES AND CORRECTIONS.

Fossils figured in the former parts of this Monograph from the Coast of Yorkshire, and attributed to the Great Oolite.

It may now be stated, as the general conviction of Palæontologists who have critically studied the subject, that the Testacea of all the marine beds intercalated with the important but local plant-bearing shales and sandstones of the Yorkshire coast, intermediate the Cornbrash and the Dogger, constitute an Inferior Oolite fauna, but that the mineral character of these deposits and their sequence are peculiar to the locality; it is found also, as might be expected in deposits so isolated in their general conditions, that the fauna of these several marine beds, although undoubtedly pertaining to the Inferior Oolite, cannot be arranged with precision upon any corresponding horizons of the same formation, either in Britain or upon the Continent. But in discarding the correlative value of the minor subdivisions, it appears that they may be assigned approximately to those groups of beds which constitute the upper portion of the Inferior Oolite, and which have been divided by Quenstedt, Oppel, and others, into two distinct stages, the lower of which is characterised by the presence of *Ammonites Humphriesianus*, the upper by *Ammonites Parkinsoni*. Upon the coast of Yorkshire these Ammonites, however, have occurred in the same bed, and the number of marine floors is so few that they cannot be considered as representing the two superior stages in the entity of their mass and of their fauna; their deficiencies are more especially remarkable in the rarity of the Brachiopoda and of the Ammonites.

These conclusions have been arrived at by an investigation of a series of details so extensive and decisive in their results as to admit of no uncertainty upon the subject. That the marine beds in question should have been assigned to the Great Oolite upwards of thirty years since by the author of the 'Geology of Yorkshire' will not excite surprise in any one who is able to recall to memory the rudimentary condition of Palæontology at that period, and the absolute ignorance which then prevailed of the Testacea of the Great Oolite; that the Palæontology of the Jurassic portion of the work in question constituted a great advance upon the previous work of Messrs. Young and Bird was at once recognised, and the author candidly stated that he assigned these marine intercalated beds to the Great Oolite solely from their position—higher than certain beds of undoubted Inferior Oolite, and lower than the Cornbrash. The progress of knowledge tending to arrange them with the Inferior Oolite, was gradual. Following the work of Professor Phillips, in 1839 appeared the two well-known memoirs of Professor Williamson on the distribution of organic remains in the Oolitic rocks of Yorkshire, in which the subordinate beds of the Lower Oolites and their organic contents are detailed with all the care and precision that might be expected from a person who had been long resident in the locality. Within the few years following appeared the elaborate works of Goldfuss, Ziethen, Roemer, Dunker, Agassiz, Deshayes, Sir R. Murchison's second edition of the 'Geology of Cheltenham,' the 'Catalogue' of Professor Morris, the memoir of D'Archiac on the Aisne, several memoirs by M. Eudes Deslongchamps on the fossils of the Oolites of Normandy, a portion of the 'Paléontologie Française' of D'Orbigny, Quenstedt's 'Wurtemburg,' and the 'Lethea' of Broun. These works, together with others which bear less directly upon the subject of the Lower Oolites, tended very materially to extend and correct the knowledge of their fossils. During the same period also the fossils of the Great Oolite in Gloucestershire had become extensively dispersed, and were compared with those from the Yorkshire coast, collected and distributed with great perseverance by Mr. Bean during a lengthened period. The first published results of influences so potential appeared in 1850, when M. d'Orbigny, in his 'Prodrome de Paléontologie,' placed many of the so-called Great Oolite Yorkshire fossils in his Étage Bajocien, or Inferior Oolite. In the same year appeared the first part of the monograph on the Great Oolite Mollusca, in the introductory remarks to which the authors pointed out the affinity of the Yorkshire so-called Great Oolite fauna to that of the Inferior Oolite, and, as a measure of precaution, were careful to keep the doubtful Yorkshire fossils distinct, both in plates and descriptions, from the Great Oolite fossils of the south of England. The various works and lesser memoirs upon the Lower Jurassic rocks published between 1850 and the present time would of themselves constitute a considerable list. Without enumerating them, it will be sufficient to mention that, in 1856-8, Dr. Albert Oppel, in his remarkable work, 'Juraformation,' placed the Yorkshire Phytiferous beds with the Inferior Oolite, and considered that they did not even represent the highest stage of that formation. In 1857 the present writer expressed, in a little work, 'The Cotteswold Hills,' convictions of similar import. In 1859 Dr. Wright enforced similar views, accompanied by extensive details and lists of Inferior Oolite fossils, in a contribution to the 'Journal of the Geological Society.' The previous Great Oolite Monograph contains four plates of these Yorkshire intercalated marine Testacea; some of which, however, pass upwards into the Great Oolite of the Cotteswolds and into the Cornbrash, as will be ascertained from the descriptions. In excluding them from the present Supplementary Monograph, the writer begs to state that he consented to their admission into the former work with great reluctance, in deference to the opinion then prevalent that they pertained to the Great Oolite, but with a strong impression (formed in 1839, upon perusing the memoir of Professor Williamson) that they constituted an Inferior Oolite fauna.

The Palæontologists of France, in their expositions of the Great Oolite fossils of that country, have, within the last few years, fully proved, by the general identity and association of species, that the fauna of the Minchinhampton beds is not exceptional or local merely, as some have supposed, but represents a very ample and characteristic series of Mollusca, a large number of which are also found in other and distant localities at the same geological horizon. Other not less interesting and important facts, confirmatory of this view, have recently been afforded by researches in English strata of the same epoch. The Oxfordshire railway sections of the Great Oolite and Forest Marble have yielded to Mr. Whiteaves a varied series of Testacea, a list of which he has kindly communicated to me, together with many of the fossils, including those which are not known in the Minchinhampton beds; the result is, that of 122 Great Oolite and 48 Forest Marble shells, in all 140 species, obtained by that gentleman in the Oxfordshire beds, upwards of 114 are also common to the Minchinhampton beds. An extensive series of Forest Marble shells from the clay beds of Wiltshire, Somersetshire, and Dorsetshire, liberally placed at my disposal by Mr. Walton, has produced a larger number of novel forms, as might have been expected from the very different lithological conditions of the deposit; nevertheless there is still a majority of Minchinhampton shells, and the entire assemblage is even more remotely allied to the Yorkshire fauna than is that of Minchinhampton. The general discordance, therefore, of the Yorkshire and southern faunas of the supposed Great Oolite within so small an area as England would lead us to infer their separation chronologically, even if we were unable to assign the northern series to that of an older and well-known era.

The following is a list of Yorkshire Testacea figured in the former Monograph which are not known to occur in any stratum more recent than the gray limestone of Scarborough, and should therefore, in accordance with the foregoing views, be excluded from the fauna of the Great Oolite:

Part I.

Ammonites Braikenridgii. Tab. XIV, fig. 1.
— Blagdeni. Tab. XIV, figs. 3 *a*, *b*.
Belemnites giganteus. Tab. XIV, figs. 4, 4 *a*.
Serpula plicatilis. Tab. XIV, figs. 5, 5 *a*, *b*.
— sulcata. Tab. XIV, fig. 6.
Cerithium Beanii. Tab. XV, fig. 5.
Chemnitzia (?) vetusta. Tab. XV, fig. 7.
— Scarburgensis. Tab. XV, fig. 8.
Actæon Sedgvici. Tab. XV, figs. 9, 9 *a*.
— pullus. Tab. XV, fig. 11.
Actæonina glabra. Tab. XV, fig. 10.
— tumidula. Tab. XV, fig. 14.
Phasiavella latiuscula. Tab. XV, fig. 16.
Natica adducta. Tab. XV, figs. 17, 17 *a*.
— (Euspira) cincta. Tab. XV, fig. 20.
Trochus Leckenbyi. Tab. XV, figs. 21, 21 *a*.

Part II.

Mytilus (Modiola) Leckenbyi. Tab. XIV, fig. 9.
Cucullæa cancellata. Tab. XIV, fig. 12.
Unicardium gibbosum. Tab. XIV, fig. 11.
Trigonia signata—decorata. Tab. XV, fig. 1.
Astarte elegans, *Phil.* (non *Sow.*). Tab. XIV, fig. 14.
Isocardia cordata. Tab. XV, fig. 5.
Myacites Beanii. Tab. XV, figs. 11 *a*, *b*.
— Scarburgensis. Tab. XV, fig. 13.
— æquatus. Tab. XII, fig. 15.

Cornbrash of the Coast of Yorkshire: its Mollusca.

The Mollusca of the Yorkshire Cornbrash offer, in their association, some marked contrasts with those of the southern counties and of the Continent upon the same geological horizon. In the southern localities the marine floors, crowded almost exclusively with Brachiopoda, is the predominating feature that arrests the attention; in the northern the Conchifera constitute the great majority; the Brachiopoda, few individually, are reduced almost to the two species *Terebratula lagenalis* and *T. obovata*, the latter being represented by forms dwarfed to about a third of the linear dimensions which the species attains in Wiltshire. The condition of the Testacea also offers some interesting contrasts. In Wiltshire the Conchifera are usually in the condition of casts, of which a large proportion are compressed and distorted; in Yorkshire the hard, dark-coloured limestone has preserved the more delicate external characters in a very perfect manner, including the thin tests of Pholadomya, Myacites, Gresslya, Goniomya, and Cercomya, together with the outer, granulated tegument of the four latter genera; and when the matrix is less hard, even their internal hinge characters may be disclosed. The Gasteropoda are few, both as to species and individuals; the Cephalopoda are, with the exception of a small Belemnite, limited to *Ammonites macrocephalus*, which affords great variety in the details of its figure and ornamentation, but which never attains to the large dimensions of Wiltshire specimens.

Its Mollusca, viewed comprehensively, may be regarded as a transitive series, a chain of life serving to connect the fauna of the Inferior Oolite with that of the Oxfordian rocks, comprising a considerable proportion of the former, perhaps an equal number of special forms, a much smaller number of species which pass upwards into the Oxfordian beds, and a still lessening proportion of forms which are recognised in the Great Oolite or Forest Marble, but these latter consist almost entirely of shells which pass upwards from the Inferior Oolite.

Minute Testacea of the Great Oolite and Forest Marble.

Only a portion of these have been selected for illustration, others, inconveniently minute, having been rejected upon that account. That some of these minute forms attain to much larger dimensions under different conditions may be inferred from the fact that many minute Gasteropoda and Conchifers associated with them are only dwarfed forms of well-known Great Oolite species, which in other beds are of the dimensions figured in the former parts of this Monograph.

Forest Marble Testacea.

The following note, kindly communicated by Mr. Walton, describes the localities of the Forest Marble cited in this Monograph:

"The principal localities from which these fossils have been obtained are Farleigh, Hungerford, in Somersetshire; Pound Pill, near Corsham, and Laycock, in Wiltshire; and Burton Bradstock, about five miles from Bridport. The lithological character of the Forest Marble is very various, demonstrating the littoral character of the deposit, which is shown also by the trails of animals and the numerous remains of what can hardly be anything but Fucoids. The best locality at Farleigh is a superficial cutting opposite Wick Farmhouse, made in forming the new Warminster Road, and the bed is a crumbly, shelly marl, and the fossils, when first found, apparently mere lumps of clay. In the small quarries near Hinton Charterhouse, Cumberwell, and Philips Norton, the rock is a hard, calcareo-arenaceous stone, and at Pound Pill it is as hard and more intractable than Carboniferous limestone. At the railroad-cutting near Laycock it is a cream-coloured clay, containing shells better preserved than usual, and from this nearly all the small shells have been procured. In many places the Forest Marble is a mere mass of broken shells, and frequently formed almost exclusively of crushed Rhynchonellæ. At Burton Bradstock the Forest Marble clay rests on the lower beds of the Inferior Oolite, and most of the fossils from that locality were picked up from a bank on the sea-shore. I have never found an Ammonite in the Forest Marble, and only one very doubtful trace in the Cornbrash."

Testacea from the Clays of the Forest Marble compared with those from the Limestones of the Great Oolite.—As might be anticipated from the widely differing mineral conditions of the two deposits, they are tenanted to a great extent by different races of Molluscs. The fossils figured in this Supplement from the Forest Marble by no means represent the whole of the additional species contained in the clay beds of that stage, but such only as from their state of preservation are suitable for our plates; a large proportion have suffered from vertical compression and consequent distortion, so that in many instances it has only been possible, even with the choice of numerous specimens, to select one or two as representatives of their respective species, and some tablets covered with shells have with reluctance been rejected when specific forms could only have been made up by the aid of doubtful restorations. Our note on the age of the gray limestone of the Yorkshire coast alludes to the general identity of species which obtains between the Testacea of the Great Oolite and Forest Marble *limestones* of Gloucestershire and of Oxfordshire; they form, in fact, but one fauna, the most prominent species of which are abundant only over very limited areas. In the Forest Marble *clays* we find that the great mass of the organic forms belong to but few genera; the deficiencies in this respect are very striking. The large collection of Mr. Walton contains not a single Ammonite or Belemnite; of Gasteropoda there is almost an entire absence of Nerinæa, Cylindrites, Ceritella, and Trocholoma, genera so abundant and varied in the limestones; these deficiencies are to a great extent compensated for by an abundance of special forms of Phasianella and of Acteonina, which is the more remarkable as the latter genus is everywhere one of the most rare forms of the limestones. The genus Cerithium is abundant, consisting of forms less dwarfed than is usually seen in the limestones. The genera Nerita, Trochus, and Monodonta, are well represented, but the two latter genera for the most part by forms special to the clays. Of the Conchifera the clays produce Tancredia comparatively in small numbers and apparently of few species, but their condition is usually such as will not admit of a rigid scrutiny; a similar paucity applies to the Arcas, Trigonias, Limas, and Pectens. Perna, Gervillia, Pteroperna, and Astarte, are for the most part represented by species special to the clays or rare in the limestones; Pholadomya, Homomya, Myacites, and Goniomya, appear to constitute the rarest generic forms in the deposit; Cercomya and Thracia, perhaps, are absent altogether. Wanting these, the clay banks swarmed with a profusion of Nuculæ and Cyprinæ, usually of forms differing from those of the limestones. Perhaps about 25 per cent. would be a fair estimate of the testaceous species special to the clays; but taking only the more common forms of each deposit, the differences between them are much more marked and important than would be inferred from such a proportion of species.

The following, probably, have not been obtained in any other deposit than the Forest Marble:

Turbo Burtonensis.
subtexata.
nodifera.
Trochus Burtonensis.
Monodonta comma.
Waltoni.
arata.
tegulata.
Onusbus Burtonensis.
Natica arata.
texata.
alta.
Acteonina Luidii.
Suessea.
fasciata.
Wiltonensis.
Phasianella variata.
Solarium turbiniformis.
Waltoni.

Pleurotomaria Bathonica.
Ostrea Wiltonensis.
Gervillia Waltoni.
Perna obliqua.
Trigonia arata.
Lucina Burtonensis.
Corbis rotunda.
Corbula Hulliana.
Islipensis.
Agatha.
Corbicella subangulata.
Cyprina bella.
Davidsoni.
Astarte robusta.
rustica.
fimbriata.
ignota.
Hilpertonensis.

Alaria parvula, p. 22. Tab. III, fig. 12; and *A. cirrus*, p. 22. Tab. III, fig. 13.

Further observations lead to the conclusion that the former shell is the young condition of the latter, and that the differences in the last volution are owing only to the stage of growth to which the specimens have respectively attained.

Index to Tab. XII, Part II, *add* figs. 13, 13 *a*, Hinge of Corbicella.

Page 95, fifth line from the bottom, *add*, and Tab. XII, figs. 13, 13 *a*.

Index to Tab. XIII, fig. 16, *for* p. 139, *read* p. 140.

Myoconcha Actæon, p. 77, Part II, *for* Tab. III *read* Tab. IV.

Tab. XIII, fig. 18, Part II, *alter* the reference to, *Pholas costellata*, p. 142.

Index to Part II, *add*, *Pholas oolitica*, p. 126. Tab. IX, fig. 21.

Alaria trifida, Part I, p. 21, *add* the following to the description:—The first two or three volutions are longitudinally costated, the transverse striations extend even upon the caudal and digital processes.

Pholodomya oblita, Part II, p. 142*; Tab. XII, fig. 5. It is now ascertained that the specimen figured was erroneously assigned to the Great Oolite; its true position is in seams of sandy marl near to the base of the Inferior Oolite, in which position it occurs at various localities in the vicinity of Stroud and Nailsworth; the officers of the Ordnance Geological Survey have also procured it from a similar position in Somersetshire. It sometimes attains very large dimensions, as is exemplified by a remarkable specimen in the Bristol Museum, which has been mistaken, as in other instances, for the aged condition of *Pholadomya fidicula*, Sow. The delicate, radiating lines are scarcely distinguishable upon the aged and inflated examples of *P. oblita*, but are always acute and conspicuous upon *P. fidicula*.

Trigonia decorata, Lyc., Part II, p. 133, Tab. XV, fig. 1, *alter* the title to *Trigonia signata*, Ag., a fine species, abundant in the Upper Trigonia Grit of the Inferior Oolite in the Cotteswolds, and more rarely in the gray limestone of the coast of Yorkshire; it occurs in a similar geological position at various Continental localities. Professor Quenstedt has figured it from Wurtemberg under the name of *Trigonia clavellata*. It has never been found to pass upwards into the Great Oolite.

Patella paradoxa, Part I, p. 90, Tab. XII, fig. 2. This rare species is the *Patella lata*, Sow., 'Min. Con.,' t. 484, fig. 1, p. 133. The compressed and imperfect specimen figured in the latter work will account for our having failed at an earlier period to identify it with the very few examples which have been obtained at Minchinhampton.

Tancredia curtansata, Part II, p. 93, Tab. XIII, figs. 7, 7 *a*, 7 *b*, *alter* the title to *Tancredia subcurtansata*; it is much less inflated, the umbones are more elevated and pointed, the posterior side is more produced, and it is destitute of the large longitudinal plications which distinguish the species of the Coral Rag; the latter is also a much larger shell, only two specimens of which have come to my knowledge, the type specimen in the York Museum, the other in the fine collection of Mr. Leckenby at Scarborough. *Tancredia Lycetti*, Oppel, from the Inferior Oolite of Wurtemberg and of Gloucestershire, is also nearly allied to the Coral Rag shell, and appears to be equally rare.

Tancredia axiniformis, p. 93, Tab. XIII, fig. 6, and Tab. XII, fig. 7, *alter* the title to *Tancredia extensa*, Lyc. In this instance the name proposed in my first notice of the Genus Tancredia, 'Ann. and Mag. Nat. Hist.,' Dec., 1850, must be retained, as an examination of many Yorkshire specimens of *T. axiniformis* leaves no doubt that it is a distinct species, which occurs in the Inferior Oolite, both in that county and in Gloucestershire; compared with the Great Oolite *T. extensa*, it is shorter, more flattened, approaching more nearly to the outline of *T. brevis*, but with much less convexity.

Tab. XV, Part II, figs. 2, 2 *a*, *alter* the title to *Ceromya Bajociana*, D'Orb.; the figure represents the usual size attained by this Ceromya in the Inferior Oolite of the Yorkshire coast; in the Cotteswolds the same formation produces it of far larger dimensions, and justifies the terms in which it is described by D'Orbigny in his 'Prodrome,' p. 274, as follows:—"Magnifique espèce courte, renflée à crochets trèscontournés, ornèe de stries concentriques d'accroisement, comme rostrée à la région anale." It is the *Isocardia concentrica* of Phillips, 'Geol. York.,' i, pl. xi, fig. 40, but not of Sowerby. The Yorkshire examples may, therefore, be considered as dwarfed forms of this really magnificent shell, the southern examples of which have the distinguishing features of the species much more strongly marked; the umbones, more especially, are larger and more elevated, the posterior extremity being also more rostrated. It is worthy of remark that this degenerated form is the only one of the genus that has been obtained from the whole of the Jurassic rocks of Yorkshire.

Anatina undulata and *Anatina plicatella*, Tab. II, Part II, *transpose* figs. 6 and 4 upon the tab.; the references to them at p. 118, and also upon the page facing the tab., will then be correct.

Pholadomya ovulum, Part II, Tab. XIII, fig. 12, *alter* the title to *Pholadomya ovalis*, Sow.; also at p. 122.

Turbo capitaneus, Goldf., Part I, p. 65, *erase* the words "Tab. IX, fig. 33," and *alter* to "Supplement, Tab. XLI, fig. 1." The index to Tab. IX, fig. 33, should be altered to *Amberleya Jurassi*, Supplement, p. 19.

Stomatia? Buvignieri, Part I, p. 85, *alter* the generic title to *Nerita*. Another figure is given, Supplement, Tab. XLI, fig. 7.

Part II, Tab. VI, fig. 15, p. 67. I agree with Dr. Oppel ('Juraformation,' p. 487) in the propriety of separating this Lucina from *L. Bellona*; its title should, therefore, be *Lucina Lycetti*, as suggested by Dr. Oppel.

Cerithium Roissii, Part I, p. 32, *alter* the generic title to *Fibula*. See p. 10 of this Supplement.

Myacites crassiusculus, Part I, p. 112, *alter* the generic title to *Homomya*. See p. 89 of this Supplement.

Myacites Vezelayi, Part I, p. 111, *alter* the generic title to *Homomya*. See p. 88 of this Supplement.

Myacites gibbosus, Part I, p. 138, *alter* the generic title to *Homomya*. See p. 88 of this Supplement.

Corbula involuta, Part I, p. 97, *alter* the title to *Corbula Buckmani*. See p. 63 of this Supplement. *Corbula Buckmani* will be found refigured, Tab. XXXIV, figs. 6, 6 *a*.

Part II, p. 123, *erase* the first reference to *Pholadomya Sæmanni*, Tab. II, fig. 1, which is *P. solitaria*.

Part II, p. 28, Tab. IV, fig. 12. This little shell, erroneously ascribed to the *Modiola pulcherrima* of Roemer, has been rectified by Professor Morris, 'Catal.,' p. 210, under the appellation of *M. Lycetti*. Compared with the allied species of the Hilsthone, it is smaller, more inflated, the radiating lines are more narrow or more distantly arranged, the test is very thin, and the specimens are usually imperfect.

Mytilus (*Modiola*) *tumidus*, Part II, p. 37, Tab. IV, fig. 5. It is stated that the rude figure of a Modiola, Young and Bird, 'Geol. York. Coast,' pl. vii, fig. 10, is intended to represent this shell, and that Professor Phillips inserted it in his list of Yorkshire fossils, 'Geol. York.,' i, p. 171, in the following terms:—"*Modiola ungulata, Coralline Great* and *Inferior Oolite*." It is not uncommon in the upper stage of the Inferior Oolite in the Cotteswold Hills.

Purpuroidea Moreausea, Part I, p. 27, Tab. IV, figs. 1—4, *alter* the title to *P. Morrisea*. The publication of the splendid work of M. Buvignier on the Palæontology of the Meuse has shown that we were mistaken in assigning our Minchinhampton species to that figured in a very indifferent manner in the little memoir by M. Buvignier in 1843. The new specific name selected for our shell by the latter author should therefore be adopted.

Part I, Tab. II, figs. 3, 3 *a*, p. 12. The Ammonite obtained at the base of the Great Oolite, and referred doubtfully to *A. macrocephalus*, is now ascertained to be *A. viator*, D'Orb., 'Pal. Fr. Terr. Jurass.,' tab. 172, of which numerous specimens are now in the British Museum, obtained from a similar geological position in Somersetshire; in some of these the last volution quite conceals all the others, leaving only a small umbilical orifice; the absence of costæ upon the inner portion of the last volution distinguishes it from *A. macrocephalus*. Dr. Oppel ('Juraformation,' p. 478) proposes for it the new title of *A. Morrisii*, which, in accordance with the above views, must remain as a synonym of *A. viator*.

Acteonina? parvula, Part I, p. 104, *alter* the generic title to *Ceritella*.

Part II, Tab. 5, figs. 18 *a*, 19 *a*. Both these figures represent the young condition of *Trigonia Goldfussii*.

Trochus pileolus, Part I, p. 66, Tab. 10, fig. 5. Additional specimens have proved that the smoothness of the surface is accidental; traces of encircling striations are sometimes visible; the shell then becomes identical with *Turbo obtusus*, Sow., of which *Trochus Bixa*, D'Orb., is also a synonym.

Nerita hemispherica, Roem., Tab XI, figs. 14, 16; *Nerita minuta*, Sow., Tab. XI, fig. 19. A comparison of very ample materials, including all the connecting forms, leaves no choice but to regard *N. hemispherica* as the adult shell of *N. minuta*. The preservation of the epidermal pattern of coloration has materially tended to this result; the older shells, as in fig. 14, with their strong, rugose plications, thickened columellar lip, and entire absence of the epidermal coat, appear at first sight sufficiently distinct, but from these we pass to specimens of less advanced growth, as in fig. 16, without plications, but still possessing the callosity upon the inner lip; some in this state, however, retain portions of the external tegument, in which may be traced remains of the two broad bands of white between the three of dark-coloured pigment, the latter consisting of transverse, wrinkled lines. From these to the smallest forms the transition is easy; the latter are most commonly more ovate, but this is by no means an invariable feature, nor are the adult shells very constant in the degree in which the spire is produced. The minute forms, which usually retain the epidermal coat, are smooth and shining; with advance of growth the shell exhibits continual and considerable increase of thickness. The two extremes of aspect are fairly represented in figs. 14 and 19. *Nerita minuta* is so inappropriate a name for the adult shell, that it seems desirable to adopt *Nerita hemispherica*, although the former has priority.

Fusus? subnodulosus, Part I, Tab. V, fig. 9, p. 23, *alter* the generic title to *Brachytrema*.

Phasianella conica, Part I, Tab. XI, fig. 30, p. 74; *Phasianella acutiuscula*, Tab. XI, fig. 28, and Tab. IX, fig. 2. An examination of numerous additional specimens has led to the conclusion that these forms should be regarded as only varieties of one species; for although some examples are even more lengthened than the figures of *P. acutiuscula*, others connect the typical specimens of each variety in a very perfect manner.

Genus *Brachytrema*, Part I, p. 24. Further information has shown that the generic description before given should be slightly modified; the outer lip was stated to be thin, which is correct as far as regards the greater number of specimens; but some species, as *B. varicosa* and *B. pygmea*, acquired at certain arrests of growth thickened outer lips or varices, as in Triton; from the latter genus they are distinguished by the shorter trochiform spire and absence of denticulations upon the borders of the aperture.

Turbo? pygmeus, Tab. IX, Part I, figs. 29, 29 *a*, *alter* the title to *Brachytrema pygmea*. The doubt as to the genus expressed in Part I, p. 65, has been justified in an example with the aperture perfect, figured by M. Piette, 'Bull. de la Soc. Géol. de France,' 2 sér., pl. xv, fig. 21, under the name of *Brachytrema brevis*; the base is strongly striated, and the aperture much contracted.

Alaria lævigata, p. 17, Tab. III, figs. 3, 3 *a*; Tab. XLI, fig. 13, *alter* the title to *Alaria Myurus*, Desl., sp. It was stated at p. 17 "that in everything excepting its smooth surface this shell agrees with the *Rostellaria Myurus* of Deslongchamps." A specimen recently obtained exhibits some encircling striations upon the upper portions of the two larger volutions; the sole distinction, therefore, that separated it from the species of Deslongchamps is thus removed. The specimen figured Tab. XLI, fig. 13, exhibits the first spine, which is monodactyle; a second and much larger spine, also monodactyle; the third and ultimate spine being didactyle.

Acteonina?, Part I, Tab. VIII, fig. 12*, is the young shell of *A. olivæformis*, p. 103.

Lima Luciencis, D'Orb., 'Gr. Ool. Mon.,' Part II, p. 28, Tab. III, fig. 4. This shell is a synonym of *Lima rudis*, Sow. The number of costæ vary from eight to eleven; the specimen figured in the 'Mineral Conchology,' tab. 214, has only seven costæ, and the figure is unusually gibbose. Its geological range is considerable; it occurs sparingly in the Great Oolite of the Minchinhampton district and in the Cornbrash of the coast of Yorkshire, but in the Coral Rag of Malton it is moderately abundant.

Sub-genus *Crossostoma*, Part I, p. 72. Of the three Oolitic species assigned to this proposed sub-genus of Delphinula, the only one which exhibits the distinctive characters is *C. Pratii;* the other two forms, *discoideum* and *heliciforme*, were formerly supposed to represent in their apertures the immature condition of that sub-genus. Subsequent observations of numerous specimens has compelled me to abandon that view, and to regard *discoideum* and *heliciforme* as adult shells, or discoidal forms of smooth Monodonta. Other examples of Monodonta allied to the Great Oolite forms, but less depressed, have been figured by Messrs. Hebert and Deslongchamps, in their 'Memoir on the Kelloway Rock Fossils of Montreuil-Bellay,' under the names of *Monodonta ovulata* and *papillata*.

Cerithium quadricinctum, Goldf., and *C. limæforme*, Roem. These two forms must be united into one species; individuals with large nodules and with only three distinct rows have been assigned to *C. limæforme*, but, even with these, indications of a fourth row are occasionally to be discovered, and the prominence of the nodules, and their number in each volution, are very variable. *C. quadricinctum* has a considerable geological range, and it occurs also in the Coral Rag of Germany.

Patella suprajurensis, Part I, p. 92, Tab. XII, figs. 9, 9 *a*. I can now only regard this form as a variety of *P. Aubentonensis*, in which the lamellæ of growth are strongly marked and the cancellated lines have disappeared. It is also not uncommon to meet with smooth examples of the latter species.

Pholadomya solitaria, Part II, p. 124, Tab. XI, fig. 1, et Tab. XII, fig. 2; erroneously printed *P. oblita* upon the reference facing the latter table. *Pholadomya oblita* is Tab. XII, fig. 5, p. 142*. The variations of figure and of ornamentation, either separately or combined, are so considerable in the cordiform examples of Pholadomya, that a large number are indispensable to enable us to legislate upon them with any confidence; probably *P. solitaria* is only a variety of *P. deltoidea*, Sow.

[*Note.*—The Author desires to tender his best thanks to Mr. West for the very careful drawings in the plates that illustrate this Monograph; and more especially for the fidelity and attention to the more minute details exhibited in the magnified figures of the smaller Gasteropoda, from the Great Oolite and Forest Marble.]

INDEX

TO

SPECIES RETAINED IN THIS SUPPLEMENT.

	PAGE	TABLE
ACTEON Bathonicum	25	XLIV, fig. 16.
— phasianoides	26	XLIV, fig. 28.
ACTEONINA brevis	26	XLI, fig. 6.
— canaliculata	27	XXXI, figs. 9, 9 *a*.
— fasciata	107	XLIV, fig. 15.
— Kirklingtonensis ...	26	XLI, fig. 5.
— Luidii	27, 106	XXXI, fig. 16; XLI, fig. 18.
— scalaris...	28	XLIV, fig. 18.
— Scarburgensis	28	XXXI, figs. 13, 13 *a*.
— Suessea	107	XLV, fig. 29.
— Wiltonensis	107	XLV, fig. 25.
AMBERLEYA armigera	20	XXXI, fig. 6.
— capitanea	95	XLI, fig. 1.
— Jurassi	19	IX, figs. 33, 33 *a*.
— monilifera	95	XLI, fig. 10.
— tricincta	96	XLI, fig. 14.
AMMONITES bullatus	3	XXXI, fig. 1.
— discus	4	XLI, figs. 8, 8 *a*.
BRACHYTREMA buccinoidea ...	5	XLIV, fig. 17.
— varicosa	5	XLIV, fig. 27.
CERITELLA fusiformis	12	XLV, fig. 4.
— Lycettea	12	XLIV, fig. 25.
— Morrisea	12	XLIV, fig. 22.
— minutissima	11	XLV, fig. 5.
CERITHIUM Bathonicum	6	XLIV, fig. 19.
— bulimoides	7	XLIV, fig. 3.
— compositum	—	XLIV, fig. 9.
— costigerum	93	XLI, figs. 11, 11 *a*, *b*.
— hemicinctum	91	XLI, fig. 17.
— multiforme	7	XLIV, fig. 20.

INDEX.

	PAGE	TABLE
CERITHIUM exscalptum	93	XLIV, fig. 23.
— ? neglectum	92	XLIV, fig. 21.
— poculum	93	XLI, fig. 24.
— undulatum	8	XLIV, fig. 6.
— Witchelli	10	XLIV, fig. 7.
— Waltoni	92	XLI, fig. 16.
CYLINDRITES exigua	24	XLIV, fig. 14.
— turriculatus	25	XLIV, figs. 26, 26 *a*.
CHEMNITZIA constricta	15	XLIV, fig. 8.
— vittata	14	XXXI, fig. 10.
DENTALIUM entaloides	28	XXXI, figs. 11, 11 *a*, 11 *b*.
EULIMA ? lævigata	13	XXXI, fig. 3.
FIBULA eulimoides	17	XXXI, fig. 5.
— variata	16	XXXI, figs. 4, 4 *a*.
KILVERTIA composita	9	XLIV, fig. 9.
— formosa	95	XLIV, fig. 5.
— pulchra	10, 94	XLI, figs. 12, 12 *a*; XLIV, fig. 4.
— spicula	9	XLIV, fig. 1.
— strangulatum	8	XLIV, fig. 2.
MONODONTA arata	102	XLV, fig. 19.
— comma	101	XLV, figs. 24, 24 *a*.
— composita	23	XLV, fig. 6.
— exigua	22	XLIV, fig. 29.
— Lycetti	22	XXXI, figs. 14, 14 *a*.
— sparsistriata	22	XLV, fig. 9.
— tegulata	102	XLV, figs. 17, 18.
— Waltoni	101	XLV, figs. 31, 31 *a*, *b*.
NATICA alta	97	XLV, figs. 22, 22 *a*.
— arata	97	XLV, fig. 2.
— Hulliana	13	XLI, figs. 2, 2 *a*.
— insignis	97	XLV, fig. 21.
— texata	96	XLV, figs. 30, 30 *a*.
NERINÆA granulata	10	XXXI, figs. 12, 12 *a*.
NERITA clavatula	98	XLV, fig. 3.
— involuta	20	XXXI, fig. 15.
NERITOPSIS Archiaci	21	XXXI, figs. 7, 7 *a*.
ONUSTUS Burtonensis	103	XLV, figs. 7, 7 *a*, *b*.
PHASIANELLA variata	104	XLV, figs. 28, 28 *a*, *b*.
PLEUROTOMARIA Bathonica	105	XLV, fig. 10.
— Burtonensis	105	XLV, figs. 8, 8 *a*, *b*.
— granulata	24	XXXI, figs. 8, 8 *a*.
— recondita	106	XLV, fig. 7.
PURPUROIDEA insignis	6	XXXI, figs. 2, 2 *a*.
RISSOA ? exigua	9	XLIV, fig. 11.
RISSOINA Milleri	18	XLIV, fig. 10.
— subulata	98	XLI, fig. 9.
— tumidula	98	XLIV, fig. 13.

	PAGE	TABLE
RISSOINA Witchelli ...	18	XLIV, fig. 12.
SOLARIUM Bathonicum	23	XLV, fig. 27.
— Waltoni	104	XLV, figs. 26, 26 *a*, *b*, *c*.
— turbiniformis	104	XLV, figs. 23, 23 *a*, *b*.
TROCHUS Burtonensis	99	XLV, fig. 16.
— Guisei	21	XLV, fig. 14.
— strigosus	29	XLV, fig. 12.
TURBO Burtonensis	100	XLV, fig. 15.
— depauperatus	99	XLV, fig. 13.
— subtexata	100	XLI, figs. 15, 15 *a*.
EULIMA? lævigata	13	XXXI, fig. 3.

BIVALVIA.

ANATINA siliqua	83	XXXV, fig. 15.
ARCA (cucullæa) clathrata	44	XXXIX, figs. 4, 4 *a*.
— corallina	43	XXXIX, fig. 3.
ASTARTE Aytonensis	78	XL, fig. 13.
— Bathonica	76	XL, figs. 23, 23 *a*.
— flexicostata	79	XL, fig. 26.
— fimbriata	77	XL, figs. 34, 34 *a*.
— Hilpertonensis	78	XXXVI, fig. 10.
— ignota	77	XL, fig. 10.
— Leckenbyi	74	XLII, fig. 3.
— orbicularis	73	XL, fig. 33.
— politula	73	XXXV, fig. 16.
— Pontonis	75	XL, fig. 31.
— robusta	74	XXXV, fig. 6, 6 *a*.
— rustica	76	XXXV, fig. 5; XL, figs. 8, 8 *a*.
— ungulata	72	XXXV, fig. 20.
AVICULA clathrata	36	XL, figs. 7, 7 *a*, *b*.
— subcostata	36	XL, fig. 24.
CARDIUM cognatum	54	XXXVI, figs. 3, 3 *a*, 2 *b*.
— incertum	53	XXXV, figs. 14, 14 *a*.
— globosum	114	XXXVIII, figs. 2, 2 *a*, *b*.
— lingulatum	53	XXXIII, figs. 2, 2 *a*; XXXV, figs. 11, 11 *a*.
— Witchelli	55	XL, fig. 36.
CORBIS elliptica	60	XXXV, fig. 1.
— Neptuni	59	XXXV, fig. 19.
— rotunda	60	XL, fig. 17.
CORBULA Agatha	65	XL, fig. 28.
— attenuata	62	XXXVII, figs. 6, 6 *a*.
— Hulliana	64	XXXVII, fig. 5.
— Islipensis	63	XXXVII, fig. 7.

	PAGE	TABLE
CORBULA involuta	63	XXXVII, figs. 4, 4 a.
CORBICELLA subangulata	70	XL, fig. 9.
— subæquilatera	69	XXXV, fig. 12.
CYPRICARDIA caudata	55	XXXVI, figs. 8, 8 a.
CYPRINA bella	71	XL, figs. 15, 15 a.
— Davidsoni	71	XXXVI, figs. 6, 6 a.
— Islipensis	70	XXXV, fig. 13.
GERVILLIA bicostata	111	XL, fig. 21.
— Islipensis	37	XXXVI, fig. 7.
— ornata	111	XL, fig. 29.
— tortuosa (var.)	37	XL, fig. 25.
— Waltoni	110	XXXII, figs. 4, 4 a, b.
GRESSLYA peregrina	79	XXXVI, figs. 2, 2 a, 2 b.
GRYPHÆA minuta	30	XL, fig. 12.
HARPAX Waltoni	101	XXXII, figs. 1, 1 a, b.
HINNITES gradus	35	XXXIII, figs. 10, 10 a.
HOMOMYA gibbosa	88	XLIII, figs. 2, 2 a; Part II, XII, fig. 14.
— crassiuscula	89	XLIII, figs. 5, 5 a.
INOCERAMUS quadratus	38	XXXVIII, figs. 1, 1 a, 1 b.
ISOCARDIA tenera	57	XXXVIII, figs. 5, 5 a, b.
— minima	56	XXXVI, figs. 1, 1 a.
— nitida	57	XXXVIII, figs. 6, 6 a, 6 b, 6 c.
ISOARCA Scarburgensis	45	XXXIX, figs. 5, 5 a.
LEDA Anglica	45	XXXIX, fig. 7.
LIMA Helvetica	41	XXXIII, figs. 8, 8 a.
— pectiniformis	39	~~XXXVI~~, fig. 1. XXXIV
— punctatilla	41	XL, fig. 32.
— rigidula	42	XXXIII, figs. 7, 7 a.
LITHODOMUS Porteri	114	XL, fig. 9.
LUCINA Beanii	59	XXXVIII, fig. 3.
— Burtonensis?	59	XL, figs. 20, 20 a, b.
— striatula	58	XXXVIII, fig. 7.
Macrodon Hirsonensis, var. rugosa	113	XXXVI, fig. 9.
Modiola gibbosa	42	XXXIII, figs. 11, 11 a.
Myacites calceiformis	80	XLII, figs. 1, 1 a.
— modica	83	XLIII, figs. 1, 1 a.
— recurvum	81	XXXVI, figs. 4, 4 a.
— sinistra	82	XXXV, figs. 17, 17 a.
NUCULA Menkei	44	XXXIX, fig. 2.
OPIS Leckenbyi	61	XXXVII, figs. 9, 9 a.
— Luciensis	62	XL, figs. 19, 19 a.
— pulchella	61	Part II, VI, fig. 3.
OSTREA Wiltonensis	108	XXXIV, figs. 1, 1 a.
— (Exogyra) lingulata	108	XXXII, figs. 2, 2 a, b.
PECTEN anisopleurus	~~32~~ 34	XXXIII, figs. 5, 5 a.
— articulatus	~~34~~ 32	XXXIII, fig. 12.
— Griesbachi	37	XXXIII, figs. 6, 6 a.

	PAGE	TABLE
PECTEN inæquicostatus	32	XXXIII, figs. 1, 1 *a*.
— Michelenais	34	XXXIII, fig. 3.
— rigidus	31	XL, fig. 16.
— Rushdonensis	38	XXXIII, figs. 4, 4 *a*, *b*, *c*.
— subspinosus	113	XL, fig. 14.
— Wollastonensis	33	XXXIII, figs. 2, 2 *a*, *b*, *c*.
PERNA foliacea	38	XXXVII, figs. 3, 3 *a*.
— mytiloides	112	XXXII, fig. 3.
— obliqua	112	XXXIV, figs. 22, 22 *a*.
PHOLADOMYA deltoidea	86	XLII, figs. 4, 4 *a*.
— lyrata	87	XLIII, figs. 3, 3 *a*.
— ovulum	84	XXXV, figs. 18, 18 *a*.
— Phillipsi	86	XLII, figs. 2, 2 *a*.
PLACUNOPSIS semistriatus	30	XXXIII, figs. 9, 9 *a*.
SOWERBYA triangularis	66	XXXV, figs. 3, 3 *a*, *b*.
— Woodwardi	67	XL, figs. 27, 27 *a*, *b*, *c*.
TANCREDIA gibbosa	68	XXXV, fig. 7; XXXVI, fig. 11.
— mactræoides	68	XXXV, fig. 4.
— similis	68	XXXV, fig. 9.
THRACIA amygdaloidea	80	XLIII, fig. 4.
TRIGONIA arata	52	XL, fig. 2.
— Bathonica	52	XL, fig. 3.
— Cassiope	49	XXXVII, fig. 10.
— clythia	48, 51	XXXVII, fig. 2; XL, figs. 5, 5 *a*.
— compta	50	XL, fig. 1.
— elongata	48	XXXIX, figs. 6, 6 *a*.
— Scarburgensis	48	XXXVII, fig. 1.
— tripartita	51	XL, fig. 4.
— tuberculosa	47	XL, fig. 6.

TAB. XXXI.

FIG.

1. Ammonites Bullatus, *D'Orb.* Reduced one half. Great Oolite (page 3).

2, 2 *a*. Purpuroidea insignis, *Lyc.* An aged shell, in which the tubercles have disappeared upon the anterior portion of the last volution. Great Oolite (page 6).

3. Eulima? lævigata, *Lyc.* Cornbrash (page 13).

4. Fibula variata, *Lyc.* Specimen with the anterior extremity of the aperture approaching to Cerithium.

4 *a*. „ „ With the anterior part of the aperture approaching to Turritella. From the Great Oolite of Kirklington, Oxon. (page 16).

5. „ eulimoides, *Whiteaves.* From the Great Oolite of Stonesfield (page 17).

6. Amberleya armigera, *Lyc.* Cornbrash (page 20).

7. Neritopsis Archiaci, *D'Archiac*, sp. Cornbrash (page 21).

7 *a*. „ „ A portion of the surface magnified (page 21).

8. Pleurotomaria granulata, *Sow.*, sp. Cornbrash (page 24).

8 *a*. „ „ A portion of the surface magnified, including the fascia of the sinus.

9. Acteonina canaliculata, *Lyc.* Great Oolite of Kirklington, Oxon. (page 27).

9 *a*. „ „ The spire enlarged.

10. Chemnitzia vittata, *Phil.*, sp. Cornbrash (page 14).

11. Dentalium entaloides, *Desl.* Cornbrash (page 28).

11 *a*. „ „ A portion of the posterior part of the shell enlarged, to exhibit the oblique striations.

11 *a*. „ „ Enlarged view of the anterior portion of the shell, in which the striations have disappeared.

12. Nerinæa granulata, *Phil.*, sp. Cornbrash (page 10).

12. „ „ A portion of the spire enlarged.

13, 13 *a*. Acteonina Scarburgensis. Cornbrash (page 28).

14. Monodonta Lycetti, *Whiteaves.* Bradfordian beds of Islip, Oxon. (page 22).

15. Nerita involuta, *Lyc.* Great Oolite, Kirklington (page 20).

16. Acteonina Luidii, *Luid.*, sp. Forest Marble, Kidlington, Oxon. A small specimen, with short spire (page 27). See also Tab. LXI, figs. 18 *a*, *b*, *c*.

Pl. XXXI.

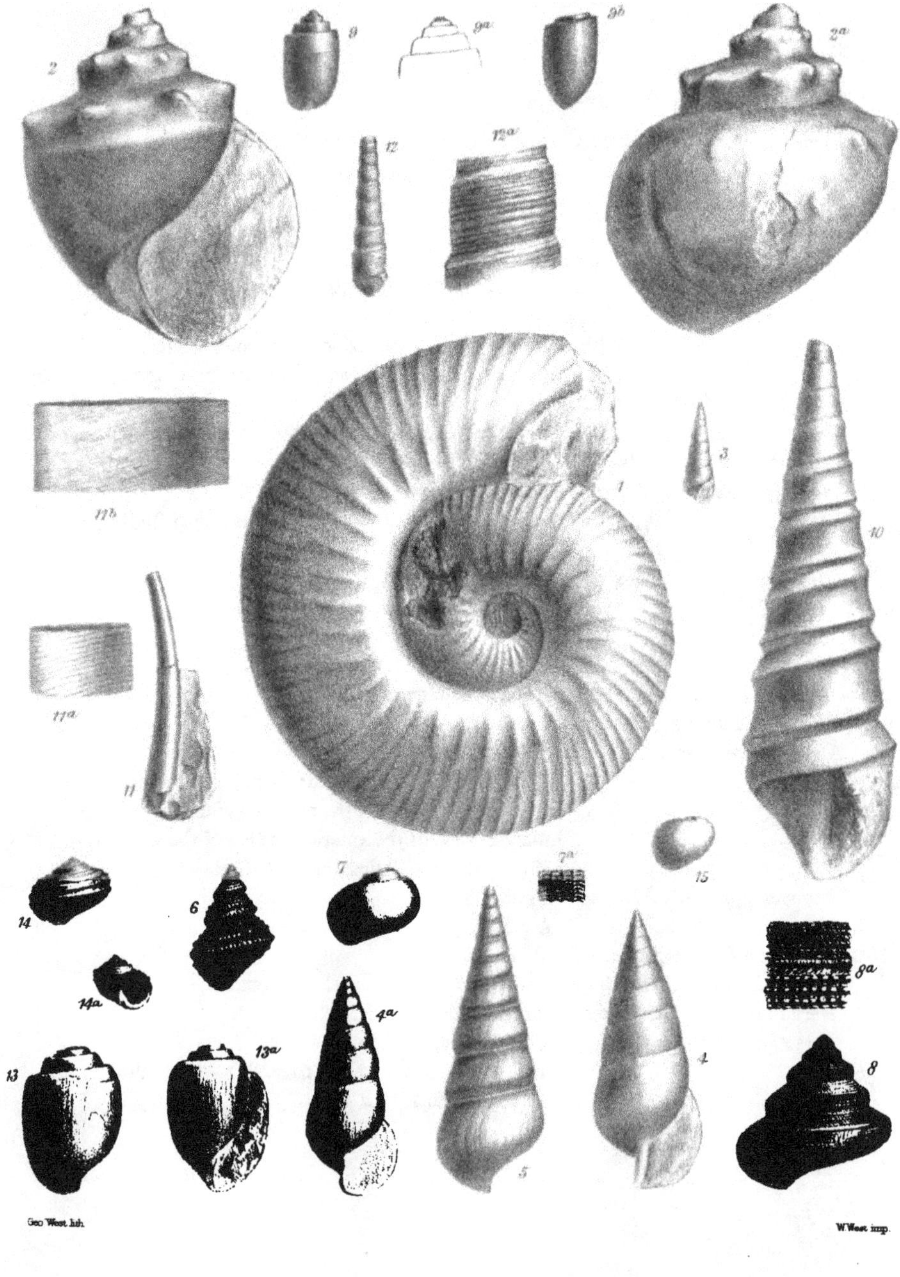

Geo West lith.

W.West imp.

TAB. XXXII.

Fig.		
1.	Harpax Waltoni, *Lyc.*	The attached valve. Forest Marble (page 110).
1 *a.*	" "	Interior of the left valve.
1 *b.*	" "	Interior of the right valve.
2.	Ostrea (Exogyra) lingulata, *Walton*, MSS.	Forest Marble (page 108).
2 *a.*	" " "	Interior of the convex valve.
2 *b.*	" " "	Interior of the flat valve.
3.	Perna mytiloides, *Lam.*	Forest Marble (page 112).
4, 4 *a*, 4 *b*.	Gervillia Waltoni, *Lyc.*	Forest Marble (page 110).

Pl. XXXII.

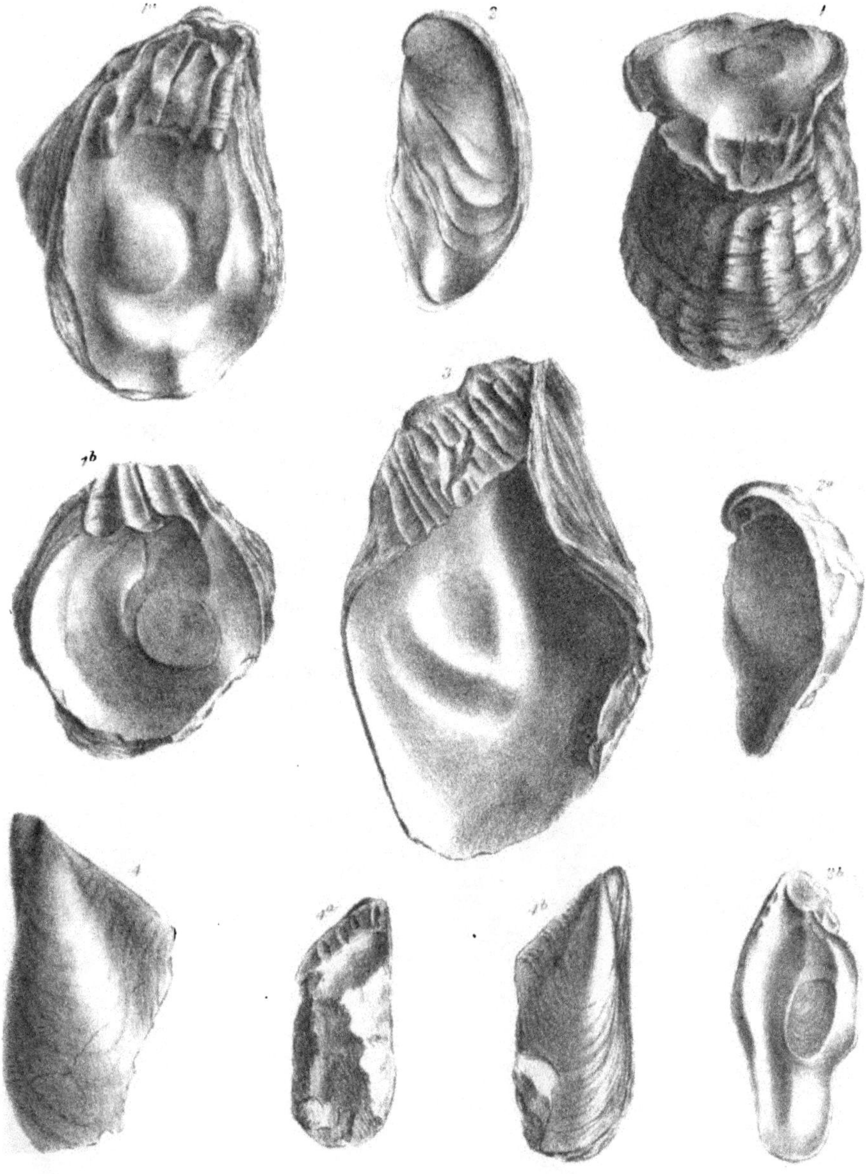

Geo West lith ad nat

W West imp

TAB. XXXIII.

FIG.		
1.	Pecten inæquicostatus, *Phil.*	Left valve. Cornbrash (page 32).
1 *a.*	" "	Right valve.
2.	Pecten Wollastonensis, *Lyc.*	Great Oolite (page 33). Right valve.
2 *b.*	" "	Magnified surface of the right valve.
2 *a.*	" "	Left valve.
2 *c.*	" "	Magnified surface of the left valve.
3.	" Michelensis, *Buv.*	Cornbrash (page 34).
4.	" Rushdenensis, *Lyc.*	Cornbrash (page 33).
4 *a.*	" "	Magnified portion of the right valve.
4 *b.*	" "	Left valve.
4 *c.*	" "	Magnified portion of the left valve.
5.	" anisopleurus, *Buv.*	Right valve. Cornbrash (page 34).
5 *a.*	" "	Left valve.
6.	" Griesbachi, *Lyc.*	Left valve. Great Oolite (page 37).
6 *a.*	" "	Portion of the surface magnified.
7.	Lima rigidula, *Phil.*, sp.	Cornbrash (page 42).
7 *a.*	" "	Portion of the surface magnified.
8.	" Helvetica, *Oppel.*	Cornbrash (page 41).
8 *a.*	" "	Portion of the surface magnified.
9.	Placunopsis semistriatus, *Bean*, sp.	Cornbrash (page 30).
9 *a.*	" "	Portion magnified.
10.	Hinnites gradus, *Bean*, sp.	Cornbrash (page 35).
10 *a.*	" "	Portion magnified.
11, 11 *a.*	Modiola gibbosa, *Sow.*	Cornbrash (page 42).
12.	Pecten articulatus, *Schloth.*	Cornbrash (page 34).

Pl. XXXIII.

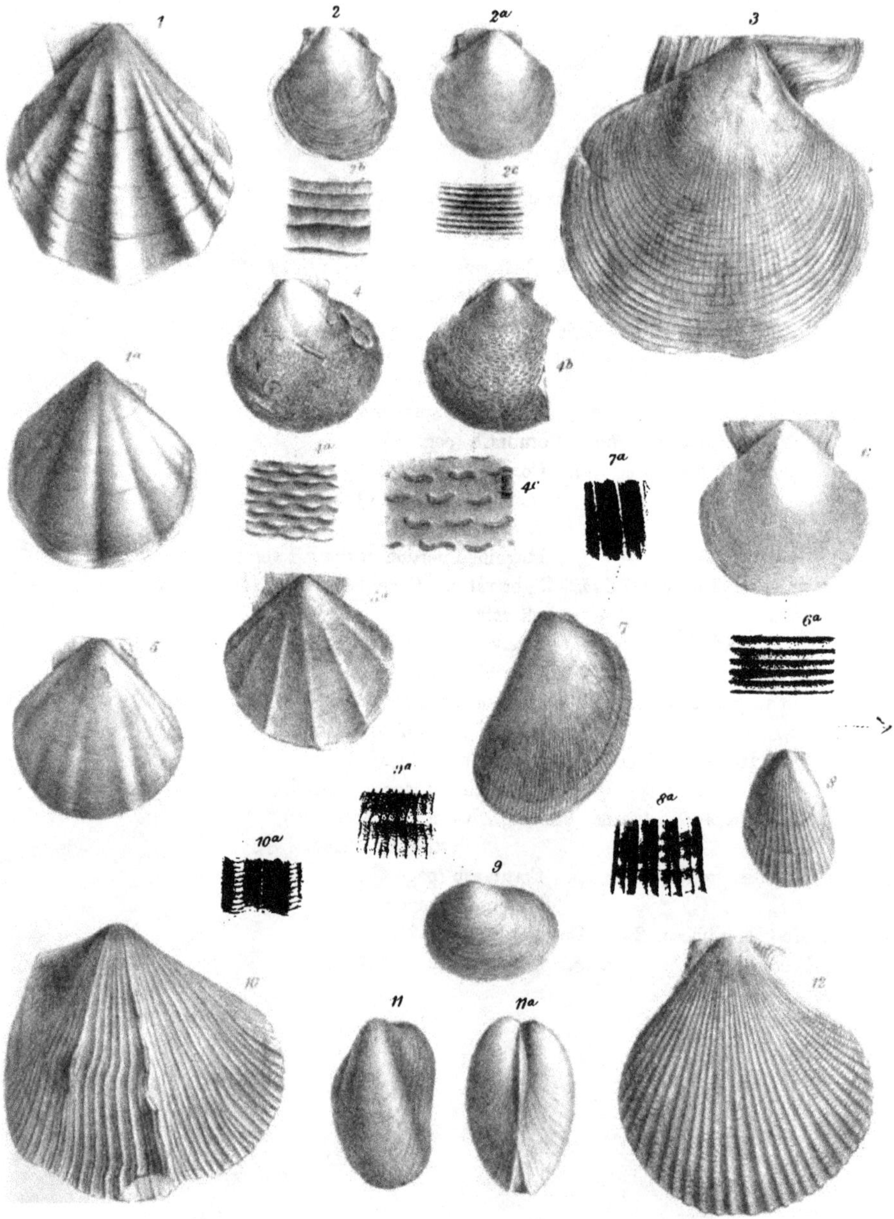

Geo West lith ad nat.

W. West imp.

TAB. XXXIV.

FIG.	
1.	Ostrea Wiltonensis, *Lyc.* Forest Marble.
1 *a*.	" " A monstrosity of the same species.
2, 2 *a*.	Perna obliqua, *Walton*, MSS. Forest Marble.
3.	Ostrea costata, *Sow.* Great Oolite. Also Part II, Tab. I, fig. 5, page 3.

Pl. XXXIV.

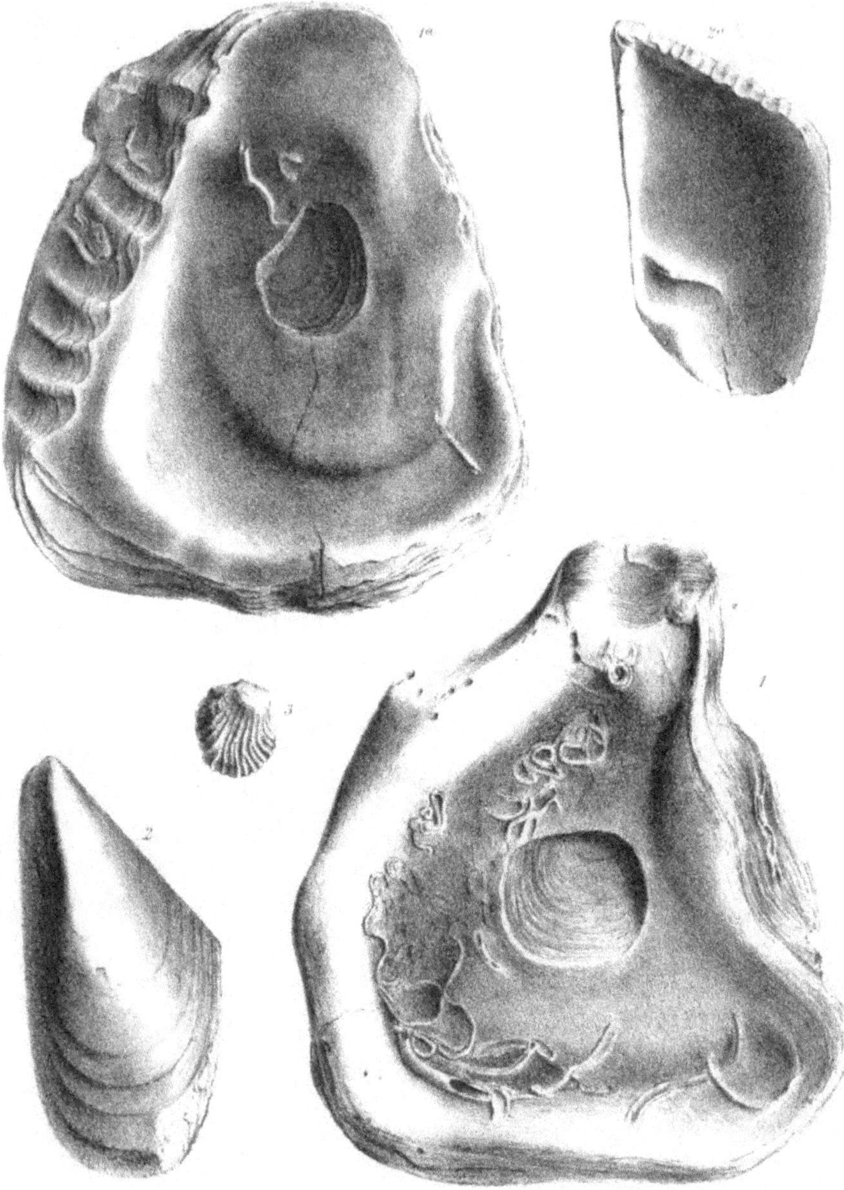

Geo West lith ad nat. W. West imp.

TAB. XXXV.

Fig.

1. Corbis elliptica, *Whiteaves*, MSS. Forest Marble. Slightly enlarged (page 60).

2, 2 *a*. Cardium subtrigonum, *Mor.* and *Lyc.* Great Oolite. See also Part II, Tab. VII, fig. 3, page 64.

3. Sowerbya triangularis, *Phil.*, sp. Cornbrash (page 66).

3 *a*. „ „ Portion of the surface magnified.

3 *b*. „ „ Hinge of the right valve magnified.

4. Tancredia mactræoides, *Whiteaves*, MSS. Great Oolite (page 68).

5. Astarte rustica, *Walton*, MSS. Great Oolite and Forest Marble (page 76). Also Tab. XL, fig. 8.

6. „ robusta, *Lyc.* Cornbrash (page 74).

6 *a*. „ „ A portion of the surface magnified, exhibiting the interstitial striations.

7. Tancredia gibbosa, *Lyc.* Great Oolite (page 68).

8. Næara Ibbetsoni, *Mor.* Slightly enlarged. Great Oolite. See also Part II, Tab. XII, fig. 9.

8 *a*. „ „ A portion of the surface magnified.

9. Tancredia similis, *Whiteaves*, MSS. Great Oolite (page 68).

10. Isocardia? nitida, *Phil.* Cornbrash. See also Tab. XXXVIII, figs. 6, 6 *a*.

10 *a*. „ „ A portion of the surface magnified.

11, 11 *a*. Cardium lingulatum, *Lyc.* An oblique specimen. Also Tab. XL, fig. 22, page 53.

12. Corbicella subæquilatera, *Lyc.* Cornbrash (page 69).

13. Cyprina Islipensis, *Lyc.* Great Oolite. Our figure is scarcely sufficiently lengthened and inequilateral (page 70).

14, 14 *a*. Cardium incertum, *Phil.* Great Oolite (page 53).

15. Anatina (Cercomya) siliqua, *Ag.* Cornbrash (page 83).

16. Astarte politula, *Bean.* Cornbrash (page 73).

17, 17 *a*. Myacites sinistra, *Ag.*, sp. Cornbrash. A breadth of two lines would require to be added to the posterior side to render the outline perfect (page 82).

17 *b*. „ „ A portion of the surface magnified.

18, 18 *a*. Pholadomya ovulum, *Ag.* Cornbrash (page 84).

19. Corbis Neptuni, *Lyc.* Great Oolite (page 59).

20. Astarte ungulata, A. lurida, *Phil.*, non *Sow.* Cornbrash (page 72).

Geo West lith ad nat.

W West imp.

TAB. XXXVI.

Fig.	
1, 1 *a*.	Isocardia minima, *Phil.* Cornbrash. Specimen with the posterior angle more strongly defined than usual (page 56).
2, 2 *a*, 2 *b*.	Gresslya peregrina, *Phil.*, sp. Cornbrash. Three varieties. See also Part II, Tab. XV, fig. 8, page 79.
3.	Cardium cognatum, *Phil.* Cornbrash (page 54).
4.	Myacites recurvum, *Phil.*, sp. Cornbrash (page 81).
5.	Ceromya concentrica, *Sow.*, sp. Great Oolite. See also Part II, Tab. X, fig. 3.
6, 6 *a*.	Cyprina Davidsoni, *Lyc.* Forest Marble (page 71).
7.	Gervillia ornata, *Lyc.* Great Oolite. Enlarged (page 111).
8.	Cypricardia caudata, *Lyc.* Great Oolite and Forest Marble (page 55).
8 *a*.	,, ,, A portion of the surface magnified.
9.	Macrodon Hirsonensis, *Arch.*, var. rugosa. Forest Marble (page 113).
10.	Astarte Hilpertonensis, *Lyc.* Forest Marble (page 78).
11.	Tancredia gibbosa, *Lyc.* Forest Marble. See also Tab. XXXV, fig. 7.

Pl. XXXVI.

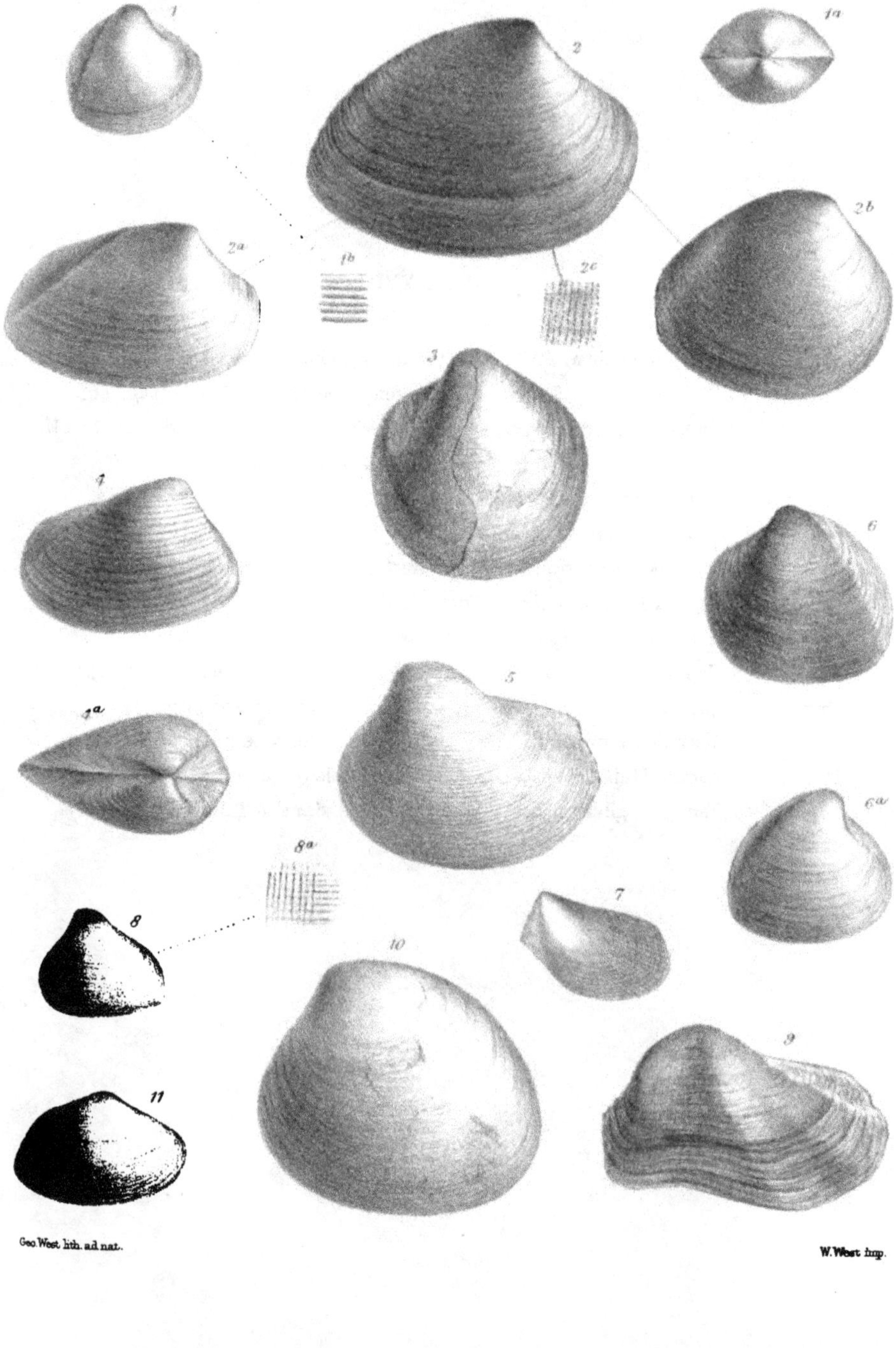

Geo. West lith. ad nat.

W. West imp.

TAB. XXXVII.

FIG.	
1.	Trigonia Scarburgensis, *Lyc.* Cornbrash (page 48).
2.	„ Clythia, *D'Orb.* Great Oolite (page 48). See also Tab. XL, fig. 5.
3, 3 *a*.	Perna foliacea, *Lyc.* Great Oolite (page 38).
4, 4 *a*.	Corbula involuta, *Munst.* Enlarged. Great Oolite (page 63).
5.	„ Hulliana, *Mor.* Enlarged. Forest Marble (page 64).
6, 6 *a*.	„ attenuata, *Lyc.* Enlarged. Great Oolite (page 62).
7.	„ Islipensis, *Lyc.* Enlarged. Great Oolite (page 63).
8.	„ Buckmani, *Buck.*, sp. Great Oolite. Also Part II, Tab. IX, fig. 6, page 97.
9, 9 *a*.	Opis Leckenbyi, *Wright.* Cornbrash (page 61).
10.	Trigonia Cassiope, *D'Orb.* Cornbrash (page 49).

Pl. XXXVII.

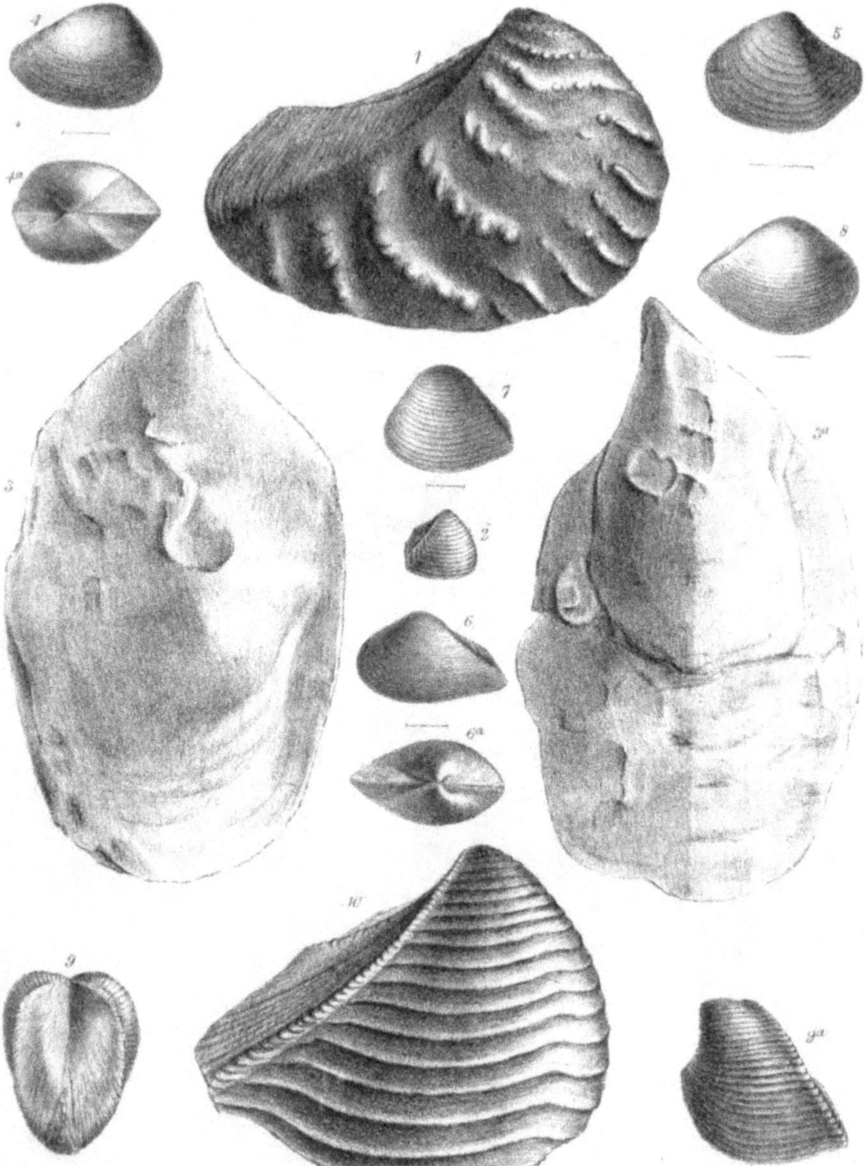

Geo. West lith.

W. West imp.

VIII.

sp. An aged example (page 38).

A smaller specimen, partially denuded of the test, and exhibiting concentric and radiating striations upon the surface of the cast.

Interior of the right or flat valve.

1 b. Cardium globosum, *Bean*. Cornbrash. The original specimen figured by Mr. Bean (page 114).

2, 2 b. " Portion of the surface magnified.

2 a. Lucina? Beanii, *Bean*, sp. Cornbrash (page 59).

3. " despecta, *Phil.* Cornbrash (Part II, p. 69).

4. " " Portion of the surface magnified.

4 a. Isocardia tenera, *Sow.* Cornbrash. Part II, p. 57.

5, 5 a. " nitida, *Phil.* Cornbrash (page 57). Also Tab. XXXV, fig. 10.

6, 6 a. " " Portion of the surface magnified.

6 b.

7. Lucina striatula, *Buv.* Cornbrash (page 58).

Pl. XXXVIII.

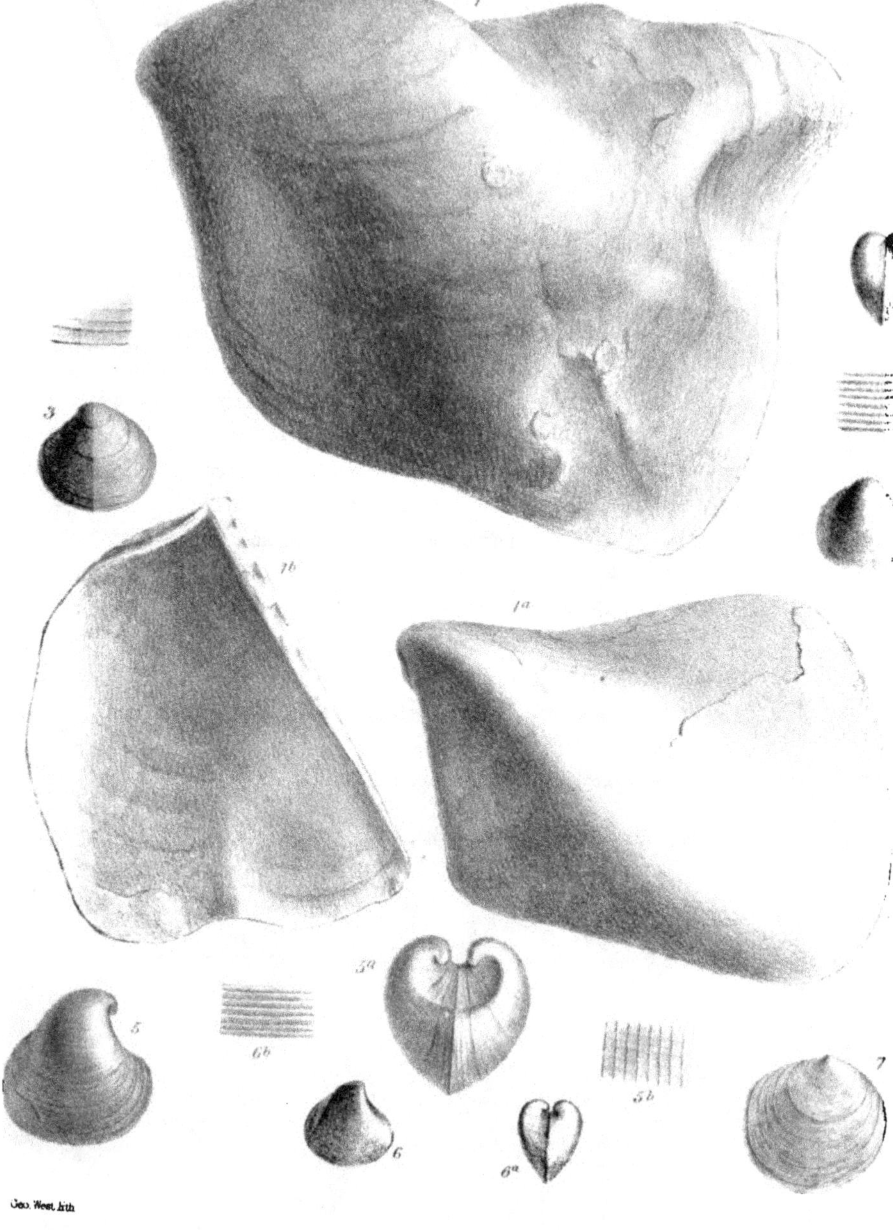

Geo. West lith

W. West imp

TAB. XXXIX.

FIG.	
1	Lima pectiniformis, *Schloth.* A large specimen, with tubular spines (page 39).
2.	Nucula Menkei, *Roem.* Great Oolite (page 44). See also Tab. XL, fig. 12.
3.	Cucullæa corallina, *Lyc.* Cornbrash (page 43).
4, 4 *a*.	„ clathrata, *Leck.* Cornbrash (page 44).
5.	Isoarca Scarburgensis, *Lyc.* Cornbrash (page 45).
5 *a*.	„ „ Portion of the surface magnified.
6, 6 *a*.	Trigonia elongata, *Sow.* Cornbrash (page 46).
7.	Leda Anglica, *D'Orb.* Cornbrash (page 45).

Pl. XXXIX.

Geo. West lith.

W. West imp.

TAB. XL.

FIG.

1. Trigonia compta, *Lyc.* Collyweston Slate (page 50).
2. „ arata, *Lyc.* Forest Marble (page 52).
3. „ Bathonica, *Lyc.* Great Oolite (page 52.)
4. „ tripartita, *Forbes.* Cornbrash (page 51.)
5. „ Clythia, *D'Orb.* Great Oolite. A specimen of advanced growth.

5 *a.* „ „ An adult specimen (pages 48 and 51).

6. „ tuberculosa, *Lyc.* Great Oolite. Magnified (page 47).
7. Avicula clathrata, *Lyc.* The smaller valve, magnified. Great Oolite.

7 *a.* „ „ The larger valve, magnified (page 36).

7 *b.* „ „ Portion of the surface magnified.

8, 8 *a.* Astarte rustica, *Walton,* MSS. Great Oolite and Forest Marble (page 76).

9. Corbicella subangulata, *Lyc.* Forest Marble (page 70).
10. Astarte ignota, *Lyc.* Forest Marble (page 77).
11. Pecten personatus, *Goldf.*, var. Great Oolite. Magnified. Part II, page 11.

11 *a.* „ „ Another variety, magnified.

12. Nucula Menkei, *Roem.*, var. Also Tab. XXXIX, fig. 2, page 44.
13. Astarte Aytonensis, *Bean.* Great Oolite (page 78).
14. Pecten subspinosus, *Schloth.* Forest Marble (page 113).
15. Cyprina bella, *Walton,* MSS. Forest Marble (page 71).

15 *a.* „ „ A shorter specimen.

16. Pecten rigidus, *Sow.* Great Oolite (page 31).
17. Corbis rotunda, *Lyc.* Forest Marble (page 60).

18, 18 *a.* Cardium Buckmani. Young specimen. Forest Marble. Part II, page 64.

18 *b.* „ „ The striated surface magnified.

19, 19 *a.* Opis Luciensis, *D'Orb.* Great Oolite (page 62).

20, 20 *a.* Lucina? Burtonensis, *Lyc.* Forest Marble (page 59).

21. Gervillia bicostata, *Lyc.* Great Oolite.
22. Cardium lingulatum, *Lyc.* Also Tab. XXXV, fig. 11, page 53.

23, 23 *a.* Astarte Bathonica, *Lyc.* Great Oolite (page 76).

24. Avicula subcostata, *Roem.* Great Oolite (pages 36, 111).
25. Gervillia tortuosa, *Sow.*, var. Cornbrash (page 37).
26. Astarte flexicostata, *Lyc.* Great Oolite (page 79).

27, 27 *a.* Sowerbya Woodwardi, *Lyc.* Left valve. Great Oolite (page 67).

27 *b*, 27 *c.* „ „ Right valve.

28, 28 *a.* Corbula Agatha, *D'Orb.* Forest Marble. Magnified (page 65).

29. Lithodomus Porteri, *Lyc.* Forest Marble. Magnified (page 114).
30. Gryphæa minuta, *Sow.* Great Oolite. Magnified (page 30).
31. Astarte Pontonis, *Lyc.* Great Oolite. Magnified (page 75).
32. Lima punctatilla, *Lyc.* Great Oolite. Magnified (page 41).
33. Astarte orbicularis, *Sow.* Great Oolite. Magnified (page 73).

34, 34 *a.* „ fimbriata, *Walton,* MSS. Forest Marble (page 77).

35. Gervillia Islipensis, *Lyc.* Great Oolite (page 37).
36. Cardium Witchelli, *Lyc.* Great Oolite. Magnified (page 55).

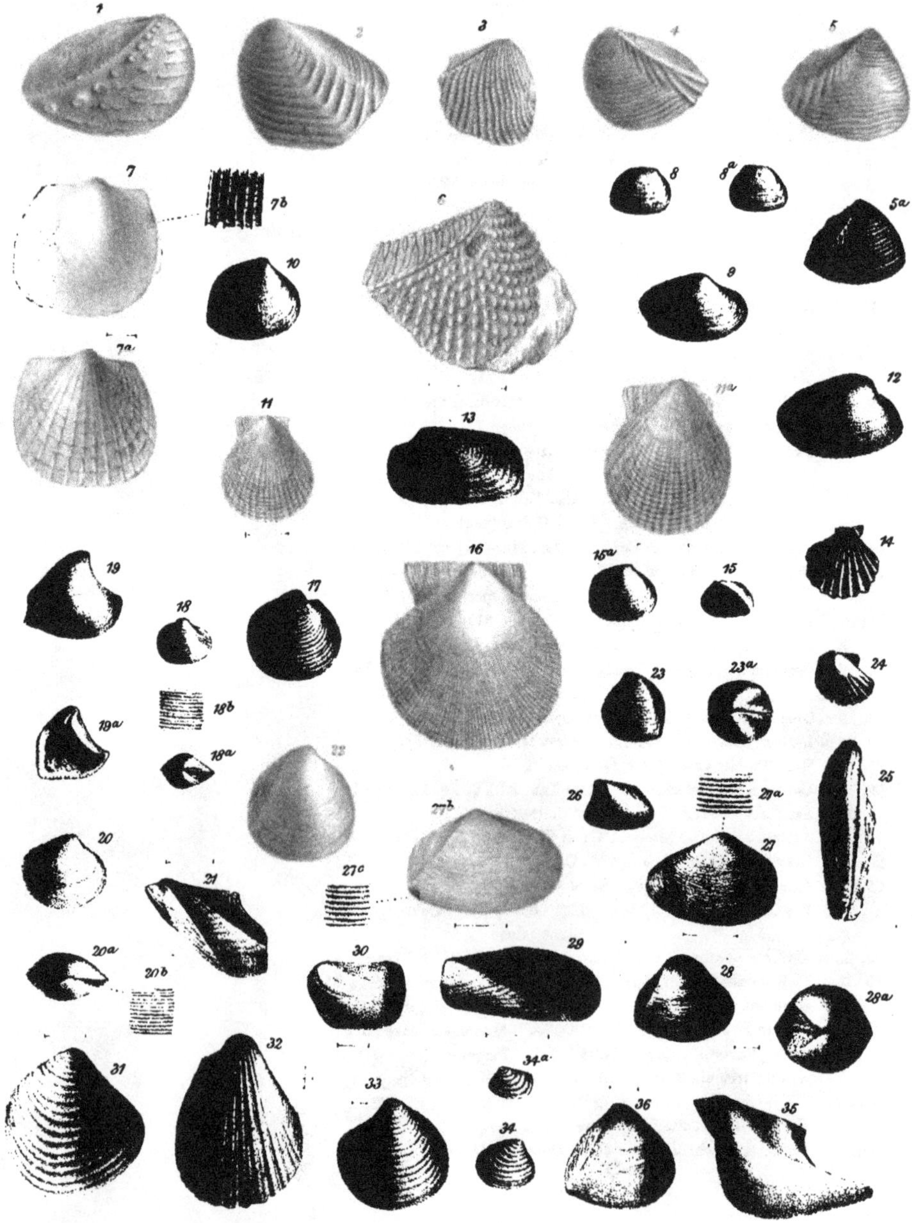

Geo West lith. ad nat.

W. West imp.

TAB. XLI.

FIG.

1. Amberleya capitanea, *Goldf.*, sp. Forest Marble (page 95).

2, 2 *a*. Natica Hulliana, *Lyc.* Great Oolite (page 13).

3. Amberleya nodosa. See also Part I, Tab. V, fig. 19.

4. Acteonina olivæformis. Great Oolite and Forest Marble. See also Part I, Tab. VIII, fig. 14, and fig. 12*.

4 *a*. „ „ A specimen of more advanced growth, with the spire more produced.

5. „ Kirklingtonensis, *Lyc.* Great Oolite (page 26).

6. „ brevis, *Lyc.* See also *Cylindritis? brevis*, Part I, Tab. VIII, fig. 13, page 26.

7, 7 *a*. Nerita Buvignieri. Examples of two stages of growth. See also *Stomatia Buvignieri*, Part I, Tab. IX, fig. 32. The specimens now figured are from the Forest Marble of Laycock.

8, 8 *a*. Ammonites discus, *Sow.* Forest Marble. Slightly reduced (page 4).

9. Rissoina subulata, *Lyc.* Great Oolite. Enlarged (page 98).

10. Amberleya monilifera, *Lyc.* Forest Marble. Enlarged (page 95).

11. Cerithium costigerum, *Piette.* Variety with flattened volutions and oblique costæ (page 92).

11 *a*. „ „ A portion of the surface enlarged.

11 *b*. „ „ Specimen with shorter, more inflated volutions, and perpendicular costæ.

11 *c*. „ „ A portion of the surface enlarged.

12. Kilvertia pulchra, *Lyc.* Great Oolite and Forest Marble. For the form of the aperture see Tab. XLIV, fig. 4, pages 10 and 94.

12. „ „ A portion of the surface enlarged.

13. Alaria myurus, *Desl.* See also *Alaria lævigata*, Part I, Tab. III, fig. 3.

14. Amberleya tricincta, *Lyc.* Forest Marble (page 96).

15. Turbo subtexatus, *Lyc.* Forest Marble.

16. Cerithium? Waltoni, *Lyc.* Forest Marble (page 92).

17. „ hemicinctum, *Lyc.* Forest Marble. Enlarged (page 91).

18, 18 *a*. Acteonina Luidii, *Mor.* An adult specimen, with the spire moderately elevated. Forest Marble. See also Tab. XXXI, fig. 16, page 27.

18 *b*. „ „ A specimen with the spire elevated.

18 *c*. „ „ Specimen with the spire elevated and the last whorl unusually lengthened.

Pl. XLI.

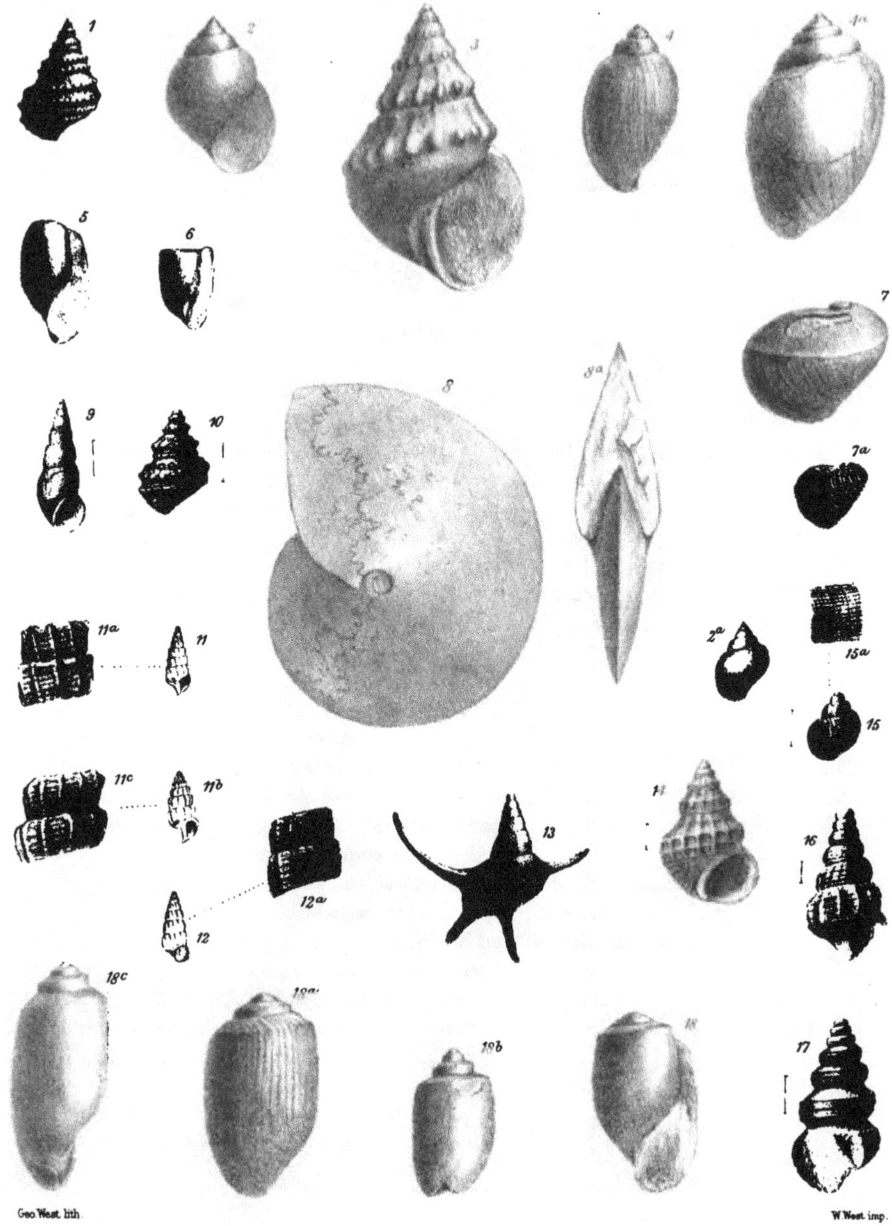

Geo. West lith. W. West imp.

TAB. XLII.

FIG.

1, 1 *a*. Myacites calceiformis, *Phil.*, sp. Cornbrash. Specimen with the test preserved (page 80).

2, 2 *a*. Pholadomya Phillipsi, *Mor.* Cornbrash (page 85).

3. Astarte Leckenbyi, *Wright.* Cornbrash (page 74).

4, 4 *a*. Pholadomya deltoidea, *Sow.* Forest Marble (page 86).

Pl. XLII.

Geo West lith

W. West imp.

TAB. XLIII.

FIG.

1, 1 *a*. Myacites modica, ***Bean***, sp. Cornbrash (page 83).

2, 2 *a*. Homomya gibbosa, *Sow.*, sp. (Page 88.)

3, 3 *a*. Pholadomya lyrata, *Sow.* Cornbrash (page 87).

4. Thracia amygdaloidea, *Lyc.* Great Oolite (page 80).

5, 5 *a*. Homomya crassiuscula. An adult specimen, with the test preserved. Part II, page 112; Supplement, page 89.

Pl. XLIII.

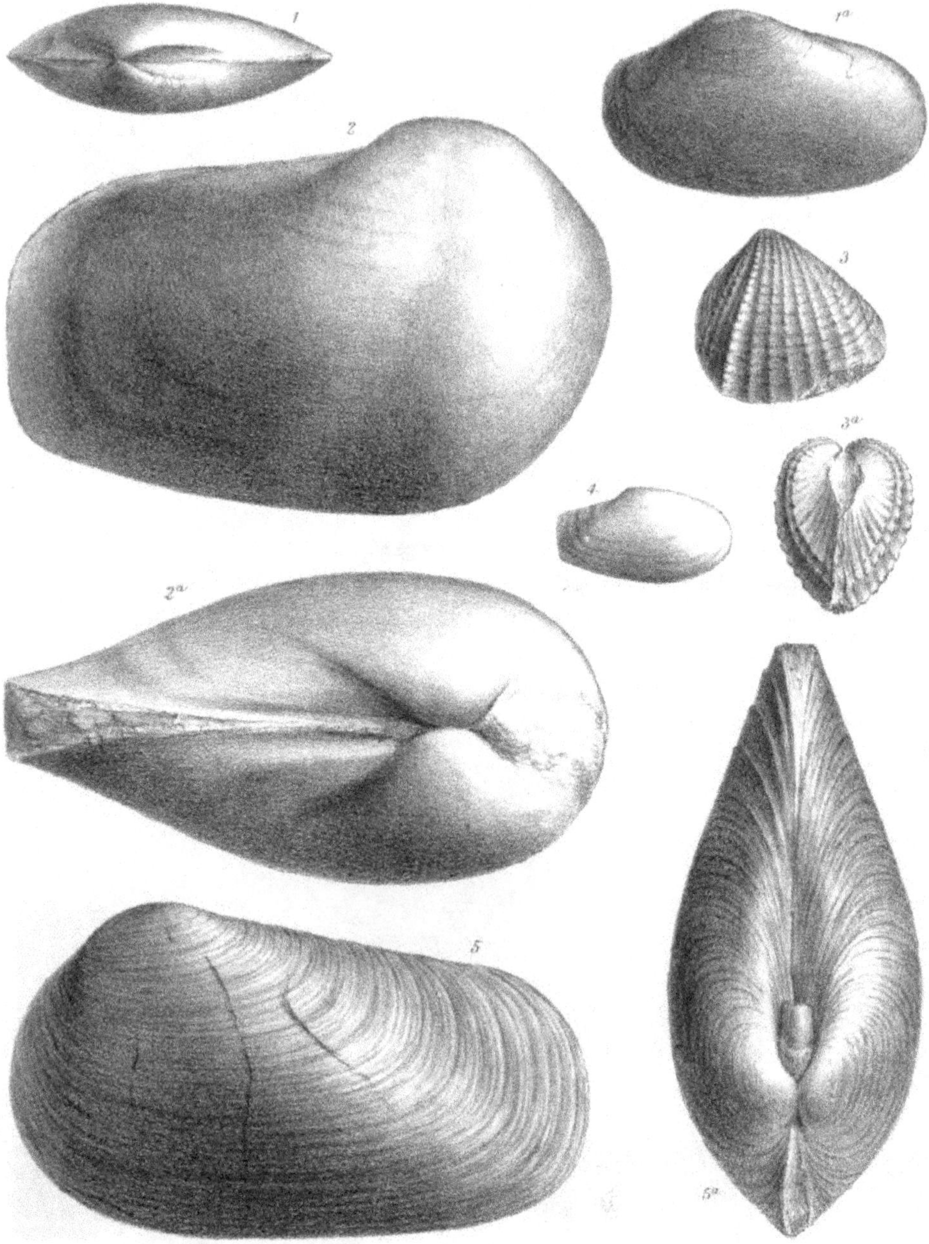

Geo West lith

W. West imp

TAB. XLIV.[1]

FIG.

1. Kilvertia spicula, *Lyc.* Great Oolite. Enlarged (page 9).
2. „ strangulata, *D'Arch.* Great Oolite. For another variety see Part I, Tab. IX, fig. 18.
3. Cerithium bulimoides, *Desl.* Great Oolite. Enlarged (page 7).
4. Kilvertia pulchra. Great Oolite. Enlarged. See also Tab. XLI, fig. 12, page 10.
5. „ formosa, *Lyc.* Great Oolite. Enlarged (page 95).
6. Cerithium undulatum, *Desl.* Great Oolite. Enlarged (page 8).
7. „ Witchelli, *Lyc.* Great Oolite. Enlarged (page 10).
8. Chemnitzia constricta, *Lyc.* Great Oolite. Enlarged. Printed Kilvertia by mistake at page 15.
9. Cerithium compositum, *Lyc.* Great Oolite. Enlarged (page 9).
10. Rissoina Milleri, *Lyc.* Great Oolite. Enlarged (page 18).
11. Rissoa? exigua, *Lyc.* Great Oolite. Enlarged (page 9).
12. Rissoina *Witchelli.* Great Oolite. Enlarged (page 18).
13. Rissoina? tumidula, *Lyc.* Great Oolite. Enlarged (page 98).
14. Cylindrites exigua, *Lyc.* Great Oolite. Enlarged (page 24).
15. Acteonina fasciata, *Lyc.* Forest Marble. Enlarged (page 107).
16. Acteon Bathonicum, *Lyc.* Great Oolite. Enlarged (page 25).
17. Brachytrema buccinoidea, *Lyc.* Great Oolite. Enlarged (page 5).
18. Acteonina scalaris, *Lyc.* A small specimen from the Great Oolite (page 28).
19. Cerithium? Bathonicum, *Lyc.* Great Oolite. Enlarged (page 6).
20. „ multiforme, *Piette.* Great Oolite. Enlarged (page 7).
21. „ ? neglectum, *Lyc.* Great Oolite. Enlarged (page 92).
22. Ceritella Morrisea, Orthostoma, *Buv.* See also Part I, Tab. IX, fig. 14.
23. Cerithium exscalptum, *Lyc.* Great Oolite. Enlarged (page 93).
24. „ poculum, *Lyc.* Great Oolite. Enlarged (page 93).
25. Ceritella Lycettea, Orthostoma, *Buv.* See also Part I, Tab. IX, fig. 7.

26, 26 *a*. Cylindrites turriculatus, *Lyc.* Great Oolite. Enlarged (fig. 25).

27. Brachytrema varicosa, *Lyc.* Great Oolite. Enlarged (page 5).
28. Acteon phasianoides, *Lyc.* Great Oolite. Enlarged (page 26).
29. Monodonta exigua, *Lyc.* Great Oolite. Enlarged (page 22).

[1] All the fossils upon this Tab., excepting No. 15, were obtained by crushing shelly portions of the Great Oolite.

Pl. XLIV.

Geo. West lith. ad nat.

W. West imp.

TAB. XLV.

FIG.

1. Monodonta Lyellii, *D'Arch.*, sp. Young shell. For the adult condition see Part I, Tab. XI, fig. 4.
2. Natica arata, *Lyc.* Great Oolite. Enlarged (page 97).
3. Nerita clavatula, *Lyc.* Great Oolite. Enlarged (page 98).
4. Ceritella fusiformis, *Lyc.* Great Oolite. Enlarged (page 12).
5. „ minutissima, *Lyc.* Great Oolite. Enlarged (page 11).
6. Monodonta composita, *Lyc.* Great Oolite. Enlarged (page 23).
7. Pleurotomaria recondita, *Lyc.* Great Oolite. Enlarged (page 106).
8. „ Burtonensis, *Lyc.* Forest Marble (page 105).
8 *a*. „ „ The base.
8 *b*. „ „ Portion of the surface magnified.
9. Monodonta sparsistriata, *Lyc.* Great Oolite. Magnified (page 22).
10. Pleurotomaria Bathonica, *Lyc.* Great Oolite. Magnified (page 105).
11, 11 *a*. Onustus Burtonensis, *Lyc.* Forest Marble. Slightly enlarged (page 103).
12. Trochus strigosus, *Lyc.* Cornbrash (page 29).
13. Turbo depauperatus, *Lyc.* Forest Marble. See also *Pleurotomaria pagodus*, Part I, Tab. X, fig. 9.
14. Trochus Guisei, *Lyc.* Great Oolite. Magnified (page 21).
15. Turbo Burtonensis, *Lyc.* Forest Marble (page 100).
16. Trochus Burtonensis, *Lyc.* Forest Marble (page 99).
17. Monodonta tegulata, *Lyc.* Forest Marble. Specimen with fine striations (page 102).
18. „ „ Forest Marble. Enlarged.
19. „ arata, *Lyc.* Forest Marble. Enlarged (page 102).
20. „ „ Variety with the encircling lines more distantly arranged.
21. Natica insignis, *Lyc.* Great Oolite. Enlarged (page 97).
22. „ (Euspira) alta, *Lyc.* Forest Marble (page 97).
23. Solarium turbiniformis, *Lyc.* Forest Marble (page 104).
23 *a*. „ „ A portion of the surface enlarged.
23 *b*. „ „ The lower surface.
24, 24 *a*. Monodonta comma, *Lyc.* Forest Marble (page 101).
24 *b*. „ „ A portion of the surface enlarged.
25. Acteonina Wiltonensis, *Lyc.* Forest Marble (page 107).
26, 26 *a*. Solarium Waltoni, *Lyc.* Forest Marble. Upper surface and profile (page 104).
26 *b*, *c*. „ „ Forest Marble. Lower surface.
27, 27 *a*. Solarium Bathonicum, *Lyc.* Great Oolite. The upper surface and profile (page 23).
27 *b*, 27 *c*. „ „ The lower surface of a smaller specimen.
27 *d*. „ „ A portion of the upper surface magnified.
28, 28 *a*, 28 *b*. Phasianella variata, *Lyc.* Page 104.
29. Acteonina Suessea, *Lyc.* Forest Marble (page 107).
30, 30 *a*. Natica texata, *Lyc.* Forest Marble (page 96).
31, 31 *a*. Monodonta Waltoni, *Lyc.* Forest Marble. Enlarged (page 101).
31 *b*. „ A portion of the striated surface magnified.

Pl. XLV.

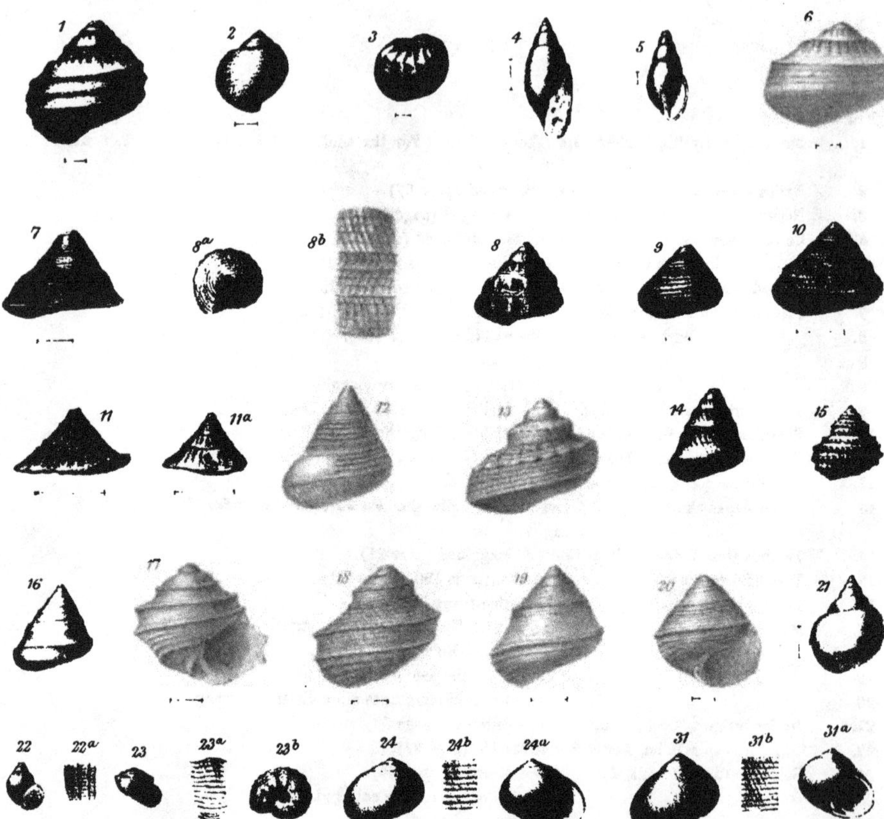

Geo. West lith. ad nat.

W. West imp.

CPSIA information can be obtained
at www.ICGtesting.com
Printed in the USA
LVHW040423110522
718423LV00002B/494

9 783375 002046